AfterShocks

ALSO BY JESS WELLS

Run, 1981

The Sharda Stories, 1982

A Herstory of Prostitution in Western Europe, 1982

The Dress, The Cry, and A Skirt Wtih No Seams, 1984

The Dress/The Sharda Stories, 1986

Two Willow Chairs, 1987

AfterShocks

a novel

Jess Wells

Third Side Press
Chicago

Cover design by putnam clark design group
Cover illustration by Brian Clark
Interior design and production by Midge Stocker
  Text set 11.5/13 ITC Korinna

Printed on recycled, acid-free paper in the United States of America.

Library of Congress Cataloging-in-Publication Data

Wells, Jess.
  Aftershocks: a novel / Jess Wells
    p. cm.
    ISBN 1-879427-08-7 : $9.95
    I. Title.
  PS3573.E488A68 1992
813'.54—dc20   92-7959
                                                           CIP

This book is available on tape to disabled women from the Womyn's
Braille Press, P.O. Box 8475, Minneapolis, MN 55408.

Third Side Press
2250 W. Farragut
Chicago, IL 60625-1802

First edition, May 1992
10 9 8 7 6 5 4 3 2 1

Dedicated to
Rachel, who taught me to speak my heart;
Ralle, to speak my mind;
Renate, to speak my characters;
and, forever, to Sharon, who listens to it all.

Acknowledgements

Many thanks to those who have patiently and astutely lent their assistance on this book. Thanks to Billie, BG, Irene, Midge, Betty, and Alice, for both fine editing and honest support; to Kay for the use of her get-away and the presence of the wolf; to my father John for his love, guidance, and joyful presence; to Kristie, Laurie, and Araya for their love; to Lesléa and Michelle, for their comraderie; to Daniel, for the love and faith of all these years; to Craig, Debi, Linda, Margaret, Charlie, Toni, and Nettie for the beauty of family. Special thanks to Rachel for the astounding gift of her wisdom and the tools she has given me to face the aftershocks in my life; to Renate, mentor and editor, whose insightful guidance has brought me the gift of a new form, voice, and genre; and to Sharon, who patiently watches the rise and fall of the art and the artist, struggling beside me to find ever-deeper love, freedom, and trust. I offer this and all else to the pantheon, whom more than ever, wrap their blue cloak around me and quiet my storms. My love to you all.

*A*rriving home to find the city of San Francisco decimated, Trout did not expect to be plagued by the desire to throw a cloth over her flat as if protecting a woman who has run naked into the street.

Dumbfounded, the nails of one hand digging into the flesh of her neck, she regarded the one-story Victorian apartment as if she were looking at something obscene. The front of the building was a pile of lathe and plaster, seeming more to have frayed than fallen. Slabs of sheetrock that had been her foyer lay in the street, while sections of the remaining walls hung in clumps from supporting cables, and the coveted hardwood floor, bleached no less, was covered in debris. Only the hallway walls and a few pillars holding up the roof remained standing.

The dressers were smashed, the contents of all the cupboards and closets spewed out. A coat worn inside out, she thought as she began to shake, and that could not be done. The hallway, though (she turned, drawn to it), was only slightly disheveled, as if someone with too many drinks in them had stumbled down its length, tipping the pictures with a careless shoulder.

This much disarray, it meant the lake was coming in on her, a canoe on its side, her father face down in the water, all the white tags of recipes and things not done piling up to her neck. The entire house was lost. Trout closed her eyes and put her hand deep into the mass of her wiry blonde hair, as if her hand might be capable of holding her up. She opened her eyes and stepped over a broken door frame and a mop head.

"Patricia!" she shouted, then shuddered at the silence.

"Henry, Jack!" she screamed, frantic to find her neighbors, some assurance that everyone had gotten out safely. Their part of the building, the back flat, was destroyed as well. Where had they gone? Especially with Jack so sick. Maybe he had already been in the hospital, she thought, aware that that would not have been good news on any other day.

Trout stared at the back of the building as if willing Henry to step out from behind a pillar. What she wouldn't give to sit and laugh with him. Where was everyone? Why was it so quiet?

Trout's hand reached out then pulled back, shaking, as if it could right a vase that had already fallen and smashed, or straighten a row of books that had tumbled from the shelf and lay under bits of wall and window. She wanted to scoop everything into a big drawer, or turn around and press her back against a huge closet door that might keep it all inside. She imagined someone summarily demanding their dog get off the sofa: "Cabinet! Off the china, right now!" It couldn't be ruined, not all of it, not everything but an umbrella stand and a couple of posters. Her breath came in shallow bursts. Trout put her hand over her mouth, wounded by the items that had managed to stay intact, in their places, where everyday life had insisted they stay, in its silly conviction that there was nothing more important than how candlesticks were arranged or the exact positioning of a little picture on a wall.

Where are my files? Trout wondered, turning frantically from side to side. All that work *couldn't* be scattered from the paperwork closet to the bathroom and the street. Those file drawers mustn't be disturbed: they worked like a clock, every bill not just on time, but three days ahead to arrive on precisely the due date, scheduled to maximize the interest on her checking account, with overdraft protection. She had fallen behind on her paperwork once before, and her father had slipped away, vanished. Not this time, though. She had exact tabs on all the folders, stationery in separate drawers, and four years of tax papers, with ledger entries.

A bile collected in her mouth and she shook her head. It couldn't be this way. Where was her little china fish? She struggled to find the remains of the bookshelf. Too precious to pack, the fish had ridden in her purse through every move, on every vacation. It was a gift from her father. And now it lay crushed between volumes of books: she saw the tail and the white dust of the crushed porcelain. The end of everything had come like this before; it had happened. She had been a child, and then she had pulled some cans out of the water, rubble like this, and suddenly she had had no childhood left, she had no father. Stumbling over the shattered remains of her front wall, Trout vomited onto a pile of books.

She clutched the briefcase to her chest and looked from side to side to see if anyone had noticed. She couldn't breathe. Her chest was tight. All her work, her grand design, these structures made things work. Panting, she wiped her mouth with her hand, shook her hand, and stepped away. All the planning, my God. She had to leave. She couldn't stay. Trout groped forward, tearing her pantyhose and scratching herself on a piece of wall that had been the living room. Her white sofa lay on its side like a vanquished Roman column. With boot marks on it too: every time she went on a business trip, she thought scornfully, Patricia put her feet on the couch.

Along the street, Trout saw houses without their Victorian facades, cornices, false brick fronts, chimneys, stairs. On the corner, a brick building had fallen into a pile of blocks, leaving industrial washing machines and steam presses twisted and half-buried.

Trout turned her back on her apartment, put her arms out, trying to stop the disorder behind her like a traffic cop clearing an intersection. She still had her raincoat slung neatly over her left arm, hand still clutching her briefcase, appearing as she did on any ordinary day while assuming the persona of Tracy Lynn Giovanni, businesswoman in a brown houndstooth suit so expensive she wouldn't even pet a dog in it, white silk blouse, work pumps, pantyhose. What about the East Bay? Evelyn and Maria in Oakland?

She turned to what sufficed at this point for a street, the pavement littered with roof tiles and odd scraps of people's belongings. A young boy running by stopped to grab her arms without knowing her: it had been an 8, he had heard it from a radio in a car. One hundred times worse than the earthquake of 1989. This had been it. An 8.0 hit at 2:13 p.m., with an epicenter at Mussel Rock Beach. Her 'friend' hadn't been home, a neighbor woman said, and no one else had been seen near the building either, Trout remembered, with fear on her face nonetheless. Henry and Jack hadn't been home, she thought with a sigh of relief Patricia was working in the Mission District, wiring a house. Trout wasn't expected back from the sales meeting until the next day. Patricia wouldn't even look for Trout because she wasn't expecting her. What if Patricia had been on a ladder when the damn thing hit, or the quake caused a surge of electricity and. . . . No, she thought. Patricia, in a time of disaster, thinking Trout was still in Omaha, would do what? Would immediately look for her daughter, of course, and Beth lived in the Mission as well. Dumbfounded, Trout wondered if the BART transit system were running. She wouldn't turn around, couldn't see any more of her house. No point in trying to rescue it. She had to get to Patricia. She'd look for more sensible shoes, even though she'd be sure to discover bills due jumbled in with cereal boxes. She had to walk to the Mission to find Patricia.

Then Trout saw her neighbor, Mrs. Williamson, shooing her children around the side of what had been her house. Tears poured down her face and made her bend even closer to the ground than her stooped shoulders generally made her. Mrs. Williamson patted her children, some of them taller than she, touched each one as if to be sure they were there, barked orders at the older girls, then headed back to the house.

"Don't go in there!" Trout shouted, dropping her briefcase and striding down the street toward the woman. "Mrs. Williamson!"

Mrs. Williamson stopped for a moment, put her hands to her mouth, her eyes wide. "The baby. She's in the house," she stammered.

Trout turned to the other children, hoping Mrs. Williamson had simply miscounted.

"We were all in the yard," Mrs. Williamson said, her voice breaking. "We were putting up the laundry. God only knows why I made the boys do it too. But it hit, such a sound you wouldn't have believed and then the house . . . the house just crumbled. The baby was sleeping." She started to cry. "She's in there, she's alive, I know it but I can't get to her. Tracy, you've got to help me. My baby."

"Where is she?" Trout tried to summon calm for her voice.

"In there. I've been listening to her cry. There, there she goes again. Better that than silence," she breathed.

Beams, drywall, cement, pipes, and the shredded contents of the house, a pile six feet deep, lay between the women and the sound of the baby. Trout could hardly imagine that all this could have been used in making the Williamson's home. It had been just a tiny square box.

"Here. Over here," Mrs. Williamson shouted, waving Trout over with short, frantic sweeps of her little arm.

Trout tried to crawl over the top of the first layer of rubble, but her skirt stopped her. She looked down at her ridiculous pumps.

"Oh Christ," she said. Mrs. Williamson, in slippers and a waistless housedress, looked at her, then tottered to the other side of the building to pick through the plaster.

"Here. Jason's pants." She held up a dusty pair of Chinos and some sneakers. "You need shoes for Christsake."

Trout twisted her voluminous hair into the collar of her blouse, took off her skirt and pantyhose and flung them aside, clambered into the pants and shoes. She started over the pile, seeing the small progress that Mrs. Williamson had made trying to move it all, piece by piece.

"Wait here until I find a way in," Trout admonished, suddenly clear-headed and forceful, relief in her voice now that Mrs. Williamson had chased away thoughts of her own house and father. Mrs. Williamson wrung her hands.

*A*t the time the earthquake hit, Patricia was standing back from the wall, one thumb looped into her tool belt as she admired the straight line of pipes she had just assembled. Proof of Master Status in Pipe Bends, she thought, with a longstanding habit of capturing thoughts in headlines. The conduit was ready for her and Mark to pull the wires, but what fool was driving into the side of the house? Patricia turned as the shaking continued, fiercer now. The walls began to sway. Patricia threw down the bender in her hand and headed out the garage door, deafened by the screaming sound of the roof tearing away and collapsing into the room where she had just been. Debris hit her on the ankles as she ran into the street.

"Mark!" she shouted. He was inside the house, barreling down the front steps as they swayed from side to side and collapsed.

The two electricians, in the street with their arms around each other, tried to steady themselves, then fell to the ground from the shaking. They covered their heads with their arms and stayed down.

The shaking stopped, as suddenly as it began, and a visible shudder ran through Patricia. She and Mark sat up. Patricia tentatively unfolded her long legs and climbed to her feet. Million-Dollar Hovel Collapses: Conduit All that Remains of Mansion, she thought.

"Christ," Mark said, still sitting. "My God."

"You all right?" she asked. He didn't answer. All around them people screamed and ran into the street, dashing in one direction, then turning back to their houses, mothers calling to their children. Beth, Patricia thought.

"My daughter!"

Patricia took her tool belt off and wrapped it over her shoulder as she ran down the street, pushing people aside. If the house she had been working on had fallen, what had happened to Beth's dump?

Three blocks, only three blocks and it's taking forever, she thought, despite the way her six-foot stride threw the sidewalk behind her. As she ran the last hundred yards, she screamed her daughter's name at the top of her lungs, feeling her Kentucky background rising to the surface, making her sound like women who stood at the base of Southern mountains during a mining disaster and called a man's name. Beth!

The house was standing. The steps had crumbled and all the windows were cracked, but Patricia scrambled up the loose pile of boards into the building. She bolted for the back flat. Pounding on the door and calling her daughter's name, she finally threw herself against the plywood door until it gave way. There was no one inside. Thank goodness, Patricia thought. It's all here, and still standing. Please God, Patricia thought, aware of a plea to someone she never called on, please keep her safe.

Back in the street, Patricia stood completely still, staring at the tips of her work boots. Where to go? She had no idea where Beth's friends lived or what Beth might be doing at this hour: the goddamn kid was unemployed, as usual, and as far as Patricia knew, barely went out of her house except to buy cigarettes. MTV Addict Considers Earthquake Surround-Sound, Patricia thought. She turned in a circle. She wanted to throw her tools down, stomp her foot and make her daughter eight years old again. It made no sense to let them grow up, she thought: what did you have with a child that's old? Somebody makin' twice as many bad decisions, and twice as hard to keep track of. Trout, of course, was off on one of her business trips and couldn't offer any suggestions. Mothers pushed by her, dragging little ones by the hand as they raced away from the elementary school, the community playground. Patricia smelled children's wet panties and perfume mixed with acrid sweat. Those mothers knew where their children were, but not her. Beth is fine, she told herself, lying. Beth always takes care of herself: two years ago when she broke her leg, she didn't even bother to call. Patricia rubbed her forehead. Where to look? Earthquake Exposes Mother: Own Child A Mystery, she thought.

She grabbed a man by the arm as he rushed by. Had he seen . . . a young woman, my daughter. She lives here, she said. He struggled free, shook his head. As he rushed off, Patricia pushed up the sleeves of her cotton shirt like someone ready to argue, then dropped her arms and turned back to Beth's house. She pulled Beth's picture from her wallet, trotted down the street presenting the photo, walked backwards when people wouldn't stop, went into shops and asked everyone in every aisle. She turned down side streets, asked children. "She was probably wearing a black leather jacket, her hair was white, bleached," Patricia explained, showing the picture of an adolescent, a photo years old, not depicting the punk her daughter had become. Why didn't she have a current picture? Why didn't she know who Beth's friends were? Other mothers did. Other mothers didn't stop asking questions of their daughters, didn't give up the way she had. They didn't abandon their children to their own goddamn lives, then lose them in rubble.

Patricia walked for hours in widening circles around the block, then returned to the house, calling the girl's name. She walked on long, sinewy legs as if she cut through space with her hips.

In Beth's apartment for the third time, Patricia pounded her fist against the door, kicked the wall so hard she broke through the sheetrock, then shook her head at the ceiling, disgusted with her own anger. Beth would come home like anybody sensible, Patricia admonished herself in a mirror above the fireplace. She expected parts of her face to have crumbled like the house. She had high, angular cheekbones and a chiseled nose, jet black hair (a mystery to her mother and so her only clue to what her father had looked like). It fell forward from the severe position behind her ears where she kept it, parted in the middle, cut just below the ear, and in its almost Asian- or Native American-straightness, it always fell forward onto Trout's face whenever Patricia leaned to kiss her. Her eyes were dark and close-set (beneath eyebrows the girls wanted to run their tongues over, Trout had teased), and the whole collection was covered with skin so fine a stranger didn't notice half the brittle things Patricia said. The skin gave her permission, and so did her round, firm breasts. People stumbled around at the sight of her beauty when they should have been standing their ground. This part of her demeanor Patricia knew for herself and she counted on it, frequently. Without her looks, people would have discovered that she was a bird of prey, a raven, Trout had told her once: she scanned the landscape when she talked, eyes darting, never lighting, never staring, rarely committing themselves to an object or a person. One would expect a beak to appear above your lips, my dear, she heard the voice of her lover say. Today she didn't smile. Only vultures would do well in this, she thought, as she leaned on the mantle, then turned away. Her body never settled either. She would lean on door frames, lean against parking meters and bars, and put her hands flat on the roof of a car when she talked to the driver. Even her image was in flux: Patricia's slash-back boots, cotton shirt, silver buckle, were part of an acquired look, she admitted to anyone who took the time to ask why a girl from Kentucky would look like a Texan. Usually when asked she would push her hands into her jeans pockets and the girls were too fascinated by how little room there was to actually hear anything about coal mining towns and the Blue Ridge Mountains.

She looked around Beth's flat, at the cobwebs and the dirty cups, the wine glasses that had rolled into the corner by the windows. There were dirty clothes under the dresser and plates with hardened food on the end-tables. None of the lamps had shades. Patricia got up and walked through the apartment. Look at this, she grumbled. Nobody taught her to lower herself like this. The kitchen counter was covered with paper bags and styrofoam containers, and the roaches had all come out of hiding. Patricia went into the bedroom, stared at the mattress on the floor, the old sleeping bag strewn among the socks and dirty underwear, the cigarette butts in tuna fish cans. By the pillow, she saw a used condom, still full, attracting ants. Patricia turned away, hurried into the living room, grabbed her tools, and bolted out the door. She's in danger, she must be, Patricia thought, otherwise she'd be home. Where else does she have to go? Goddamn kid, anyway. Precious little thing. Living like this and with . . . men.

*V*alium had seemed a reasonable alternative, Cherice thought, throwing her arms out at the pitch dark of the elevator: here's this guy with a broken foot, a lot of pain, and they're stuck between floors. She'd already pounded on the door and screamed. Where had everybody gone? Bailed out without noticing the hyena in the elevator, that was pretty clear. Just like the company to build insulated elevators so even gossip won't leak out unless it's billed to somebody's account. She had tried the telephone and left it dangling off the hook, hoping it might send a signal to a control panel somewhere.

The whole time this guy had still been on the floor, writhing around and cussing, their feet getting all tangled together. At least the shaking had stopped. The elevator was not taking them toward the lobby or anyplace else, but at least the walls weren't vibrating like the whole thing was a trash compactor and they were yesterday's pork and beans. The guy had said he didn't know which was worse, the pain from his foot or the fear the whole thing would dive-bomb into the car park.

"I've got something for us," she said firmly.

"What, a thirty-story forklift in your purse?"

"I've got to find my briefcase," Cherice said, turning, her legs twisting under his.

"Spare us the stock tips," he said, through clenched teeth.

"It's here. No, this one must be yours. How did you know I was in the market? Mine's boxy. Here it is. What are these papers all over the place? You take work home? It'll kill you, taking work home."

"Mine? Christ, I suppose all the envelopes have opened up."

"I think so. There's little slips all over the place."

"Shit," Jacob said and banged his head against the elevator wall. "I hate people with their receipt envelopes at tax time," he grimaced. "Like an accountant should record every fifty-cent purchase from the 7-Eleven store. Ah, that's my foot, my foot!"

"I'm sorry," Cherice said, clambering off him. Jacob rocked on the small of his back, trying to grab his ankle but only bumping heads with her. She landed on his hand with her knee, her palm leaning all her weight into his chest.

"Ah, lady, God!"

"I'm sorry, really," Cherice snapped. "It's pitch black. I can't tell your chest from the floorboards."

"My weight trainer will be pleased," he murmured.

"Here, take . . . one of these."

"What are they?" Jacob asked.

"Valium. I'm taking two. Maybe you should take more, you're in pain. Low dosage . . ."

"I don't take drugs," he said. "All right, just give them to me. But move slowly for Christsake."

God, she hated bossy men, but she reached for him carefully, setting her hand on his rib cage to orient herself, finding his arm, then cupping his big hand in hers and laying the pills in his palm. Hairy hands. How strange, she thought. Nice cotton shirt, though. She retreated to a corner of the elevator, pulling her legs underneath her and downing the Valium.

"Of course these elevators get air," Jacob said quietly.

"Sure," Cherice said without assurance, waving his fear away with her hand. "They don't build them like that anymore. It'll just be a matter of minutes. The emergency power will kick in—we'll be blinking at the sunlight in no time."

"Wait a minute. I have a lighter," he said, struggling to withdraw it from his pocket. He snapped it on, and the two of them studied each other's faces.

Maybe she reacted that way because she only saw his face for an instant, or because she was looking at it in the muted tones of a single flame, but when she saw his face her lips parted, she cocked her head in surprise. He was gorgeous, and she'd admit it to anyone who asked, she thought. He had big, broad shoulders, jutting chin, a nose like a toucan curving smoothly above his thin, bow-shaped mouth. His skin was flawless (maybe it was the light, she reasoned) and sculpted by high cheekbones. His jet-black hair cascaded to his shoulders, though it started from a place far back from his forehead. My God, Cherice thought.

"Let's look at your foot," she said nervously.

Dead in the water again, Jacob thought. He tried to drive the pain out of his mind long enough to complete a full thought. Could a day get any worse than this? Could a life get any worse than this? Laid out flat, his foot screwed but good, yet another client's account thrown into total disarray. Thought he could rush home and figure out a way to fix it, work all night if necessary, but not now. All right, you win, he thought acridly, looking toward the darkened ceiling, what do you want me to do, shout it from the rooftops? I'm a lousy accountant, a goddamn lousy failure as an accountant, and considering how accountants stack up in the world, that doesn't say much.

"Hold the light down here," Cherice said irritably. "Can't you sit up? I don't know anything about these sort of things. I wasn't even a Girl Scout. Oh shit, it's starting to swell."

"Don't touch it."

"Well, we have to do something. It may just be sprained. We need a . . . you know, one of those wraps." She lifted his foot gingerly. "Does that hurt?"

"Yes!"

What was it about her face, he wondered? A small nose, round face, medium height, medium breasts, hair of no distinct color, eyes that in this light could be any hue at all. She didn't wear make-up, didn't wear lipstick. You looked at her and couldn't find anything to remember. Like someone you met at a party and struggled to memorize her brooch so that when she waved at you in the street you'd know who she was. A woman like this could change her blouse and start a new life, he thought. He let the flame go out, put the lighter in his pocket.

"Do you have a scarf on?" Cherice asked in the dark.

"No."

"Well, we need something to bind your foot. How about an undershirt?"

"Yeah, OK." Jacob struggled to sit up. Cherice put her arms around the middle of his back and helped him up. He leaned on his palms, grimacing.

Stuck in a tin box, but where the hell was he going to go if he got out? He felt Cherice nervously unbutton his shirt, her hands shaking slightly, her fingers fumbling with the buttons, abandoning the task, then seizing the front of his shirt gruffly. Should he go back to the office to feign interest? Jacob thought. Abigail. God, he hoped she was all right. He sighed. That was the reason he was taking the account home, for one last glimpse of her, for one last chance to say something totally original and convincing like 'but why do you have to leave me?' Of course she'd be with that Malcolm bastard, that shit-bag lawyer, Mr. Tort. Now there's a man who was proud of himself. Malcolm was probably helping her ransack his apartment right this minute. He certainly would not head for home, not now. Bad enough to walk in with your heart limping behind you but to literally hobble in, dragging a briefcase full of disaster . . . no, he wouldn't go home. He hoped Abigail wouldn't try to take his art prints. So, he had said that the nudes looked like her, that didn't mean she could take them. But he knew, he'd be left with the marks on the wall where the frames had been, nothing in the bathroom but one of her pink razors and a tube of Speed Stick. You don't communicate, Jacob, she had said caustically, and pulled out her valise. God, it was a death sentence, like leukemia. Men don't grow, they don't change, you could see that decision in a woman's face. Women pronounced you one way or the other and that was it. Admit this about communication to someone new and it'd be all over. They'd take their Bloody Marys and move down the bar so fast the celery leaves would blow in the goddamn wind.

*T*rout scrambled over the first obstacle, lost her footing and fell. Mrs. Williamson screamed and crouched down, clutching the front of her dress to her face. Plaster piled against Trout's foot and pieces of wood fell from the ceiling.

"It's all right," Trout said. "It's all right," as much to herself as to the baby and Mrs. Williamson. She clung to pipes, nearly lost her balance several times, calculated each move, while the smell of fear rose from her body. She stuffed wisps of her hair back into her blouse to prepare herself.

She could make this work. She had to, she thought. She clearly wasn't going to be effective at home, what home she had left. She should have had something constructed, she thought with chagrin. Not just bought a safe: the entire paperwork closet should have been specially reinforced. She grabbed a pipe as if wanting to break it off. She hadn't taken care of business. The irritation made her step more boldly toward the inside of the house.

She dropped into a trough between the first stack of debris and a second.

"Where's the baby's room?" she asked in what she hoped was Mrs. Williamson's direction.

"In front of you. In the middle," Mrs. Williamson said, pointing toward the sound of Trout's voice.

"Get some pants for yourself," Trout told her.

Mrs. Williamson ignored her suggestion and tried to climb over the pile, Trout describing where to step, what to hold. She was too short and stooped over to reach half the handholds, Trout thought. Mrs. Williamson faltered several times, too frightened to continue, and cried, then tried to smooth her housedress from where it had climbed onto her thighs. On the other side of the pile, the two women lifted the pipes that lay crosswise over the crib. Then the other wood began to shift, so they set the pipe down again. Trout wiped her forehead, trying to think. There was no sound of the baby.

"Which direction does the crib face?"

The two women began slowly lifting boards from the end. As they made progress, they worked more feverishly, tearing at the pile, straining all their muscles.

"Is this it?" Trout said, excited at the sight of a little bear decal. The baby's bed was under a lean-to created by a fallen beam. Plasterboard walls had tumbled against the beam, pipes on top of the plasterboard, like a pencil on a stack of cards. Trout worried that lifting any of it would break the drywall and send the wood crashing through the unsupported areas into the crib.

"Becky!" Mrs. Williamson called, and the baby began to cry again. "Mommy's here!"

As the women touched the crib, the debris on top began to shift and the baby screamed. They backed up slightly. Trout turned to Mrs. Williamson.

"Do you have a saw?"

"In this mess? Oh dear."

"I can't come up with anything else," Trout lamented.

"The tool room. Charlie's tool room. I can't tell where it is anymore. Here, it's over here." The two women scrambled through the two-by-fours, oblivious to the cuts and bruises, the wiring tearing at their clothes.

"A screwdriver! The saw's got to be here," Mrs. Williamson said.

"Hang onto that screwdriver. Gather any tools you can find—they'll be needed. Somewhere," Trout said, aware of her presumptive, authoritative tone. Mrs. Williamson put tools into the pockets of her dress.

"Here it is. Is this it?" she said.

"A hack saw. That's not right but it'll do. You keep looking." Trout went back to the crib, undid the screws and took the blade out of the hack saw. Mrs. Williamson had joined her with the screwdriver. Trout poked a hole into the crib back and began sawing. Mrs. Williamson started to poke a hole on the other side.

"No, make another hole on this side. We'll cut a space just big enough for her."

Trout reached in. "There she is."

Mrs. Williamson pushed her aside and thrust both hands into the hole, scraping both of their wrists against the jagged side of the crib wall.

"It's not big enough," Mrs. Williamson wailed.

"Move. Let go of her!" Trout said. "Move!"

Trout sawed furiously until Mrs. Williamson dove at the baby, pulling her into her arms, crying into her neck.

"Is she all right?"

"My God, she's bleeding. Becky!" The baby had wet her pants, and blood oozed from her leg, soaking her sleep suit.

Trout bit her fingernails, then straightened to tackle the next task. Getting Mrs. Williamson over the rubble had been difficult enough: it had required crawling and hanging from pipes. How were they going to do it with a baby? And one that's obviously hurt? I'll just deal with the logistics, Trout thought, backing away from the child. Mrs. Williamson gingerly opened the baby's clothing to inspect the wound, but Trout fiercely grabbed the woman's hands.

"Strap her to the front of you," Trout directed sharply. "We're taking her to the hospital." The woman's housedress had nothing to secure the child. The two looked around for something to use. There was no cloth in sight, even in the crib.

"It was too hot for a blanket, and I was . . . washing the sheets," Mrs. Williamson said apologetically. "The weather was so strange today."

The baby's dresser was buried. With a sigh, Trout stripped off her shirt and put the baby in it, tied the sleeves around Mrs. Williamson's neck, the tails around her waist. Trout's hair seemed to balloon out, covering her shoulders. Bare-chested now, without a bra, Trout scowled and Mrs. Williamson averted her eyes. The monograms on the cuffs peeked from behind Mrs. Williamson's head. Well, damn it, Trout thought, the culture that taught Trout to climb stacks of wood was the one that taught her to go topless. For the first time since they started the endeavor, they faced each other as neighbors, a lesbian and a heterosexual mother of seven, acquaintances in the day-to-day through an accident of proximity, partners now because of a disaster.

"I'll go first," Trout said, "and guide you." Mrs. Williamson looked at her breasts, then looked away.

*P*atricia wandered through the Mission flashing the picture of her daughter, presenting it to lines of people at the groceries where women carried away shopping carts of canned goods, filling bags with anything they could get their hands on. As the bins of vegetables began to empty, people pushed their way into the shops, shoving Patricia aside. Women with their children, handkerchiefs tossed over their heads, some with rosaries already out, joined large crowds trying to get into the churches. Patricia followed the flow of people drawn down 24th Street without an idea of where she was going but with a vague sense of moving toward the hospital. As she neared Portrero Avenue, she pressed her way through the crowd, showing the picture of Beth, chewing her lip with guilt, then making her face hard and closed against possible criticism. She searched the faces around her and was reassured by the sight of all those needy people. At least she had company.

"You seen her?" she repeated, then just held up the picture to any face that would turn her way. "Older. A punk," she said.

"There's some punks," a man said, gesturing with a cigarette.

Beth leaned against the cement wall in front of the hospital, one hand behind the small of her back, the other intently fingering a cigarette that was already down to the butt.

"Beth!" Patricia shouted, pushing people aside, nearly knocking down small children.

Christ, she isn't even upset, Patricia thought as she plowed toward her. Child Pulled from Plane Wreckage Asks for Refund on Movie. Kid'll take any occasion to lounge around. Patricia should have known the reunion would not be like it was in other families. She rushed to Beth, gathered her roughly in her arms.

"Are you all right?"

"Yeah. Sure," Beth said, a bit incredulously. "You OK? Man you should see some a' these people, Mom. They just keep comin'. I saw one man walk through here, his little girl didn't have a leg."

She grabbed Beth by the shoulders and shook her. The girl's white hair barely moved and as she closed her eyes, Patricia saw the smudges of black eyeliner. The kid smelled a little like dust and a lot like tobacco. Patricia started to cry, turning away.

"I've been looking for hours. Christ, I couldn't find you," she said fiercely.

"I'm OK, Ma," Beth said softly, and pulled away.

Child's Last Words as Mother Says Jump from Burning Ship: 'Marijuana'll Get Wet,' Patricia thought. "Where you been?"

"Here. I've been . . . precisely . . . here," Beth said slowly. Patricia stuffed her hands into her pockets: whenever she wants me off her back she makes her language tight and proper, tells her mother to stop sounding like Kentucky. Well, it's true. No matter where she lives, you scare a woman deep enough she goes right back to her home town, acts like she did at her mother's dinner table.

The women faced each other, not certain what to say. With clumsy hands, Patricia reached out and touched her daughter's face.

"The garage I was working in collapsed," Patricia said. "Right after I got the goddamn pipe up."

Beth said nothing, looked down at her boots, then looked over the crowd. A man next to Beth elbowed her and Beth turned away from her mother to talk. She cleared her throat as she turned back.

"Look, Mom," she said hesitantly, "some pipes at the Chevron refinery have broken. There's a big oil spill and a bunch of us are goin' to go wash the ducks."

"What?"

"You remember. I'm part of a group that washes ducks whenever there's an oil spill," Beth said warily. "We show up from all over the place. Anytime there's oil, there's us."

"You can't leave, Beth," Patricia said, remembering how her daughter (during a Sunday dinner!) had jumped onto a bus for parts unknown and had once spent her own money for a Greyhound to a spill site. She'd hear of a disaster on the radio and walk out the door.

"It's OK, Mom."

"It's not OK, goddamn it."

"You can't tell me what to do, Ma. You go all kinds of places without me, remember?"

"You're not going anywhere! The whole city is a mess."

How absurd, Patricia thought. Devastation, and still the two of them are going over the same old ground, haggling about Beth and her goddamn 'freedom.' Patricia sighed.

"I've been looking for you for hours. How many times do I have to say that? Where are you going to sleep? The city is very dangerous right now, you know. People are crazy when shit like this happens."

"I'll be on a boat, Mom. It's real safe. We set up a station on the shore, trap the birds, wash them, warm them, set them free in another part of the bay. You know, I've done it before."

Patricia closed her eyes and rubbed her forehead. She had met that boy a couple of months ago (was he the one? she wondered). He was a reasonable kind of guy, but for Beth to leave, that wouldn't do: to be running off for a cause that was not her own, with a man? Fate of Aquatic Animals Ranks Higher Than Mother's Love.

Patricia turned away, shifted the weight of the tool belt on her shoulder, then turned back and saw the look in Beth's eyes. She knew the girl would go anyway, regardless of any arrangement she had made with her mother. Never discussing it with her, agreeing with her, working on it together, just . . . vacating, as Trout would say. She had done it more times than Patricia could count and every time Patricia had been left feeling worse than a fool. The only time things seemed to work out well was when Trout intervened and soothed everyone's temper. Today, it seemed better to let her go with her mother's blessing than to create the mess of another fight between them. Besides, this work thing with the ducks seemed a bit like sending the girl to camp or getting her a job. God knows she didn't want to discourage that. Better Beth should be up to her elbows in duck suds then hanging out on the streets where she could get into trouble. First time the kid saw stereos carted out of broken display windows, Patricia would be spending all her time getting Beth out of jail. Boats were pretty safe during

earthquakes, weren't they? All right, go, be out of
temptation's way, but for God's sake be safe, she thought,
realizing it was the second time she'd called on that figure
she usually disdained.

"Where will I find you when you come back?"

"At home!" Beth said, incredulously.

Patricia stared at her. Beth turned her back and, at the
shoulder of the boy, walked Portrero Avenue toward Army
Street, without turning around. Patricia watched until Beth's
black jacket and white hair disappeared, a damnable echo of
all the other times her daughter had disappeared from her
life, the times she had stood and watched the distance pour
between them like muddy water into a springtime creek.
Patricia turned and headed toward her own home.

*L*ouise folded her arms tightly across her big chest and
bent double when she discovered the damage to her
bar. Slept through the whole damn thing, she muttered,
knowing that she was being generous with herself. She had
passed out on the bar again, that was the real story. She
could see herself: her head heavy on her arm, one hand slid
down the pillar of a Glenlivet bottle. She was still seated on
the high stool behind the bar where she usually sat with her
arms folded, surveying the customers.

Last night Sabito's had been packed, the women tumbling
in the doors, wild and challenging at pool, smitten, daring,
like that bulldagger who crossed the room in big confident
strides. The woman had wedged herself sideways against the
bar between that blonde femme who appeared from nowhere
and a woman Louise surmised was not with her. It was that
stride that had done it, Louise thought. The goddamn butch
looked just like she had looked twenty years ago, when there
was still some sex in her thighs, some energy like the stuff
that last night had pushed the youngster across the floor.
Even the same damn styles in again as then; the baggy
pants, cardigan sweater, hair back from the forehead but
now in the '90s without the pomade. Louise had stopped

ringing up a set of drinks and watched the woman walk. The evening had gone downhill from there. She had been distracted, her tally came out short, she had poured too many free ones. Closing time was closing time and she was usually pretty strict about it but she had let a few stragglers sit at the bar with her. She owned the damn business, or what was left of it, and she could put it in jeopardy if she wanted. She had known she was heading for trouble when she bought them all a round, and poured herself another one, but it hadn't stopped her, had it? she thought, kicking at the remnants of the wall of her bar. The kids had stayed 'til four, if she remembered it right, and she'd cleaned up, sat down pretending to read a paper, walked around, jimmy-rigged the jukebox and played a stack, racked up a couple games of pool. Insomnia. Funny how it sounds so close to insanity, she thought. Why couldn't she have amnesia instead? Maybe they were opposites: either no remembering, or the torture of too much remembering. How many times had she prayed for it, this fuckin' amnesia? Must be a beautiful feeling, floating around with no clue of how you had grown, where your belly had come from, or who had put the scars on your legs. Couple years ago she had scrawled it in on her own ladies' bathroom: Amnesia = Nirvana.

The sun had come up but no matter how many times she'd poured one from the bottle she couldn't sleep. She'd even fixed a couple chairs and taped up the vinyl on a barstool and had taken to just wandering through the place, weaving in and out of the tables like a pinball scooting through the shoots. She'd picked up a copy of the Bay Times that some sloppy bitch had stuck under a table leg to keep it from wobbling. "The New Celibacy," the cover story had read, and Louise had howled, still holding the Glenlivet bottle so that it slopped out onto her shirt. The New Celibacy? Shit. Why hadn't they interviewed her? She'd been at it for years. But what would she tell some smart little dyke with a notepad at the ready? Wasn't even a legitimate reason. No broken heart after twenty years of marriage, no lover healing from incest, it was cowardice, she thought today. She picked up a cement fragment and wondered from what spot it had fallen. After being bedded by stone butches had gone out of style, she had simply packed it in.

Of course that wasn't the image she had in the community, and she wasn't about to set anyone straight. She was a businesswoman, after all. She was big and impressive, in Ben Davis pants and plaid shirts when they were the style, and lately in the little earrings or lapel pins she thought fitting on a butch, occasionally even a few shirts with epaulets and colored buttons: it was the '90s after all. She had a big wide face and short brown hair that was gray at the temples. Christ, you could see her blue eyes clear across the room, the girls always said. The women came and flirted sometimes, and there were a few young femmes who thought her strong and secure (she laughed to herself about that one!). Sometimes (the blue moon is what you're talkin' Louise, she thought), sometimes a straight woman would arrive waiting to be turned out, and she'd comply, once, always only one time apiece. It had happened more in the '70s than now. Sign of the times.

Look at this place. Half the wall crumbled down. Boys running down the street toward each other, pulling objects out of their pockets, pointing at buildings, then running back down the street together, and the sirens.

"What you lookin' at?" she said and put her hands on her hips when a dusty man, big like a construction worker, stopped in front of the gaping hole that had been the best side of the bar. He turned and walked away. Jesus, Louise, she thought, whaddaya think he's lookin' at? The damn wall is gone. But wasn't that what you were supposed to say? Some big-guy looks at a lesbian, you say "what you lookin' at?" Now she wished he hadn't gone. There wasn't anybody to talk to, to hear her say, "Mother of God, the wall's gone. Tumbled down here. It was nice, real nice this wall." The glass Bud signs and the Schlitz mirror and those Nagel posters that the feminists didn't like—but then, they didn't drink much anyway. There was a piece of one, poking out from under a pile of that god-awful dusty cement. The landlord's gonna love this. She stepped to the edge of the jukebox and leaned out into the alley, turned to look at the main street, pulled back in surprise and ran to the door, unlatched it, took off the 2x4 bracing (they never would have gotten in to save her if something . . . terrible had happened, she thought), and went into the street. People were jammed onto the sidewalk as if it were the 24th Street Fair. She heard someone shouting a block away. Jesus, Louise breathed. The pavement was cracked around the parking meters, and the neon sign for the Jefferson Tamale Parlor had fallen into the street. It came and went and you were passed out, she thought. Another night spent impaled by her past, squirming on the stick of what was, pinned against what should have been but wasn't. Shit. The burning in her stomach that others called a hang-over, she called a hang-on, damn sickness caused by thoughts that won't wash away like bad memories ought to.

"There! In there," Louise heard a woman's voice say in a pinched and panicked tone. Louise, standing on the street with her arms folded, feeling out of place in the daylight, turned with alarm, trying not to throw herself off balance. Two women, one with her arms around another, bolted into Sabito's as if it were the only door out of a threatening fun-house. Louise trotted after them, veering slightly as she walked.

"Oh, look at the pool table," one of the women said, walking slowly, as if she were studying a difficult shot. Louise, alarmed suddenly, quickly strode to her prized possession.

"Oh, Jesus, I was so . . ." Louise breathed, "upset about the wall, I didn't even . . ."

"Coffee," Louise said, breaking away from the little cluster before they could smell her breath. The women glanced at each other as if Louise had looked at a dead man and thought about carnivals. She didn't care. Coffee was what she needed, badly.

The table, set in a side room all its own, was covered with a fine white dust and a huge chunk of plaster from the ceiling. "Help me with this," Louise commanded, barely noticing the woman's face.

"I'll make the coffee," one of the women said. Louise pointed toward the kitchen without looking up.

Screw the wall, the damn neon, here was something worth saving, Louise thought. They lifted the big piece and Louise heaved it to the floor, too near her feet. "Oh, God, don't scrape anything, don't brush anything across the surface." Mahogany, bought from a bar in Cincinnati that had gone under, the table had been transported like gold bullion by a youthful Louise on her way to the City. It had been strapped into the back of a truck, displacing all her clothing and books into the front seat where they threatened to topple onto her. The table was perfectly level, beautifully carved, with legs more graceful than a race horse. She had polished it and brushed it for fifteen years; she'd growled at more than one moxy bitch who thought it cool to roll a cue stick across its surface to prove she could play. Now look at it.

"Get a garbage bag," she growled, then looked at the floor. "Forget it," she said, and started carefully lifting plaster shards and throwing them onto the floor.

The two women worked on the pool table with reverence, as if it were the flag of a special country, the official seal of a coveted society. Honor, achievement, sex appeal, Louise thought, macha stand and maturity: it had all been flaunted here, like no place else.

"Don't you usually cover this?" the woman asked.

"You think a canvas cover would'a been any match for an earthquake?" Louise said caustically, knowing the woman was right. If she hadn't been drunk, it would've been covered. She was damn lucky she had managed to lock the door, secure the till, though she couldn't remember doing either.

More women arrived as Louise vacuumed the table. The second group seemed to announce the beginning of a deluge. Women arrived without shoes, women wringing their hands, or worrying about a backpack left behind. Groups of women milled around what had been a tiny dance floor. They stepped into the building hesitantly, then, at the sight of other survivors, burst into little groups to ask questions: "Where were you when it hit? Did your house fall down? Did you find your lover? How bad was this one, really? Do you know anyone who was hurt?" Some told their stories with hysterical anxiety, in high-pitched tones and quick words.

Thousands were dead, they said. Buses had been turned into ambulances and were still so busy they wouldn't stop for you anymore. Whole areas of the city looked like movies of London in the war, other parts had not been touched at all.

The growing crowd was comforting to Louise. She was freed from last night, from the many nights that had caused last night. She had customers and those were the kinds of people she knew how to deal with. Besides, the bulk of bodies in her place protected her from the gaping hole in the wall.

"There was this one place down the street that only lost the bottom floor. The others are just hanging there."

"And I saw a whole bathtub that smashed through the wall onto the fire escape . . . "

The stories went on as Louise dusted tables, inspected the kitchen, peered into her special case of Glenlivet, inventoried bottles and finally took her place behind the bar. It looked like the night of a demonstration, Louise thought, when the cops got ugly and people were surprised at how vicious the hatred was, like they all figured it out at once. They chewed on the idea of it. Chomped and mulled and turned it around. Is that really the answer? Is that possible? What does it mean? Good nights for the bar: people like to drink when they're surprised by life.

*M*ore vulnerable now with her breasts exposed, and her mass of hair dangling around her face, Trout felt something in her loosening, drawing out toward the world of flesh and wood and crying. As they crawled through the remains of the house, Trout looked back at her shirt, saw its blueness, the shirt's perfect lines and flawless cloth suddenly framing the baby like a matting around a print. When they reached the other side, Mrs. Williamson turned away from her. She found one of her husband's white shirts that was twisted in a heap in the corner and handed it solemnly to Trout, who faced her eye to eye and put it on.

The older children cried and stroked the baby, clung to their mother, as the women marched toward the hospital. San Francisco General Hospital was in the Mission. Trout would be heading toward Patricia's job site in that direction, too.

They walked as a unit, Mrs. Williamson and Trout shoulder to shoulder, clutching the hands of the children. The seven of them pushed their way through crowds at intersections, Trout occasionally putting her arm around Mrs. Williamson's shoulder to direct her as she hustled her children forward. In any other situation, Trout remembered, Mrs. Williamson would have stood one-quarter behind her husband, as if always in a portrait. Though Mrs. Williamson knew the Mission better than she, she took direction from Trout as if it were part of a natural law, a common occurrence, perhaps feeling, Trout speculated, that Mrs. Williamson's need to be guided was stronger than the gender of the arm around her shoulder. And what of her own need, she wondered, seeing again the destruction of her house and the paperwork she had abandoned?

The six-lane boulevard that had been Portrero Avenue was a sea of people who stood as if they had forgotten their destination. People held their children, staring at the brick complex of General Hospital. The earthquake had turned it into a series of frayed buildings, intact, operating, but with the cornices lying in the gardens. The mass of people rolled toward the building like a wave that had decided to come to shore, then finding nothing of value in the sand, retreating until the time to try again.

Some at the hospital cried and pushed their way toward the entrance, frantic to find relatives they couldn't locate. Where was the casualty list? Trout heard them shout. Whom had the hospital taken in? Others congregated, complete families, and those who appeared to have no one to look for, standing close to the building, facing the lighted windows. Some people talked about auxiliary power at the hospital and that if supplies would be allocated, they would certainly start here, but many waited without excuses, it seemed to Trout, knowing that proximity to help was solace enough to draw them down the side streets to Portrero Avenue. Ambulances crept through the density of humans as if facing the prospect of a stampede.

Trout pushed Mrs. Williamson and her children toward the receiving doors and turned to leave.

"I have to find . . . " Trout began, but Mrs. Williamson grabbed her arm with such force that she followed the troop into the waiting room. Trout steered Mrs. Williamson toward the pediatric ward.

People congregated in the halls, some sitting with head in hands, some leaning against walls, other pushing quarters into the candy machines and shoving supplies into their pockets. People covered with dust and perspiration lined the entrance to every room, watching. Medical staff moved quickly, frenetically, looking around with pinched expressions, appearing to Trout to be on the edge of panic over the sheer numbers of wounded coming through the door, at the clutching expressions on the faces of the watchers. Occasionally attendants would move through the crowd, encouraging people to leave, handing out a hastily constructed map of relief centers where they were promised food, perhaps shelter. Copies of the maps disappeared from the pile.

Trout stepped back at the sight of the hands grabbing and tried to smooth her hair. She could never be a nurse. She couldn't do a job like that. All the goodness and caring, all the nurturance would be drained out of her, a substance in a bottle that is finished when it is taken. She looked around for a corner to sit in, but there wasn't a space available. Love and generosity were finite things, she thought with fear, as she watched Mrs. Williamson and her brood being swallowed up by the doors of the pediatric ward. She found a narrow stretch of wall in the hospital and leaned against it, facing inward. Everyone reaches a breaking point: she had with her own father. And this now. All of it drained away. She heard his reedy little voice calling to her as it hadn't in years: Can't you do something about it, Tracy? he had said, aloud or silently—at this point she no longer remembered. Can't you do something? The question made her knees buckle and she crouched in a corner, covering her face.

She had lived alone with her father since the day she was born, her mother having died in childbirth. Trout had grown up on a lake in Michigan where the upper-class came in the summer to launch their boats and buy fishing tackle they never used.

Tracy's house was on an inlet, not sprawling across the sandy shore, open to the breeze like the modern, wood-and-glass homes of the doctors, but pushed up against a little shingled cottage along the marshy strip, where the cattails and brush stopped the breeze before it reached the screened porch off the kitchen and the little window of her bedroom. Her father insisted it was the best place for a year-round home, protected from the winter wind, circled by birds that perched on the puffy ends of the cattails, singing in the morning. It was a nice house, built in the 1950s and carefully decorated by Tracy's mother before she died, with drapes that matched the carpets, solid furniture, a sense of decor, rooms that had designated purposes and unique color schemes, not the helter-skelter mismatch of the summer renters next door.

They had coffee on the porch every day, Luke Giovanni, a lanky man with a narrow chest and expansive hands, receding brown hair and a jutting chin, and his daughter Tracy, flat-chested, all legs, lashless bright green eyes, with blonde hair that didn't seem to grow but to spin out of her head like cotton candy. Luke would intone the Latin names of the Red-wing Blackbirds and the Blue Martins. Tracy would clutch a big cup of warm milk with a dash of coffee, and lift her moustached lips to say, "Bluejay, male."

Her father owned Middle Lake Boat Sales off the highway, but would have nothing to do with the power boats he sold. His passion was canoeing, silently moving across the water before the sun had burned the mist off the lake, creeping up on the egrets and blackbirds, while the water dribbled off his paddle with a sound that didn't disturb a single wing.

Tracy was also a good canoeist, and it was a source of pride and companionship between them, until the summer she was ten. Tracy had been sitting placidly watching a young nest of blackbirds being fed by their mother when she was startled by the sound of a revving power-boat. The teen-age driver had pounded the dashboard and cursed. Tracy had hidden her canoe deeper in the reeds with a simple, noiseless turn of her paddle and had watched the kids pull aluminum cans tied with fishing wire from their motor. The cans were tangled hopelessly in the blades, battering the boat each time they tried to break away. They had shouted directions at each other, produced a knife, cut themselves free and, with an enormous surge of power that frightened all the birds into the air and stirred the silty bottom, they had cut across the lake, throwing the twisted cans behind them.

Tracy had paddled through the reeds to the cans and pulled them into her canoe. They shouldn't have been in this shallow water: they were disturbing the birds, she thought. They were lucky it hadn't destroyed their motor altogether. All the cans had had their labels carefully removed and Tracy hadn't seen any debris in the water. This could not have been simple rubbish. Who would tie cans together just to throw them away? As she held the dripping puzzle in her hands, the last can on the string caught her eye: it was a very old canister of ice skate wax, a can that was easily twenty years old, with dark red printing and bold letters on the metal, the same brand her father had always used and, dipping the last crusty bits from the bottom, had ceremoniously walked to the trash two days ago. Tracy looked across the lake at her cottage. What was her father doing? Sabotaging the summer residents? Why would he do this? Tracy covered the cans with a parka in the bottom of the canoe. If they found them he'd be ruined, she thought, furtively looking around her and suddenly filled with a fear not just of the doctors and their wives, but of her father. For the next two weeks, every day after Luke went to work, Tracy launched the canoe and pulled scores of booby-traps from the nesting grounds of birds.

"What are these?" she said softly when she returned one evening, pulling several lines of cans out of a sack. Her father turned his back on her and walked onto the porch.

"They're picking on the birds, Tracy," he said quietly.

"You can't ruin their boats, Dad," she said incredulously. "I mean . . . it's crazy."

"Starling."

"What?"

Her father sat in his chair on the porch and didn't turn around. Tracy stood behind him, holding the cans.

"Daddy, what are you going to . . . "

"Goldfinch, Martin," he said plaintively.

Tracy let the sack of cans drop to the floor in front of her and looked from the bag to the string of cans in her hand, to the back of her father's chair.

"Red-winged Blackbird."

"But tell me why, Dad."

"Barn owl, white-crested hawk."

Tracy stood very still, the cans still hanging off her hand. She wanted to turn to someone else for the answer, but no one was there.

"OK. We'll . . . take care of it, Dad," she said, with a tone she had never heard in her voice. "It'll be OK."

Today, in the hospital, Trout saw nurses trying to calm the people by talking slowly, pointing with what Trout thought were hypnotically slow movements of their arms. Don't do it, she recited as a silent plea to the nurses, don't be suffocated by them.

*P*atricia could see pieces of her home before she reached the remnants of her doorstep. Clocks and her tennis shoes, end tables, pipes and car wax and a broken basket from the kitchen lay in the street. Jack and Henry's flat next door was destroyed as well. Patricia held her hands out to the mess as if demanding an explanation, then covered her face and turned away. She opened her eyes and whirled around again with her legs spread wide for fear she would fall. The damn hallway just dared her to walk down it and call out for a beer.

It was evil, she thought, putting her hands on her hips, then dropping them to her side. It's mean and ugly, she thought. A working-class girl with a beautiful apartment, and not even a new one like a box with sloppy workmanship, but an eighty-year-old classic Victorian, with new furniture. And knowing how much she valued it (just to spite her, she knew it), they'd thrown it into the sand and turned it to junk.

"You lied to me!" she screamed, clenching her fists. She strode into the heap of her possessions and furiously threw them at the skeleton of the building, long arms flailing in the air, heaving pieces of cement and lathe, books and ashtrays down the tunnel of the hallway.

"Fucker you lied!" she screamed until her face was red and she held her hands like claws. I didn't ask for so much, she growled through clenched teeth. Something new. Something that's mine. Mine because I want it. She closed her eyes when she saw her living room furniture. Not because someone says what I can and cannot have, but because I wanted it. Something they couldn't take. She had been sure of it: it was secure; it was permanent. She had paid for it, goddamnit. And they'd taken it anyway. She didn't need to see anymore. What was there to see? All her clothes turned to rags? Everything she owned lookin' like garbage?

Where were Henry and Jack? Christ, how were they going to recover from this with Jack at death's door? And all her friends in the East Bay, where the faultlines were as numerous as freeways. She couldn't call them, couldn't take the BART to the other side of the bay. What tiny community of friends she had managed to build was now divorced and isolated. It was just her and Trout, if Trout could even get back. Why did she have to pick East Bay friends? What good were they when they couldn't get to her? She turned on her heel and walked away.

There really wasn't any place to go. Trout wouldn't be home for another day, at least, if there was any way she could get home. People on the street said the airport was destroyed, and there were lines at every phone booth even though the phones didn't work. Spouses Fulfill Obligation At Useless Phone: 'But Honey, I Tried,' They Wail.

Now, left alone, Patricia felt a familiar sadness overcoming her, a pain that spread through her chest and made her stop, lean against a wall. She walked again when people stared at her with frightened eyes as they hurried toward the

hospital. Did she look as terrified as they did? Patricia
wondered. The tool belt, still across her shoulder, seemed
heavier than ever. No, she might look as frightened, but not
as surprised. The world falling around her feet was
something Patricia had always expected. Whether it arrived
by nuclear destruction or mass murder or the Government
wiping out whole communities, the calm that Patricia felt told
her that devastation was something she had assumed was
around the corner. Now that it had finally happened she felt,
well, resigned.

Born and raised in a small town in Kentucky, Patricia had
grown up thinking that even the landscape was something
that took a lot and gave very little. Air was a humid glob you
had to struggle to breathe. Wind was a force you battled as
it blew coal dust on your laundry, your window sill, your shirt
as you walked through town. Winters froze the pipes,
chipped the red from the Coca-Cola signs. There was always
more snow than the roofs could bear, more rain than the
creeks could hold. Disaster poured from the sky and grew
from the earth in stinging nettles and black snakes, in coal
that settled in your lungs until your cheeks were gray and
mottled. When the mines collapsed, people shook their
heads in disbelief, but it made sense to Patricia: dig a hole,
the ground falls into it, sure as anything. No mystery. No
surprise. The earthquake felt the same way: build on landfill
and sand that shakes, you get shook.

She turned a corner, not certain where she was going,
knowing she didn't want to go back to the house without
Trout. What shit-ass luck could have destroyed that Victorian
she was working on, torn apart her own home, but spared
the junkhole Beth lived in? Home Equity No Match For
Fickle Fissures, she thought sarcastically.

Patricia crossed Mission and 14th streets and saw an
electrical transformer on fire, the flames jumping from the
metal canister like a hobo's campfire. On the street, two
women picked through fallen beams with urgency, the
women stepping back and covering their mouths, then
pushing forward with fear. As Patricia drew closer she heard
a woman's scream, shrill and tired, coming from under the
debris. The skin prickled on Patricia's arms. A woman's

hand poked above the rubble, waving despite assurances that they saw her by the people pulling away the boards. Patricia stood frozen on the sidewalk. The women threw the last board aside and struggled to pull the woman free. Her face, neck, and chest were covered with blood, running down her arms that were stiffly outstretched like a scarecrow, the hands limp. Patricia rushed to help them move the woman to the sidewalk. The other women burst into sobs and held each other as the woman lay on the cement, her skirt hiked up around her thighs, her mouth and eyes opened toward death. Her blood puddled on the sidewalk.

"Is she . . . ?" Patricia asked, then looked around. She had just been alive, and now the blood was running onto the sidewalk toward Patricia's boots; the woman's eyes rolled back in her head. The sound of the women crying and the woman's scream melded together in Patricia's ears and amplified.

"I'll just . . . get something to cover her," Patricia mumbled, and turned back to the house whose staircase had crumbled. In an alley beside the building, Patricia found a piece of green plastic. The crying of the women seemed to get louder, but as Patricia turned to address them, they were more than a block away, leaning on each other as they walked.

"Wait. You can't just . . ." she called. Patricia looked down at the body, saw the blood puddling around her boots. She covered the woman with plastic and stepped away, walked briskly in the opposite direction of the sobbing women. It wasn't her responsibility, she thought nervously. She should stay. What if . . . children ran across . . . it? What could she do anyway? The woman was dead. She'd tell the police if she ran into them. That was enough, wasn't it? Besides, it was up to those other women. They had found her. Maybe they were neighbors, or even relatives? Who could tell?

Patricia's long stride gobbled up the sidewalk. She didn't even know where she had been. What were the coordinates? The cross-street? Was it two blocks away? How could she tell the police where to find the body if she . . .

"Flowers?"

Patricia turned to a woman whose flower stand had lost its roof and one of its sides. She held out a small bouquet to her.

"You may as well take them," the woman said. "They won't sell on a night like tonight."

Patricia backed away, clasped her hands behind her.

"Glass of water? You could try a local phone call," the woman said, pointing at the rest of her offerings. "Spreading good cheer is my business . . . and you could use some."

Patricia looked at the daffodils, smelled the roses from where she stood. She was thirsty, and she should try to call Evelyn and Marie, but she shook her head and continued down the street. Flowers, she thought with disgust. Definitely not a time for flowers, no matter how nice they were.

Looking up from the pavement, a familiar site caught her eye: Sabito's, the dyke bar in the Mission, looking suddenly incongruous. Sensible enough she would wander this way, and reasonable enough there should be a dyke bar in her path—this was San Francisco, after all—but in the midst of this destruction and loss, a bar, not crumbled. And safe. At least it was someplace she knew well, she thought, thinking of how much she could use a beer.

*I*n the financial district, 36th floor, the earthquake took even the veterans by surprise. They had felt the floor rolling on its specially-engineered struts, subject to a strong wind. Life up this high was like living on a willow branch and one simply got used to the sway, grew accustomed to seeing newspapers as a new species of bird floating on a breeze between the buildings. Those who weren't acquainted with the unique geography that existed thirty stories up would stop their work when the wind went by and take nervous inventory of survival items—shoes, coats, wallets, and bags. This one, however, even the San Francisco natives knew immediately was the Big One. The building shifted violently, dipping the entire floor as if bending to touch the sidewalk, and throwing everyone in the office onto desks or the floor.

Lynn was not there to see her desk move across the room and smash into her coveted glass door. The meeting had gone poorly and she was just now taking her lunch in MacArthur Park, sitting on a stone bench that was protected by a circle of leafy trees. Across the park, the falling glass tore whole branches. The shards of glass dug into the ground like knives, their blades pink from the eerie light. Lynn saw the glass rain into the street, moving the suspended arms of a sculpture that was yards in front of her, making the metal beams moan. She saw people falling to their knees, their blood spilling around them. She whirled in a circle, still holding her sandwich, then dove underneath the stone bench.

All those coveted window offices were exploding. Mine, too, Lynn thought. Papers blowing out the windows. Nothing left of any office, all the work ended now. My God, right this minute, millions are being lost.

People who rushed outdoors in fear the building would fall now darted back inside as the glass formed lethal piles on the sidewalk.

Lynn's mind felt like a rotor in an engine, spinning and striking, igniting on its own insides.

I'll just stay here, she thought, curled under this cement bench. Let it all fall down, they won't miss me. I'm the boss but they won't notice. 'Trade with China,' they said at the meeting. 'An incredible market to be penetrated,' and they didn't notice this blonde was one of 'them,' you know. I couldn't say my father was a serviceman, my mother half-Chinese: I should have said it. Sitting in the meeting on how to negotiate, the man said they're like the Indians, with their ritual of gifts. They laughed, 'Just like the Indians, bring 'em some beads,' they said, my peers, some of them my own employees, and I didn't say a thing. I don't ever talk about this . . . being Chinese.

Lynn never ventured too far down Montgomery or Post because she'd be there, at the base of the Pyramid building, at the Holiday Inn, and the walkway that could deposit her at the community grounds of Chinatown where the men played checkers during the day and the old women walked round-shouldered on their hobbled feet, a single item in a plastic shopping bag. On the other side of the Pyramid, people boiled eggs in tea and hung ducks by their necks. Her father would never have permitted that. Her family had brushed away the little bits of red paper that firecrackers left behind on their doorstep New Year's Day. Mother had learned Mexican cooking and the secrets of potroast.

The sound of destruction from Chinatown brought it down the street to her, though, rumbling like engines in a huge train yard as the brick buildings collapsed and their wood frames tore apart. The meeting she had just attended brought images of Beijing sailing from the glassless window frames like the lethal spikes, down to her in the park. It wouldn't let her wander with her blinders on, or allow her to walk around the fringes of Chinatown, through MacArthur Park and up into the glass spires. Now that the company was opening trade with China, and she was on the negotiating team, she would either have to pretend ("Are the Chinese like that?" she would have to coo, "How interesting") or become visible.

Lynn especially wouldn't cross into Chinatown today, not now with the glass piled around her like a sea. On both sides of her, above her in her glass office, and up the street into Chinatown, the shattered buildings made it clear she was Chinese. She would be exposed either way, she thought: either to the whites in the office as Chinese, or to those who really knew as a Chinese woman ignorant of her own culture. This tremble has gone inside me and won't stop coming out, she thought. Lynn pressed her face into the moist grass and covered her ears.

*T*rout stood hypnotized by the movements of the nurses dipping into a box filled with paper instructions, passing them out with the gestures of machines. The movement of providing is so smooth, so flawless. But try to end it: it's as abrupt as pulling the brake handle on a train.

Every evening of her childhood, Trout's father had gone out in the canoe and laid more traps. Tracy had gotten up in the morning and pulled them out. She volunteered to do the grocery shopping and stopped buying canned food. Luke stopped asking her about her day. In the evenings, he would sit in his chair reciting the nesting habits of the local birds, sometimes halting mid-sentence to take her hand and spend the rest of the evening in silence.

At the end of the summer, when the wind started battering the willow trees not just in the evenings but in the afternoon as well, Tracy's father would announce with great jubilance: "The egrets and we will be happy to know that the season is over!" Luke would lay off his staff, shutter the boat depot, register for unemployment, put away his canoe, and chop wood for the fireplace. Tracy would go back to school.

As the snow fell, her father would bring out his binoculars and watch the lake turn black and freeze, holding a finger up in the morning over coffee to silence her. "The ice is cracking. Two feet thick now," he would say with a smile, then rise to bring his skates out of the closet. The lake was deserted, the bars and clubs shuttered, the rental units empty most of the time, the expensive homes sitting vacant. The birds that remained stayed silently huddled in the twisted bushes. The landscape was a black lake draped in white like the couches and chandeliers in the homes of the rich.

Tracy's father would glide into this motionless landscape on a pair of old black skates, looking, she thought, like a giant crow, his arms tight at his side, hands clutched behind his back. Tracy would pick up her school books and watch him leave, never sure how many hours he would stay out or where he'd go. By then he knew the names of the birds of South America.

The Giovanni's nearest year-round neighbor was a woman named Maggie, secretary at the Lakeside Chamber of Commerce. The next spring, Trout had watched Maggie load an overnight case and her purse into her car when Luke strode across the lawns and clambered into the passenger seat. Maggie had shrugged her shoulders, palms up, as if confused but resigned, and had driven off with her father.

Four hours later, Maggie had screeched to a halt in
Trout's driveway and burst into the house, dragging Luke by
the arm.

"Your daddy's a lunatic, do you know that? Crazy as a
goddamn loon," Maggie had said confrontively.

"You OK, Dad?" Tracy had asked.

"He makes us go into this antique store, I don't know why
and I don't think he does, either. He finds this lamp, a
dancing hippo. Pretty soon, he's skating around the place,
laughing like a maniac."

Tracy had smiled.

"This is no laughing matter, my dear. I had to drag him
into the street, he was laughing so loud. People stepped into
the street to avoid us. Like he was Manson in a cutlery shop
or something. I'm tellin' you the man is touched."

"Hippo's figure eight," Luke had announced, skating
around the room and holding his arm up like the hippo lamp.

"What in the name of God is goin' on here?" Maggie had
asked incredulously. She looked at the secretive little girl in
front of her. Tracy had been standing with a screwdriver in
one hand, the door of a small cabinet in the other. A
jumbled pile of mail cascaded onto the floor at her feet,
envelopes of bills and past due notices covering the ends of
her shoes. Maggie had turned and stormed through the
house. She opened all the kitchen cupboards and found
them empty, inspected the dirty refrigerator, scowled over
the state of the oven. She opened all the crusted metal
canisters. Maggie checked the sheets on the bed and pushed
her way into the laundry room, where the dirty clothes were
piled so high they kept the door from being opened.

"Lord God, child, who's been takin' care of you?" Maggie
said. When Tracy didn't answer, Maggie rubbed her face with
her hands and walked around the kitchen.

"Dad," little Tracy said softly, "go onto the porch and
watch the birds. I saw an egret this morning."

"Egret," Luke said, dropping his arm and striding to where
his binoculars hung from a peg, hurrying onto the porch.

"We can manage," Tracy said defiantly.

"Oh, you can manage. Who's been doing the cooking?"

"We eat peanut butter. And baloney. I used to buy boxes of stuff I saw on TV but. . ."

"Oh you do?"

"And I copy what other kids have in their lunch bags."

Maggie turned away, bit her lip.

"I can take care of him," Tracy said.

"This is not about who's takin' care of him," Maggie had said angrily. "This is about who is takin' care of you. Your grandma alive?"

"No."

Maggie had put her hands on her hips. "You got an aunt, or a cousin? How about an uncle?"

"I don't know them. Maggie," Tracy said, "teach me to run the washer-dryer. Everything's got spots when it comes out."

"You're an eleven-year-old child."

Tracy had thrown her shoulders back in her wrinkled white blouse, her plaid school uniform and white socks that bagged around her ankles.

"We're learning about the food groups in school."

"The food groups," Maggie said and leaned on the counter. "Well, God knows being a ward of the state isn't any pretty way to grow up either, I'm not suggesting that. Seen too many girls turn to hookers and potheads after juvie hall," she said under her breath.

"He ever hit you, or get mad?" Maggie said pointedly.

"No!"

"Is there a gun in this house?"

"No. Just teach me a couple things, Maggie," Tracy said. "I can do the rest."

Maggie had folded her arms and sighed. "I dare say a bright little thing like you prob'ly could," she said with resignation. "But we're writing letters to your relatives." She pointed at the pile of envelopes on the floor.

Maggie had rolled her sleeves up and followed Tracy to the laundry room, pulling mounds of clothes from behind the door.

"First thing you gotta do is separate the whites from the colors," she said, beginning her instruction.

Maggie had taught her to preheat the oven, iron her
school blouses, took her to the grocery store every week and
taught her to plan meals. She bought Tracy a little step-stool
to put in front of the washing machine, to carry to the stove.

"These are your best friends," Maggie had said, holding
the instructions to the washing machine in one hand, the
recipe on the back of a box in the other hand. Together,
they hung instruction booklets from short white strings on
the knobs of all the appliances. My best friends, Tracy had
thought, looking at the small white papers that fluttered from
all corners of the house.

The nurses in the hospital were passing out sheets of
white paper, and the arms straining upward to grab them
made Trout close her eyes, clutch her stomach. Her best
friends? she wondered sadly, now that they were scattered
under slabs of plaster.

*P*atricia set her tool belt on a stool, put her foot on the
metal boot-rail and leaned against the bar. Clasping her
hands, and turning from her image in the mirror, she wasn't
sure if she should order a drink or offer to check the
electrical. Just to have found Sabito's still standing, without
dead bodies or trapped women inside was a long, cool tall
one, to her. Half the lesbos hanging against the side walls,
feeling silly with their hands stuck in their pockets for lack of
anything else to do, she thought. Everybody looking like
they're on their first date, a bit numb and dazed, Patricia
thought, kicking the bar with her boot. Despite how much
she wanted to talk about the woman who lay dead on the
sidewalk (Christ, should I have stayed? she wondered), she
wasn't going to join the wailers over by the wall.

"You can't get to Palo Alto, I'm telling you," she heard a
woman say to someone sitting in a chair with her face in her
hands. "All the roads are destroyed. Someone said the
freeway overhang fell the fuck down." The seated woman
leaned back against the wall and sobbed.

"Louise, you servin' at this point?" Patricia, noticing that no one was drinking, knew she wouldn't have said anything had she checked first. Well the whole city destroyed, daughter trompin' around after ducks, screams of women in her ears, she could bloody well have a beer in the afternoon if she wanted.

"I think that's an idea whose time has come," said Louise, hauling a case of beer from the cooler.

Louise perched on her stool and talked about damage to the bar, swigged on a beer like it was oxygen after a run, swapped a few stories, as the others had, but with caution. "I grabbed hold a'this bar and rode it," Louise said to Patricia, laying her chest on the bar and grasping the railing. "Always did say the world's safest place is behind a bar," she said, laughing.

Patricia looked at her closely. She was passed out, Patricia thought incredulously. Nobody would throw themselves on a goddamn bar. And today she was hung-over but good. Puffed up like she's got prunes for eyes and a rutabaga for a nose, she's telling me about safe, Patricia thought. She was tempted to ask Louise what it had been like to watch the bricks fall out of the wall, but she didn't. The woman'd just lie. Potato-Head Insists She Don't Grow In Dirt.

Louise looked away and grasped the draft beer spigot, knowing she was unmasked. Screw it. What a woman drinks is her own business. She functioned. That was the real test, wasn't it? As for the girl thing, well, maybe Patricia'd hang in with the code: never peal back another butch's armor.

"How about you?" Louise asked. "Where were you?"

"Working," Patricia said, then turned away. She wasn't going to describe running through the Mission looking for a daughter she knew so little about, or standing in the junk yard of her house doing as much damage with her anger as the earthquake had. She wasn't going to describe the blood on the sidewalk or leaving a dead body in the street. Louise had evened the score.

Patricia saw people on the street look on the scene with caution but not cross the line of broken glass to walk in any

sooner than they would have come through the swinging
doors on a Saturday night. The women's closed faces replied
that this was not a time for curiosity.

Now, left without lover or daughter, Patricia was at a loss,
and very frightened, she had to admit as she wrapped her
hands around the beer bottle. Beth didn't care, hadn't even
bothered to come home to her place or comment that her
mother had nearly been killed. Well, Patricia cared. She was
ruined, she knew that. Just when she finally had something.
Sure, they were just renters, but things were starting to get
better. Now they'd have to pay for the old furniture and buy
new. Hadn't a pissy nickel of savings and no way to get any
more. She shook her head, remembering Mark telling her, as
she ran by the job site again still looking for Beth, that the
garage had fallen on the truck and flattened the cab. She
hadn't even thought of it 'til now. Her truck was destroyed
and most of her tools ruined inside it. She could bet her ass
that someone who let their whole house fall down wasn't
going to worry about paying some dyke and a queen for the
thousands of dollars in labor they'd put into the house. She
was out the wages she had given Mark and there wasn't a
lot of opportunities to make it up: with the earthquake, the
union would be down at City Hall watchin' every single
building permit and the inspectors would be doin' double
time. Everyone rebuilding would need electricians, but the
world didn't work like that. She was a good electrician, but
an unlicensed one. You could remodel someone's house or
re-wire their kitchen without anyone being the wiser but when
it came to building a house from the ground up, it took
contractors and licenses pasted all over hell and back. And
the little jobs, well, there might be a lot of those, but the
permit department would put all the paperwork for major
construction ahead of remodel jobs and she'd go broke
waiting for the high sign to start. You got one chance at
things, if that many, Patricia thought, taking a long pull on
her beer. Life had made it clear to her that she got slightly
less than one.

*N*ice cologne, Cherice thought, perspiring slightly as she slipped his cotton shirt off one arm, then the next.

"Can you get your. . ."

"No," Jacob said sharply, holding his foot off the ground with both hands cupped under his knee. "What are you, a nun or something? Just take my damn shirt off." What's the matter with this woman, Jacob thought?

Cherice frowned. Bastard. She yanked the cotton undershirt from inside his pants and pulled it over his head. He scrambled to get his arms out without letting his foot drop, but it banged against the floor anyway. Cherice tore the shirt with her teeth.

"I need the light," she said gruffly. Jacob leaned against the wall and fished in his pocket. In the sudden light, Cherice's face was pulled into a fierce scowl. Jacob flipped the light off.

"All right, I'm sorry," he said, then flicked the lighter again. Nice lips, he thought. They look very soft, and very full. He wondered how he'd missed them the first time he looked.

Cherice glared at him. "I need the light here," she said pointedly, and took off his shoe, removed his sock. "Ooh, God," she said.

"Is it horrible?"

"Well, you're either very black and blue or there's some weird-ass shadows in here. Now hold still."

She wrapped his ankle until he balked.

"Lay down," she said, "we've got to keep this elevated."

"I thought you weren't a Girl Scout."

She cradled his foot in her lap, took the lighter from his hand and watched him settle himself on the floor.

"Do you want your shirt back on?"

"No. I don't know whether it's the Valium or the wrap, but that feels better."

She extinguished the light. "Now what?"

"Well where's this auxiliary power?" he said. "Must have been a hell'uva quake. You have anyone worrying at home?"

Cherice was silent.

"Me either. Jacob, Jacob Lefkowitz," he said, tentatively putting his hand out in the dark.

"Nice to meet you," she said. "Cherice Butler."

Jacob dropped his hand, since it couldn't be seen in the dark and it had met no other flesh. Cherice leaned against the wall, his foot heavy in her lap. Jacob lay back down on the floor. In the darkness, they felt themselves alone, and yet listened closely to each other's breathing. Their movements took on larger-than-life proportions. As the hours went by, Jacob fell asleep, and Cherice listened to him snore. She must have dozed off herself, then woke when Jacob flinched as he awoke.

Cherice reached behind her for the phone.

"Pepperoni, double mushrooms," she said, then covered the mouthpiece with her hand. "Whadd'ya say, medium? I don't think we could finish a large."

"Very funny," he said, not lifting his head from the floor. Jacob heard the receiver bounce against the wall.

"Is it the dark, or did you lie about the dosage?" Jacob said. "I feel like I'm trapped at an office party after too much Scotch."

"And you know it will come up during your salary review tomorrow."

"Oh Christ. . . So," he said, hoping conversation would push away the darkness pressing on him, "what do you do for a living?"

"You already guessed. I'm a stock broker."

Jacob snorted, chewed the inside of his lip for a moment. "Check the time, will ya?" he said, flicking on the lighter.

"7:10. We've been in here more than four hours!" she said. He flicked off the light.

"I'm an accountant," he said to the darkness. "And not a very good one," he said with more hostility than defensiveness.

"Oh, that's probably not true," she said without conviction.

"No. It is true," he said. "Especially true on Valium. And I'm not a saxophone player trapped in an accounting firm. I'm just not very good."

Cherice was silent, the darkness filled in with the sound of her unasked question.

"Well," he said, his voice rising, "what's wrong with that? You never met a man who admitted he was mediocre?"

"No," she said softly, surprised by her answer. "Come to think of it, I haven't."

"Neither have I." King of the Hill, all that, he thought.

"The few, the proud, the accountants," he said. So what do you do when you're just a poor schmuck with no talent? I don't know. I don't care. "Try tellin' the boys that at racquetball: I have no desire to be vice president. You know what they say when you talk like that? They tell 'ya to get laid."

Cherice snorted, turned away.

"Seriously," he said. "Like pussy's the problem. Sorry, sorry," he said, touching her arm in the dark. "But they're your drugs, you know."

"They always used to feel like low dosage," she said dreamily, leaning her head against the wall.

"So, you've met your first man who's not on his way up."

The elevator suddenly jerked forward, the lights flickering on. Both Cherice and Jacob let out a yell, Cherice clambering to her feet, dropping his foot with a thud. She pounded on the door.

"Not up, down, you asshole!" she shouted, as the elevator slid smoothly up the building.

*T*rout knew she should be rushing through the city to find Patricia, but where? She watched people hesitantly leaving the hospital, gripping their maps with white-knuckled hands. Maggie says these papers are your best friends, she chanted, but a voice inside her didn't believe it any longer.

The summer of Maggie's discovery, Trout's relatives had arrived in a steady stream. They had sat on the edge of the sofa, wringing their hands, cajoling Luke to enroll her in a boarding school. He just laughed and leaned toward Tracy, nodding his head toward Uncle Sid.

"He's a horny owl," he whispered, and Tracy tried not to smile.

Relatives had timidly offered to send her themselves, but she wouldn't go, not to a school, not to their homes, even

for a summer, she said. They had looked at Tracy with
cautious eyes. Mental illness was hereditary, wasn't it, they
had seemed to ask. Foster homes were out of the question:
middle-class children did not go to foster homes, and if they
did, the child would never be middle-class again. No, the
family would have to make the best of it by themselves.
Besides, their concern and their half-hearted attempts to
make a difference had been met with the closed face of a
wild-haired girl standing resolutely behind her father's chair,
one hand protectively on his shoulder.

"I can do this, Aunt Grace. I can take care of it," Tracy
had said in a fierce voice.

Numbers had always been something to rely on, Trout
thought as she groped toward a bus-stop bench in the street.
Always, one could count on the numbers. Years ago, her
father's lawyer had sold the boat business and the check
had more numbers on it than Tracy had ever seen. Relatives
sent money. Distant cousins arrived to hesitantly inspect the
cupboards and refrigerator as if a box of insanity might jump
off the shelf and spill on them. A few days after their
departure, they sent a check. The dividends from her
mother's life insurance arrived in small manila envelopes:
From the account of Lucille Giovanni. Tracy would hold
them to her cheek as if they were a kiss.

As the pile of mail grew on the hat-rack table and her
father sat deeper in his recitations, Tracy learned to forge his
signature and pay the bills. She sat on a footstool in front of
him and checked his teeth, scheduled his dental
appointments and took him shopping for new clothes,
ushering him around with a magazine picture in her hand.

In the evening, Luke would pull out a map of the lake and
begin his winter's plotting: "There's a gap in the ice here," he
would say solemnly, warning his daughter away from the
area. Every day the circles changed, carefully drawn in
pencil and then erased. Tracy regarded him with a
suspicious eye. If he had spent the summer sabotaging
boats, what was he doing in the winter? When the two or
three ice-fishing shacks sent up a thin plume of smoke on a
Saturday morning, Tracy brought out her own skates to
check for markings of another secret campaign.

Each day that winter, she watched her father sliding across the ice with a feeling that he slipped further away, pushing across a lake that expanded every morning, taking him deeper into a world where no one heard the rhythmic scratch of his blades on the ice. When was he going to lose track of the fissures and fall in, lost in a place that was forbidding, uncharted, governed by rules he couldn't see, just like the world he inhabited above the ice?

Very much like the world she inhabited today, Trout thought as she pushed her way through the crowd at the hospital, out onto the street to find Patricia. Houses didn't stay standing, and the straight yellow street lines were buckled and torn. What simple law of logic governed the world now?

As she hurried toward the Mission and what she hoped was a safe and secure Patricia, Trout saw people in the street in clothing not suited for the time, without coats or the things they generally held to occupy their hands. A woman slipped into a man's jacket to cover her torn blouse, and a child was wrapped into a pair of women's shorts. A gay man, showing the irony of it all, Trout smiled, sauntered down the street with a broken umbrella held like a parasol, Auntie Mame in a demolition zone. The winos and homeless smiled as the streets filled with people muttering to themselves. Some people had returned to their homes, their wives back from jobs, their children nearby, and they threw themselves into work, the men shoveling piles of sand and brick-dust in methodical, unseeing gestures. Women tried to fit lock to door to roof. Groups of young men in shirt sleeves, deciding to work together, tried to reconstruct the houses they lived in, while a woman with a crying baby sat on what had been a stoop. Women frantically searched for something to enclose what was theirs and keep out what was not, so futile when the earthquake had shaken apart the lines that separated a family from what belonged in the street. Everywhere she walked, Trout saw the bars filling and she began walking faster: these people knew their fate, and hers was yet to be discovered.

The neighbors at Patricia's job site hurried to tell her that 'the lady worker' had escaped and gone off to find her daughter. Trout inspected the destroyed truck and double-checked the details of Patricia's safety, afraid to peer into the collapsed garage.

As she continued farther up Market Street, people congregated at cable car turnabouts and rapid transit stops, the lines inoperable now but still drawing people as if they were the litmus test of the city's health. Trout stood with people staring at the subway opening, waiting to ride anywhere, in any direction, under the assumption that the lines only ran to safer places.

Weaving among the groups of would-be travelers, a juggler and a mime set out their baskets and performed to stunned silence, as if the audience thought it sacrilege to interrupt the somber fear that kept them all staring at the metro line. Then the people shifted. "We're standing up, after all," a woman said with a strained metallic din in her voice. Their children were frightened but safe, and here were these entertainers. She mentioned to any adult who would catch her eye her anxiety, "would there, wouldn't there" be a train to take her to someone's house in the avenues or a destination she hadn't yet chosen, "don't you know." The travelers looked down Market Street toward the financial district, where the sun glinted off piles of glass and the red flash of ambulance lights shot the piles with the look of blood. They turned to the mime and the circling balls. The performers didn't mind sharing the same street corner, their faces told each other, glad for once to share this audience suddenly ready to suck whatever distraction they could from the deft little hands and the white face paint.

This was insurmountable, Trout thought, as the striped and spotted balls were flung against the gray sky. It was all irreparably damaged, and as she said it vehemently to herself, with a jaw that clenched down on the words so tightly, she nearly growled out loud. Her stomach clenched and she turned away from the circling balls for fear she'd vomit again. What were they going to do without a home, without a plan? What was she going to tell Patricia? That she had run out of ideas? Preposterous. Out of stamina, suddenly drained of ability? Was she stalling for time by strolling through the Mission?

The longer they had lived together, the more complex the machinery had become. To start over now, with new appliances, new due dates for carpet cleaning and fire alarm battery checks . . . Trout stepped away from the crowd. It's not that they owned more stuff than other people, just that she was, well, responsible. Until now. She couldn't understand the fatigue she felt. She was probably in shock, she thought (What is the statistically-average duration of surprise, she wondered), but this seemed deeper, a voice she had listened to before, with disastrous consequences. Trout shook her head, and began walking again.

Like a loud clap that stops a barking dog, the crack of the earthquake had stopped traffic and trains, making the mime's and silent juggler's stage seem large. With the electricity cut in parts of the city, the workers poured into the street, marching resolutely toward their homes, flagging down the sporadic truck lucky enough to be salvaged and tough enough for the broken streets. The men and women filled the backs of pickups, hung off the sides and the bumpers, charging forward as if going to war, as if heading toward victory or manhood, Trout thought. She heard their jittery, overly-loud shouting, their calls across the streets at passers-by and thought that the men hanging from the running boards didn't seem to know, honestly, if they were courageous. All their lives they had prepared themselves to be capable of great bravery. All of their games and guns and fighting as boys had been to make them of the stuff for heroic deeds and great rescues. Instead, those who thought they would be brave were tested and judged by a rumbling that lasted less than sixty seconds, given barely time to remember how they felt, let alone how valiantly they had reacted. When the city collapsed, they were not pulling their wives from cliff tops or beating a man bigger than they. The men of the city were working, heads down. Trout frowned. Cheated of the moment they had longed for, the brave seemed surly and resentful.

Trout arrived at Beth's house but found it empty. Neighbors said the girl had sauntered out of her house as if checking the weather. Sounds like she's healthy and in her usual mood, Trout thought. Patricia would take Beth to a *rescue center*, as the people in the street had called it. No doubt the kid had no money or food. The nearest center was Dolores Park. Trout pulled her hair into a neat bun, secured it with a pencil, as if hoping that would tidy what she considered her shameless hesitation. Plan or no plan, she said resolutely, finding Patricia was the most important thing in the world.

*P*atricia, almost her entire torso stretched across the length of the bar, looked out at the street, at the brick and the picture frames that had been the side of Sabito's. This was where she had started, downhearted in the ruins. Success had taken an off-ramp before reaching her Kentucky town, inventions and opportunities finding the winding two-lane freeway over the mountains too much an effort to settle in a town as small and gray as hers. Life, where things moved and changed, well, that was television, jungles where birds grew as big as rabbits, and deserts stretched farther than camels could walk in a month. She stared as if the pictures could bring the textures to her, and she imagined the feel of the sand against her skin, the smoothness of the leaves of an exotic plant.

Patricia and her mother had lived in town, a geographic position her mother defended like cans in the pantry and socks without holes. They weren't going to live in a holler, her mother frequently said with her hands on her hips. "No tin roof over my baby's head," she'd say, shaking a spoon at Patricia to make her grateful for what they had. "What are you complain' about: there's no chickens outside your bedroom winda'." They lived above the hardware store whose downstairs windows were festooned with U-joints and garden gloves, the stairway to her front door smelling faintly of WD-40 and the oily covering on nails. As a child, she had sat in her front window when she wasn't watching television and pushed aside the polyester lace curtains, peered over the window box of plastic flowers and watched the men come and go with their little brown paper sacks, their lengths of pipe and wire tied with string. Was that one my father? she had wondered. Was his nose my nose? Do I walk like he does? Who's got some of this black hair of mine?

The father of her memory had been the circus, popcorn in striped boxes, tigers walking in a circle. Her father was the hairy hand who steadied her step up the bleachers. He was the light that swept the tops of the canvas and shone on the woman in sequined tights. Her father was a ride with the windows down and a man's deep laugh as the night blew her hair in front of her face. When she came home from seeing him on his evenings for custody, her father was her mother rocking in the overstuffed chair, the back rhythmically bumping into the kitchen table as the woman smoked cigarettes and didn't turn to look. Then, her father was the sound of truck tires scattering stones in the street as if fleeing disaster. By the time she was six, there was no sound of the truck at all.

That was what he had been, Patricia concluded as she leaned on the bar in Sabito's, the sound of little stones under a truck making a get-away. It sounded too much like today: no cars, no trucks on the street, only the cry of frightened women, the shriek of children who don't understand where everything's gone.

Patricia's mother had been a secretary for the Catholic church and its two-room school, typing funeral notices and letters to the owners of the coal mines asking for donations to the coal fund, the clothing fund, the book fund for the poor. She wasn't Catholic, but seemed to fall into that category of people whose "hardship" meant she didn't have to practice the religion. She was a "good works" that kept the priests' balance sheet of giving always in the black, her mother said bitterly.

One spring morning, Patricia had been standing in the schoolyard holding Meredith's hand, the wind whipping at the hem of her mother's new flowered dress and raising goosebumps where the neckline V-d toward her breasts. The head nun had walked over to her and, without looking at Patricia, had said with a forced smile, "Meredith, dear, you'll catch your death in that . . . outfit. Why don't you dress more . . . sensibly? Perhaps a wool skirt from what we've gathered for the church. . ." she had said under her breath. Meredith had tightly gripped her daughter's hand, turned to the nun with her nostrils flaring. "I don't wear second-hand clothing, Sister Marie." She had turned on her open-heeled shoes and, striding faster than Patricia could run, returned to the office.

"You take a lesson, there, girl," Meredith had growled, "underneath all the blessings—the sharp teeth of real people." Sisters of the Oozing Pity, Meredith had mumbled under her breath.

Where the hell was Trout? Patricia thought, grabbing her beer as if tempted to throw it against the wall. Their whole life had just been turned to church bazaar items, stuff for a fifty-cent grab bag. There was no sense to it, but then accepting the logic of things had never been her strong suit. That was Trout's forte, and Meredith's.

Patricia's mother had seemed in an endless struggle to make sense of things, then to finally give up and cross over the line into simple categorization. Her mother would recount the plots of soap operas and talk shows as she did her ironing, as Patricia did the dishes.

"Jason Finds Love in the Law Office," her mother said, pressing the iron into a cotton shirt. "Melanie Lost Without Purpose After Baby Dies." She listed events and motivations like the contents of flash-cards, grocery lists.

Music could be captured in four or five words: "'Heart Lost in Marina Del Ray.' Hand me that pilla' case. 'Man Leaves to Drive with Friends,' God, I'd beat the bastard said that to me." Soon, it was: "'Daughter Gets C in English.' Any stupider, you won't even make it as a waitress. You know how to spell 'toast'?"

As she grew into high school, Patricia stood two feet taller than her mother. Meredith looked up, needle and thread in hand. "P.D. Sprouts to Six Feet," her mother said softly. Patricia grew out of her desk at school, her long legs jutting out like uncovered roots. "Young Patty Deneane Joins Track Team, Cashes In On Lanky Legs," her mother said. At high school graduation, her gown barely covered her knees.

"Miniskirt Fashion Saves Graduate from Embarrassment," her mother whispered to herself as she sat with proud tears collecting in a hankie.

Most days, Meredith would be home when Patricia returned from school, greeting her daughter with her evening call as the child climbed the stairs. "Shake that dust off before you come in here. I got somethin' special for dinner." Some nights, though, Meredith would return late, having crossed from their dry county into one that clustered its bars on the street just beyond the reach of the voter's jurisdiction. When she came into the apartment, anger would cling to the woman's hair like smoke, its heaviness pulling her red hair from its banded ponytail. She would flop into her overstuffed chair as if she had struggled her way through an incredible blaze. The smoky haze that clung to her mother would color the events of the day, until it wasn't the priest or the nuns she railed against, but a waitress who hadn't brought cheese for her eggs, and a traffic light that wouldn't, goddamnit, wouldn't turn green.

Patricia had developed a stormy temper of her own, sometimes bursting in the door after school and heaving her books down the stairs, stomping into her room and tearing a shirt from collar to cuff. Her mother would speak to her very gently and continue to set the table for dinner, sometimes might even brush her hair. Anger was soothed, and it seemed only right, Patricia had thought, there was a lot in the world to be angry about. Tenderness: that was pickin' shattered coffee cups from between the canisters, under the stove.

*B*eth slouched down Portrero Avenue with her black
leather jacket hanging open, pinching the end of her
unlit cigarette with her teeth. Army Street was wall-to-wall
cars, people swarming between them. The access ramps to
the freeway had collapsed and there was no going southward
except on foot, people said. Suits me fine, Beth thought, I'm
headin' toward the ocean: Michael said the boat would pick
them up there.

Two boys on motorcycles pulled up in front of Beth and
Michael, screeching to a halt inches from their feet.

"My motorcycle," he shouted. "Shit, I thought someone
stole it."

"They did, man," the boy on the bike laughed.

"Take us to the ocean," Michael shouted over the roar of
the engines. "China Beach."

"Where the fuck is that?"

"C'mon, let's go!"

Michael motioned Beth on to the back of one of the bikes
as he jumped onto the other. The four of them inched their
way through the city, driving on sidewalks, swerving between
cars, over the hills, past Twin Peaks and finally through the
Presidio.

Beth stood at the railing of the China Beach Recreation
Building, lighting her cigarette. Why had all these people
showed up by the side of the ocean? The place was in good
shape, still the long, low pink building that was covered on
the weekends with sunbathers and families with hot dogs.
She had come here a few times, but just walked through
with her friends, six of them in black pants, safety pins,
leather jackets, scuffing their boots along the cement. Today
there were no families. On the lawn Beth saw a group of
Fairy People holding hands in a circle.

"You're never going to believe this," Michael said,
suddenly standing at her elbow and making Beth jump.

"Shit. You scared me. Where's the boat?"

"It's pickin' up people south of the city, not here," Michael
said. "Look at this." He pulled a huge roll of bills from his
pocket. "The bike, man, I sold the bike."

Beth pulled the cigarette out of her mouth. "Why the fuck
did you sell the bike?" she said, incredulously.

"Are you kidding? Can't you see all this cash?" he said, in hushed tones. "Five times what I paid for it! For that I can skip out on the payments and look . . . profit. Pure and simple."

"How we gonna get to the boat, you asshole?"

"Fuck the boat."

"Then why are we here?"

"For the bike, bimbo! The deal. Cash!"

Beth turned away from him, took a few steps backward. Turning in a slow circle, she said nothing, took another drag of her cigarette and pitched it with a flick of her fingers. Another lyin' bastard, she thought. Beth looked back at the group at China Beach. Pointless to argue and a waste to stay.

She walked slowly through the forested Presidio, toward the city. Truckloads of reserve soldiers, called back to a deserted Presidio, were shipping out in trucks with flapping canvas sides. With a sudden burst of energy, Beth jumped onto the fender of one of the trucks, pulled aside the canvas back and, discovering it empty, hauled herself inside.

"Hey girl," a voice inside called softly from one of the dark corners.

"Who's there?" Beth said cautiously. A woman leaned forward, a young punk in old black pants, kerchief over her head, bright red lips. She handed Beth a small flask.

"Think they'll get us outa here?" the girl asked. Beth sniffed the mouthpiece, took a long swallow, shrugged her shoulders.

The women rode through the city without concern for their destination, finished the whiskey, stumbled out of the truck as it veered from Army Street, away from the freeway, toward Third Avenue.

A little woozy from the drink, and disoriented from the sudden bright sun, the women stood near the overpass and stared. People struggled up the broken structure like rock climbers on their first foray, all heading south, away from the City. Behind them, houses built on the bedrock of Portrero Hill were still standing, but the huge green water tower above the Projects had burst a seam and it spouted like waterfalls in movies of Brazil. Beth's view of the houses and roads below the tower was obliterated by the white cascade.

"Let's go," Beth said, and the women joined the caravan of people.

Beth slung her leather jacket over her shoulder and rolled up the sleeves of her white shirt. They wove their way between the cars, at first joking about the leather upholstery, the dangling mirror ornaments, the doilies on the back ledge. Soon, the cars seemed a blur, just another obstacle. With increasing frequency, men selling goods appeared at the sides of the crowds, clambering up the embankment with a sack of apples or a jug of water. The crowd pushed toward the sellers, suddenly animated. Beth and the punk girl (named K, she had said), pushed their way toward the water, then fell back. One dollar a glass, the man said, and took in fistfuls of money despite protests from the walkers. Beth angrily pushed people aside and left the circle. She hadn't thought about water, or food, or how long it would take her to get to the boat.

The girls looked at each other and started walking, past the men who were gathering at the side of the road, hawking pieces of plastic, empty bottles, ropes. Beth found a milk crate lying by the road and snatched it up. K took the other side and they walked with their eyes on the shoulder, grabbing things that they thought they could sell, tossing them into the box. They kept collecting as they passed Levits Furniture showroom where people dragged mattresses across the pavement and laid them side by side in the parking lot to install clusters of their children and stake a claim.

They had a couple of glass bottles, a pair of pants, three socks, a piece of wire, several plastic six-pack tops that Beth was convinced could be twisted into rope. They kept gathering, wandering through the crowd.

"What do you have in there?" called out a man standing with one foot inside his Jaguar, the sleeves of his tailored shirt rolled up and his tie askew.

"Rope," Beth said.

"Any food?"

"No."

"How about selling me your jacket?" the man said, reaching for his wallet.

"Not a chance."

"Well, how'd you like to stay in here tonight? It's real leather, you know. But just you, the cute one."

"Fuck off," Beth said as she pushed her way through the crowd on the other side of his car.

"Hey cunt, you'll do worse before this is over," he called to her. Beth flipped him off.

"Where are we going to sleep?" K asked Beth in a small voice.

"How the fuck do I know? Does it look like any of these people know the answer to that?" Beth said irritably.

"I'm so hungry I'm startin' to wish for my mother's shitty cookin', can you believe that?" K said.

"Shut up, will ya?" Beth said.

They rounded the corner at Silver Avenue where the exodus slowed. At the top of the hill, the two women could see for miles. Thousands of people stood in front of Candlestick Park, facing the stadium, crouched on every inch of the shoulder and meridian and parking lot, people covering the terraced hillside at the Industrial Park next to the Candlestick, and the structure itself, with all its lights on, glowing like a space station.

"Dead people in there," a man beside her said under his breath. "They're bringin' 'em in by helicopter. Aren't lettin' anybody in to see who they are."

"Helicopters?" Beth asked.

"Army helicopters," the man said. "You know, the ones for transport of soldiers and such. I don't wanna go in, I'll tell you that much. If she's dead, she's dead. I don't need to see no thousand other dead ones to find out. But those people down there, see 'em by the entrance, they came in with the ambulances, when they could still get down here, and now there's nowhere for them to go."

"Jesus," Beth said.

"I'll give ya that," the man said. "You ever been there for a game? It's piss-chillin' cold. Always did say you had to be a stiff to take it." The man snorted at his own joke and walked away.

Beth picked up one end of the milk crate and called to K. They kept walking. As the dusk began to settle, the southern

city was especially dark. Foster City was in worse shape
than San Francisco: built on land-fill, houses had lost their
foundations, and the residents streamed out of the area like
war refugees. All electricity to this section of the peninsula
had been cut and the travelers understood that the glow
from Candlestick was from emergency generators. They
hurried away from it as they would ordinarily have been
drawn toward the light.

*T*rout surveyed the people along the streets, watching
their struggles, feeling portions of their confusion inside
her. As long as she remained unable to marshall her energy,
incapable of devising a plan of action, she was a woman
turning her back to an oncoming truck. The eighteen-wheeler
of their life together was without a driver, and Patricia was in
the passenger seat. Patricia would be waiting for Trout's
strategy. Never yet met a butch who could really pull out the
stops in a difficult situation. Fix it baby, is all she had ever
heard. Until today, it had always made her feel needed.

She had nothing on her: her briefcase was back in the
jumble of her home, her clothing gone, her silk shirt under a
baby's butt. Her hair, usually confined to a french twist, a
bun, anything to control the wildness of its curls, blew
around her face. Now she walked in the kind of attire she
had worn years ago, before she had decided that money was
important and succumbed to wearing pumps to get it. She
walked more loosely in the flat shoes, the white shirt rough
against her nipples.

Dogs crossed her path, with their quick, light walk on
pads that seemed to keep them above the ground. Trout
recognized several from the park. She had been going to the
dog parks for two years, carrying coffee and a newspaper to
appear as if she were just there for the morning or evening
air. She would sit on the benches and watch the dogs scout
through the bushes, stand frozen across a stretch of lawn,
then charge toward one another. She would sip coffee,
smiling at the way they challenged each other by standing

side by side, heads held still with their eyes on each other, waiting for one of them to flinch. She discussed worms and techniques against barking with the owners who stood in a circle, their animals romping around them, as if they were at a PTA meeting. "Hi, I'm Coco's mom," "I'm Chester's father," they would say to her and she would shake their hands as if she were the owner of one of the dogs herself. The dog owners never questioned her, just said, "Oh, I see, you're thinking about getting a dog." She always said yes, though she knew she was thinking about dogs, but never about getting one.

This evening, however, masters and mistresses had fled, were caught outside the city, or preoccupied. The gates and fences and dog runs had been destroyed, and the dogs banded together. Packs of dogs darted into the fallen buildings as if they were slipping into the brush, investigating with their noses to the ground. Kitchens had been destroyed; cupboards were lying unguarded. Now no one laid claim to the pantries, and the dogs jumped over concrete piles and devoured entire larders. The docile family pet, now strengthened by its repossession of clan life, was a force to be contended with. When a large pack of dogs marched down the street as if in formation, shoulder to shoulder, legs stiff and heads erect, women picked up their children and the neighbors stepped aside.

Trout stopped to watch a Schnauzer tear open a box of corn flakes, then toss the box back and forth while it gripped it in its teeth. She thought she had her life organized like a pantry, but in fact, it was simply a pile. The papers and file folders to keep everything in order, the timely payments on her possessions had not saved it all from destruction. There was no assurance in what she realized now was her own unceasing scrutiny. So much of her life had gone into protecting things and preventing events, she thought as she kicked a faucet and a child's toy aside with a haphazard swing of her foot. She was so tired. So tired of it all. It had gotten so bad that every day had grown into a plague. Her feelings that the safety and success of everything depended on her and her alone had gotten to the point where it was torture to go on business trips: Trout had developed a fear of airplanes. Her life was based on the necessity of maintaining a tight rein, and so she had become convinced that the plane's safe landing also depended on her. As long as she gripped the arms of the seat, got white in the face, sweated into her palms and shirtwaist and thighs, the takeoffs and landings would be smooth. She was sure of it.

Only the absence of all those possessions and projects to worry about showed her that worry took an enormous part of her brain. Funny she hadn't noticed it before. She thought it was just her job, her dreadful little charade where decisions involved no luck or chance, or at least no recognition of them, needing only a constant industry related to the control of money and people. It had infected her, she thought, wiping her forehead with fatigue as if taken by a fever. She had had a calendar with the dates marked for the oil changes on their cars, the days the meter reader came by, the months for dental checks and mammograms and pap smears, the dates the filters had to be changed in the heater, the water purifier, the kitchen fan, and the coffee maker cleaned with vinegar, the last time she had new heels on which pumps, the times for quarterly financial statements and graphs of how their cash flow fluctuated during the year, the day all the wools should go to the dry cleaner and be packed for the season, when the trees needed fertilizer and were expected to bloom. It was a maze, a calendar one expected for the launch of a Naval battalion or a major retail store. Everything was in writing. She should march back to the house and dig it out. How were things going to run without it? She shook her head: what was left to run? And after all that careful planning, that amazing control of the subtlety of her life. She prided herself on it: It was an incredible skill she had and when people stepped aside and let her run things she knew it was because she was good at it. People could see it. They relied on her to orchestrate things, and why not? She had leveraged it into a decent income.

On the other hand, she thought warily as she paced down the street, startling herself with the notion that there even was an other hand, she had worried about the sofa going gray, her credit rating maintaining itself. She fretted over brushing her teeth, keeping the roots of her hair dyed. Was she advancing at her job fast enough? Should the sod get more water or would that cause disease? Were the walls in the house getting scuffed and the bedspread covered with grime? Could she get better interest rates by moving all her accounts? Did she and Patricia have enough sex? Would the Socialist Party ever be something to be proud of? Should she rotate her tires again? Didn't the car door have another scratch? What about Patricia's cholesterol level and her own crows-feet? Were their heating costs being wasted on drafty windows? Did she give enough to charity? Were the white pots and pans getting scratched and yellowed? Was her consumer debt too high? Was success really possible? Was she preparing for her retirement soon enough? Were mid-life crises and bouts of infidelity inevitable? Did documentaries count as 'watching television'?

Maybe it was just the plague of being in her thirties, Trout thought, unsure of whether the heat rising through her was a sense of relief or fear. It was natural to have worked so hard to keep things in order, wasn't it? Earthquake or no earthquake, everyone reaches a point, she heard herself thinking without conviction, when you realize you're not young enough to be innocent nor old enough to be wisely confident. This was just . . . mid-adulthood . . . wasn't it? A reasonable sense of disillusionment, depression, an anxiety over too much ambition and no indication of the outcome. The white couch was lying in the dirt with scuff marks from Patricia's boots. Her spectacular calendar was a doily under twenty-thousand pounds of plaster. Well who cares about scuff marks? she thought crossly. Everything was a big scuff mark, the whole city. Jesus. Maybe she should go back there and burn the sofa like an effigy of everything white and worrisome. Maybe this was real beauty, the sight of dogs shredding what they weren't allowed to touch. A German shepherd scratched at the front of a refrigerator that was now lying on its side. The dog clawed at the rubber seal on the freezer.

"You can do it," Trout called brightly.

The freezer door sprung open and the shepherd dove on the foil-covered meat, tearing away the aluminum with its claws. Other dogs joined him and Trout laughed at the frenzy.

"37 Fletcher Street," she called. "We've got fillets in there!" That's what she wanted to be, she thought, a dog rolling her spine around in the rotting life she had led. Just enough brains to know her name and when to lie on her little rug, all the rest of her gray matter devoted to smell, to sex, to the feel of sun in the afternoon. Not a bad trade-off.

They were busted, she thought with a wry smile. The whole city was caught in the act: there were husbands on the streets in jockey shorts with women who looked too guilty to be their wives. Porches and decks that carpenters guaranteed were now a pile of tangled boards. Word was that a couple of municipal buildings had fallen and were finally unmasked as the boondoggle the liberals had always claimed them to be. Engineers will be put on trial and politicians'll lose their careers; landlords (hers included) will finally be forced to put in before they take out. Sweet justice, she thought. The crooks now had nowhere to hide.

"Hey, I believe them: we're survivors," a man's voice said behind her. Trout turned toward a group of people gathered around a radio at a street corner. His friends silenced him and bent closer to hear: Trout stopped to listen as well. Pressure from the San Andreas Fault, building since the last big quake in 1906, had finally been relieved.

"Look, the whole damn city's been worrying about this one for more than a century," the man continued to his friends. "I say we're lucky, we're alive, and we're free from the worry. Frankly, I feel great."

"To survival," said a man in the group and raised a beer.

"To the end of worry," said a woman, and clinked cans.

*P*atricia watched the women in Sabito's the way she had regarded stories of desert life and rain forest animals: the way this one swung her hips, the way the other ran her fingertip over her lips when she was thinking. Hell, they'd always been her fascination. Her mother, Meredith, never could figure it. Fresh out'a childhood, Patricia had abandoned her post in front of the upstairs windows, had taken to going into the hardware store every day after school, coming home with two little washers for a sink that wasn't dripping, nails for a project that never materialized.

Patricia had been watching a dark-haired girl behind the counter slip dimes between her thumb and first finger into the change drawer, stand on a chair to hang brackets from display posts, crawl around in the display window placing the bales of wire and the wooden clothespins in a mysterious design. At night Patricia had lain in her bed imagining that the girl's perfume was wafting up through the floorboards.

By mid-summer, Patricia was a regular, with a stool behind the counter. A pencil fell off the ledge of the register and Patricia's eyes had followed the rounding and rising of the dark-haired girl's ass as she bent to retrieve it.

"Patty D?" her mother had said gruffly as she stepped from behind a stack of wire bales, a couple of new sponges in her hand, "time . . . to fix dinner."

When had she come in? Patricia wondered, reddening. Had the others in the store seen her watching as well? Now they knew for sure. Christ, Patricia had never been expected to fix a dinner in her life: it had always been the garbage and window washing, fixing the cords on lamps. Patricia climbed off the stool.

When they reached their flat, Meredith rocked furiously in her overstuffed chair. "It's about time you think about boys," she had said through clenched teeth.

Patricia's baby had been fathered behind the local pharmacy on a night when the invitation for sex seemed as lack-luster as saying, "Let's walk to the gas station for a soda."

Meredith had come home drunk the night after Patricia told her she was pregnant.

"Only one time in my life I ever jeopardized my livelihood, you hear me, girl?" Meredith had said, slouching nearly horizontal in her chair. "One time. Priest took on this broad-chested blonde man. Clyde. Priest gave him a truck. Picked up low-grade coal as a donation from the companies and distributed it to the poor."

Meredith had struggled to sit up. "Three months a' work an', the priest had me draw up papers. The two of us went to the man's home in the hills—a shack, sweetie, could see right through the walls—to give him his own set of keys and ownership of the truck. Well, what a ceremony," she said, waving her shaking hands in the air. Meredith leaned forward drunkenly. "Place was filled with beds, six of 'em, jutting from every wall, filling the entire place. There was one tiny table with one chair, the stove, and six beds, all made up. I'm tellin' you the truth. In between the beds were paper sacks filled to the tops with men's underwear, and that's when I knew why the priest had brought me." She smiled, wiped her mouth with the back of her hand. "No nun would have entered such a place and a priest never travels anywhere unaccompanied. This Clyde, he filled the room with the smell of a man's skin. Odor of dampened chest hair—now I know you know what I'm talkin' about—the fragrance of a man's thighs." Meredith looked at her daughter to see if there was a reaction, then turned away. "I didn't hear the conversation. I looked at the pigs in a pen outside the window, two chickens warmin' their neck feathers in boxes beside the stove. Idyllic Home Scene in Country Shack. I wanted those beds, little girl, wanted to be snowed in with this man and sweat into every one of those beds. Two weeks later, m'bra dangled over the edge of them paper bags and three weeks later I was grinnin' at the nervous chickens. You understand me, girl? Four weeks later, priest meets Clyde's coal truck at the driveway and the man never came into the office again. Two Beds Blessed, Four Lost Forever as Catholics Boycott Love Shack. That's what I said, watchin' from the office window, and that's what I say to you now. It's a Boycott of Love Shack."

Pleasure is danger, Patricia had grumbled as she lay in bed that night.

Wasn't that the truth, Patricia thought, swigging on her beer like she wanted to wash down the acrid taste of her mother's pronouncement. Joy Boycott Beats No-Grapes As Longest Running Protest. What joy she had found in her life with Trout was now crumpled under her television and the stuffing from the sofa. It had been a hard fight getting this far, and now what did she have?

After a documentary on television describing the political power of the gay community in San Francisco, an hour in which her mother had rocked the baby and Patricia had tried to hide her interest by fiddling with a lock and key set, her mother had gone to the kitchen to poke at the beef stew.

"Maybe that California place'd be a good spot for you, Patty D," her mother had said.

Patricia had packed her bag, her baby and bought a ticket West. Patricia had worked the soda counter at the local drug store, she worked the office of the feed store, saved her money. She was going to a place she had seen on the television, any place. She was going where people read the newspaper to figure things out, not just recite the headlines.

Politics and travel, those were the things her mother couldn't reduce to a category. She couldn't explain away the spires of the churches in Europe or the jungle plants of Africa. Politics demanded more than the simple "what" her mother recited as if it were the sum of life. Baby Conceived to Cut Sunday's Boredom, Patricia had thought.

"Letters Bring Great Solace to Families," her mother had said as Patricia boarded the bus.

The last time she had had nothing, Patricia thought in Sabito's, it was with a little girl by her side, and this time it was with nobody. Duck-Janitor and Executive Leave Electrician To Sink/Swim, she thought, looking at her half-empty beer.

Years ago, when she'd been younger, angrier (maybe with more energy, she said to herself), she had looked at the world and spit. Went on welfare, worked the angles. Today, she didn't have the strength. Her furniture looked like it was straight out of the thrift store. Her house was a place a tornado had stirred up just for laughs. She couldn't pick through it. Bought all the stuff at Macy's but it was filthy now, and she was back in the kind of place she knew too well, at the bar with a beer, not looking in her pocket for fear there wasn't money for another. Here she was, hanging with a bunch of girls who didn't know what to do with themselves and she didn't know, either. Where the hell was Trout?

Trout and Patricia had met five years ago at a party, and Trout had pulled gold out of the swamp even then. Patricia's date had been an upper-class Bostonian, flitting about the room while the other partygoers took snide pot-shots at her politics. Patricia retreated into the kitchen to avoid showing her embarrassment.

"If you're looking for your date's political consciousness, may I suggest the vegetable bin," Trout had said, putting her hand on the edge of the refrigerator door just inches from Patricia.

Angel-haired Vixen Cuts Cotillion Queen To Size, Patricia had thought with a smirk, and hung one of her thumbs through her beltloop.

"My name is Trout."

"Patricia."

"It's going to be divine, I know it will," Patricia's date had called back to the living room as she came into the kitchen. Trout took her hand from the refrigerator and stepped back. "Are you sure you don't want my car, Patricia?" the Bostonian had whined. "They'll just strip it in my neighborhood. Saab, '79. I'm going to Inn-dee-ya for a year," she had said, turning to Trout. "Isn't that great? Eight hundred dollars, Patricia."

"Gee . . . ," Trout had said to Patricia, feigning nonchalance, "why don't you and I take it for a test drive? I'll be the impartial observer."

Patricia had fought another smile, then held her hand out for the keys. The Bostonian had chortled with triumph, dropped them into Patricia's hand and returned to the living room.

"Let me guess," Trout had said softly. "You're upper-class Boston just like her, right?"

Patricia had snorted, taken her by the elbow and led her out the door.

"Woman thinks it's 'quaint' that I grew up over a hardware store," Patricia had said fiercely.

They had climbed into the front seat, and Trout immediately extracted paperwork from the glove compartment.

"I don't trust this," Patricia had said slowly as they pulled away from the curb.

"Well, you can't trust her, but you can always trust good paperwork," Trout had said. "Registration's up to snuff. No parking tickets. Look here, regular oil changes. She's got quite the paper trail," Trout had said, waving the paperwork in the air.

Now there's a woman who could make it right, Patricia thought, twirling her beer bottle between her fingers. She'll dig out some paperwork, and we'll be up and runnin' in no time. Trout'd run or crawl or commandeer any vehicle that operates to get here. Patricia smiled. Whatever it took was whatever Trout would do. Eternal Optimist Finds Hidden Route Through Mud Slide, Patricia thought, knowing that at Trout's arrival she would shake her head over the woman's moxy and say, "How did you have the guts to convince them to. . . ." Trout would just look at her with those bright, lashless eyes and say, incredulously, "Well, it needed to be done." Didn't matter what it was, from the simplest suggestion to the most complicated change, all Patricia had to do was tell Trout she wanted it, and in two days (if Trout was busy) Trout would present a file folder with facts, schedules, price comparisons, and with a tenderness in her eyes, outline a plan of action.

Patricia sipped her beer while she glanced to the side. Trout would set her file folder on the table and Patricia would grasp her hand before it left its task, pull her forward and slide a hand across the small of her back. Hell, Patricia'd take her down, right there, wherever they were, in the kitchen, the hallway, and Trout would always say something like "but . . . don't you want to hear about . . . the interest rate?" just before Patricia covered her mouth with her lips. Builder of Fireplace Marries Woman Bearing Fire. Such a duo. She wasn't even sure why or how it happened, but the sound of the vacuum or the smell of dinner in the oven, it set her off. The roll of the filing cabinets and she'd get a little grin on her face, check to see if the bed was made. She'd slip her hand into that mass of angel hair, ready to get lost. Nearly six feet tall, it made her happy to pull Trout in, wrapping her in long arms and legs, draping her in her black hair. Trout deserved it. It's complicated, all that stuff she invents, and the more complex her solution was, the more complex Patricia made her love-making. Imagine what she's going to think up for this situation, Patricia thought.

She needed to imagine it, she thought sadly, to imagine a file folder (and what a folder it would have to be), to fix this mess, and then the taste of skin, the feel of Trout's hands gripping her forearms, the breathy sound she makes just before she comes. That would drive away the sight of a woman's hand waving. She needed her arms around someone, her face in cotton-y hair, her tongue behind an earlobe.

*T*he elevator stopped with a jolt and the doors slid open. Cherice stepped out. Wind sucked through the building with a force that pulled her down the hall. She screamed. The floor-to-ceiling windows had been blown out. Her legs moved but couldn't fight the current that took her toward the 36-story drop. She slid farther down the hall, her arms flailing as she bent forward against the wind. There was nothing to hang onto, nothing to break her. The papers that had spilled out of Jacob's briefcase whipped by her and out the windows. Her breath caught in her throat as she was pulled, her coat and jacket yanking on her shoulders. Three feet before the lethal window she grasped a doorknob with both hands. The door flung open, and the force of the movement pulled her off the ground, hurling her pumps out the window. She scrambled inside and fell against the wall.

"Jacob!" she screamed, leaning only slightly toward the open door. "Don't come out."

"I can't stay here, for Christsake!"

"Just hold on. Stay there."

Cherice turned to look at the office and her mouth dropped open. Penthouse suite, top floor. All the windows intact, not a single item out of place. Mahogany, a huge desk, crystal and mirrors everywhere, a leather couch and a creamy rug. So this is where the bastard stays, she thought, knowing the office belonged to the head of the brokerage firm. Probably reinforced against bomb attacks and assassination attempts. It was legendary. 'Going up to 36' the top brokers said when they went to meet the boss. She had never been there. She'd only seen him in pictures. He had never bothered to come down to her floor to meet the junior brokers. Worker bees, that's what they were. And here was the nest of the queen.

"Cherice!"

"OK, OK. Hold on." She wasn't going back into the hallway to get him and he would never be able to fight the wind on one foot. She picked up a small Asian rug and threw it into the hall to increase his traction, but as soon as she put it down and flattened herself against the wall again she saw the wind slide the rug down the hall and out the window.

"Jesus!" she exclaimed.

"What's over there?" he called.

"Heaven," she said, more to herself than him as she lunged forward and slammed the door. A rope. A rope to tie me to something so I don't fall out the window, and to tie to him. Yeah sure, lots of rope in the suite of the King and Consort, she thought sarcastically. She barreled through the room in her stocking feet, considered taking down the drapes but couldn't spare the time to take the cord from the fabric. The drapes themselves were too gossamer: they'd never hold his weight. She opened a door: it was a closet filled with tailored suits and monogrammed shirts. She opened a door nearest the windows, in the corner of the room, a door papered the same as the walls.

"A bedroom, oh, bad boys," she said and strode over to strip off the sheets. Opened a closet and pulled out several others. She tied them together as she crossed the room, knotted the end to a heavy credenza, wrapped it around her waist. She opened the door and braced herself.

"I'm going to throw you this sheet," she shouted above the sound of the wind. "Tie it around your waist. Drag yourself in here with it."

Jacob slunk into the hallway and cursed as the wind pulled him toward the windows. Cherice dug her toes into the carpet and pulled him into the room, shut the door and locked it, leaned her head against the door in relief.

"So," Cherice said, pressed against the wall but throwing her arms out, her electric blue coat and suit jacket making a web, "still no pizza. Jesus, delivery's slow."

"Very funny," Jacob said, struggling off the floor until he towered over her, and undoing the wrap. "Really," he fought for breath. "You're a very funny woman."

"You're kind. Most people say strange," she said, bugging out her gray eyes and stroking her pale white throat. She stripped off the sheet and strode into the room.

"You take these Valium on a regular basis?" he said.

Cherice nodded. "I'm a stock broker, remember? Terrible problems with stress and hypertension," she said in mockery.

"I see."

"Don't complain. You're better company as a result."

"The Jell-O-man. Christ, will you look at this place," Jacob said, hobbling over to the leather sofa, regarding the enormous modern paintings and beveled mirrors, the book cases with accent lights shining on Asian statuary. The desk near the window was six feet of art deco wood. He shook his head with disgust and admiration, then settled onto the sofa, his foot up on the arm.

Cherice walked slowly along the bookcase wall, dragging her fingers across the gleaming surface. She ran her fingers through the thick ash-blonde hair that hung blunt-cut at her shoulders. She stripped off her blue coat and threw it like a challenge across one of the leather chairs. The gesture pressed her high, round breasts against her silk shirt, a revelation not lost on Jacob.

"Hey," she said, smiling, putting her hands on her hips.

"What?" Jacob said, suspiciously. The last time she had an idea they had wound up drugged on the floor of an elevator.

"Let's trash the place," she said, throwing her arms high into the air, then lacing her fingers behind her head. "C'mon. Let's have a party in here."

"We can't stay here . . . we should . . . go. We should leave. What's with you, you have no home?"

"I am in no mood to brave that stuff again," Cherice said, pointing at the door. "Besides, you said yourself, neither of us has anyone to rush home to. I don't even have house plants to worry about."

Jacob sighed. "Well, that's a point."

"Have a drink," Cherice said.

"Have you no scruples?" he asked, only half seriously.

"Scruples? I'm a stock broker, remember?" She crossed the room in front of the desk, regarded the finely-papered, blank wall. "We drink a little of his brandy, he'll write it off as a donation to the Earthquake Relief Fund. With an extra six zeros behind the price." At a seam, she pushed with flat hands and the wall sprung open. "Ah, the obligatory bar," she said snidely. She stepped sideways, pressed the wall again. The panels opened. "And the executive kitchenette. This boy has it all."

"Food? They can't begrudge us a little food."

"Of course they can't," she said triumphantly throwing out her arms. "Besides, all we have to do is leave the door open when we leave. It'll look like the proverbial hurricane came through."

"One of those statues flies out the window it could kill someone," Jacob said solemnly.

"That's a point." Cherice gestured at the kitchenette like a game show hostess. "No Cup-a-Soup in the executive suite. And there's always leftovers 'cause when the boss entertains, the peons are too frightened to eat. Well, their torture is our gain. A small wager on paté?" She held the handle of the refrigerator, waiting for his reply.

"Just serve lunch," Jacob said, noting the sparkle that had come into her eyes and the way she flung her hair around when she was excited. She took up a lot of space, this woman. How could he have thought she was nondescript? She hadn't been moving, he reasoned.

"Voilà. Do I know corporate lifestyle or what?" she said, sticking her head into the refrigerator. "Paté, brie, Chardonnay. God, this guy has no originality. Ooh, caviar. We're in for a good one, my man."

"Fantastic. I didn't know how hungry I was until we walked through this door."

"Crawled, Mr. Lefkowitz. We crawled through. Fruit salad, de rigueur, and green salad," she recited. "Another wager on Balsamic vinegar? I hate corporate shitheads."

"So why do you work with them?" Jacob said.

"Because I get paid for being irascible. Stockbrokers are supposed to be obnoxious. Don't tell me you enjoy your job."

"Bring us the wine, waitress," Jacob replied, sidestepping the issue.

"Hey, now, none of that, Peaches."

"Peaches?" he said with disgust.

Cherice laughed, looked back into the refrigerator, glad she had found something to acknowledge his beauty. Love calling the boys by a woman's endearment: they can't stand it.

"Eat up," she said authoritatively, and set out the food on the glass coffee table in front of the sofa. Jacob caught a glimpse of Cherice eating, surprised at the way her lips gently touched the rim of her wine glass, the sheen of moisture the wine left on them, the tender way she touched her lips with her napkin. The words she uses are like steel, but her lips, that is a different matter, he thought. They devoured their dinner until the color-coordinated plastic containers were empty. Cherice sauntered to the bar like she had nowhere to go and a year to get there.

"An after-dinner drink? I'll bet there's some good brandy in here." She continued to the window, parted the curtains.

"Jesus it's dark out there," she said, surprised. "Jacob, there are no street lights."

Jacob struggled off the couch, jumped on one foot over to the window, leaned his palm against the window frame just above Cherice's head. They were silent, looking at the darkness below them where freeways and city streets usually glowed orange, up the hills to the neighborhoods where the porch lights and living rooms of homes had always twinkled. Jacob looked down at the streets of the financial district that lay directly below them.

"Glass?" he said.

"Oh my God," Cherice said, suddenly frightened.

*T*rout walked through the Mission with a spring in her step. Could that be possible? Was she nearly skipping? How could that happen when she didn't even know where she was going? Somehow to be walking around without a purpose or destination, freed of some monumental task that needed to be done or damnable work to be completed every minute of every day, well, it was a new feeling, one that hadn't visited her in a long time. There literally was nothing to be done. She couldn't dig out her house: that would take a bulldozer. She couldn't call the office: there weren't any phones operating for miles (more than half a dozen people had stopped to ask her if she had found one). What would she say when she got through anyway? It's all turned to shit so start over somewhere else, without me? No, she had nothing more important to do than wander around looking for Patricia, who would show up at her daughter's flat sooner or later.

Besides, it was all insured. That was the beauty of it. Years and years of meticulousness had paid off: they had earthquake insurance on the contents of their flat, at replacement value. She ticked off the list to herself: health insurance, dental insurance, life insurance, disability insurance, credit card insurance. Christ, they could hide under a rock for months and their lives would continue because of all the money they'd pumped into insurance companies in the past five years. All the policies had separate folders, color-coded filing systems and check-tracking procedures. Some were even automatically withdrawn with special arrangements to dump the money from one account to another when it got too low. It was a well-oiled machine, her paperwork system. So what if all her copies were ground into the dirt? The machine could simply click into place and work anyway, couldn't it? She didn't have to monitor it; it was that well built. Patricia wasn't even sure how much coverage they had or how precisely she had planned it all. Trout snapped her fingers and slammed her fist into her palm, smiling to herself like a gambler who is pleased enough with the game to cash in the chips. Safe, sound, and financially secure, she thought. It wasn't really as bad as it could have been, Trout surmised, looking around, listening to radios that people had blaring from their cars. Only 2,000 dead, compared to 65,000 in Armenia, and the electricity still working in parts of the city, the water running just fine. Not a lot of fires, and the helicopters were already lifting in materials from outside the area. The radio stations were beginning "The End of Worry" campaign and playing upbeat music. Makeshift banks had been established in municipal buildings because the ATM systems were defunct.

Trout felt a thrilling sort of defiance growing inside her. The votes have been cast: one vote for human organization, one hundred votes for nature. Long live tectonic plates! She threw her head back. Power to the canines and the bits of plaster that gave up, to give us a chance to give in.

She had always liked her wicked side, she thought. She was raised in the middle-class white world, in a social class that expected her to be "good," taught her that everything a girl desired could be hers if she just behaved well. What others didn't see, though, was that, faced with the mandate to behave, a part of Trout turned the other direction, thumb on her nose. No one, including Patricia, ever saw the G-string she wore under her perfectly pressed business suit, the erotica she kept in her briefcase, hidden slightly but still able to appear at a "bad" time (though she made sure it never did). Not even her closest friends saw the way she walked the line of failure and success: repeatedly drinking too much the night before an important presentation, driving her car on empty when rushing to the airport for business trips.

Now, all of it had all fallen down. Thank the Goddess, she thought, surprised and suddenly energized by her own pronouncement. Thank you, quake, for ruining it all in a big ugly hurry.

"Give you this sausage for one of those shoe laces," a voice called to her.

"What?"

"Trade me one, we'll cut them in two and both have enough," a man said, stepping off a porch with a packaged Kielbasa in his hands. "You're gonna get hungry. You got money?"

Her briefcase. Money? she thought.

"All right," she said, "one shoelace for the sausage."

*P*atricia tipped her head back and ran her hands through her straight black hair, down the expanse of her neck and along the open collar of her shirt. She nestled one arm under her breasts and stretched the other arm down the length of the bar, leaned her head against it. If she were home with Trout she would take Trout's face in her hands, any gesture that would stop her from the fury that she had felt at the house, the anger that lived inside her. Trout may have said her hair made her look like a raven, but Patricia knew it was all that smoke that had hung in Meredith's hair, she thought. Condensed inside me. Smoke Woman Belches Fury, Turns to Screeching Black Raven. The sound of the woman's screaming seemed to be moving through her, pressing on her own lips. If she weren't lying all over this bar, she knew she could rise over the city with her beak wide open, shrieking like the bird of fury. Hurry, Trout, get back here. Just one little word from you. Christ, just some sign that the wheels were in motion and she'd settle, she'd nestle, she'd wrap Trout up and deliver her sweaty and panting.

As the afternoon wore on, sirens announced the ambulances pushing through the Mission, the police tracking looters. The back-up warning sound of large trucks could be heard on all sides of Sabito's. A short man with strands slicked over a bald spot stood at the intersection and shouted instructions into a megaphone. Patricia gathered

with other women trying to hear. A woman stepped through
the hole in the wall, crossed the street, and talked with a
woman with a clipboard who gestured toward Dolores Park.

"A rescue center," the woman said as she came back into
the bar, not smiling. "They're doling out food and building
tent groups."

"Oh good," one of the women said.

"No it's not. They're dividing everyone up. Families and
singles."

"Where are couples going?"

"Men/women get their own tents. Women/women go with
the singles."

"Well you can't have the Ritz, you know."

"Why should I sleep in a single bed with a bunch of
strangers around when I can stay here with my girl? This is
no time to be split up."

"Besides," the woman said, pushing her way back into the
bar, "you know the food'll be lousy."

Sabito's was crowded now, filling even with non-drinkers.
Patricia thought the women who came in didn't look
frightened. They looked filled with remorse as they folded
themselves onto the floor with their arms around their knees.
She knew that look, Patricia thought, like there was
somethin' they could have done: they should have stopped
playing sooner and gotten it together; or laid down the tools
and briefcase, done their hair and danced, Patricia imagined
them saying, as she leaned against the bar. Guilt of All Rests
Upon My Chest, Dyke Anthem Says. Patricia turned away
and took another swig of her beer.

The mood began to settle: it had been hours since the
women watching the street had seen anyone carrying an
injured child or rushing with an arm or hand wrapped in
bloodied cloth. Occasionally, Patricia looked down at her
feet, expecting blood to be rushing toward her shoes.

She drank another beer, listening to the stories with what
started out as a hungry interest but soon was just half her
consciousness. When the fear is gone, the story begins to
shrink. Tell it once to the first person who cares, all the
details, and then the second time there's somethin' left out.
Soon you say, yeah, you were "in it," slowly writing yourself

out of your own past. History Shortens Four-Decade Life To Single Shrug of Shoulders. Same way a relationship goes from right in front of your eyes, to a few stories that soon get old, to "Oh yeah, that was a bad one too."

"Louise," a woman said, leaning between the bar stools, "sorry about your house. God what a mess, eh?"

Louise stopped pouring, a handful of ice cradled in her palm. "You saw my house?"

"You haven't been there?" the woman asked incredulously.

"Don't answer my question with a question! You seen my house or not?"

The butch pulled back a moment but, with bad news to relay, she backed down.

"Louise, the whole thing's fallen down. You live at the corner of 19th and Guerrero, right?"

"Shit."

Patricia slid her beer along the length of the bar and joined the conversation. "Are there any walls standing?"

"No, I'm tellin' ya, it's a mess. The sheetrock fell away like cards. Nothin' left. On the corner, right? You live on the corner?" the woman asked.

Louise turned away, mixed the drink in another glass, asked the women waiting at the end of the bar if they had any money, then simply pushed the glass forward and wiped her hands on her pants. The woman with the bad news shrugged her shoulders, grabbed her beer by the neck and moved away.

Louise moved a case of Bud Light with her foot, brushing plaster dust from the lip of the bar. It's all in the street. She rested her foot on the case, folded her hands across the bar. Why should she care? What did she have in there, anyway, a stiff corduroy couch, with one indentation from one ass only, a speckled dinette set she had gotten from her mother years ago and crammed into the kitchen so there was only room for one chair to be pulled out. The rest was milk-crates. Fifty-seven years old and she's still livin' in milk-crates, people on the street would say. Wasn't a dyke in town who had ever seen the inside of her apartment. She should run down the street and show it to them now? No fuckin' way.

Go back and see it turned to trash? It was trash from the beginning, only still standing, all the legs of things at right angles.

"I'll cover for you here if you wanna go salvage something," Patricia called to her. Louise didn't move. Didn't look out the wall at the street, wouldn't turn her head when the door opened.

It was all unmasked. Turned out and exposed, like she should be, Louise thought. No, it was safer here in the bar. This was who she was, anyway. Right here behind the bar.

"Whad'am I gonna do there?" Louise asked, leaving her perch and swaggering toward Patricia. "Pull flannel shirts out of the dirt?" She pulled a beer from the trough. "Rescue a couple a' neckties?"

Patricia snorted, smiled a little. "What about tables or chairs?"

"Particle board. The Lee Press-On Nails of furniture."

Patricia looked Louise in the eye.

Louise smiled grimly, turned away.

"Worst thing at my house," Patricia said as Louise moved down the bar toward her, "is that the stuff isn't even paid for. No, that's not true, just barely. Finally out'a the hole. And now this."

"Next couple'a years," Louise said, "all the middle-class dykes'll be in Chinos and shirts with holes, secretly working on re-building their stock portfolios before their wardrobe. The working-class girls? You'll find them at Breuner's home furnishing goin' into debt. Christ, give the Republicans twelve years and even the dykes shave their legs."

Where was Trout, goddamnit? Patricia thought. Tell her the problem, any problem, she'd say: 'Let's put it on the agenda' and it'd be done, anything from taxes to dish soap, and the lists would start growing.

Some of the lesbians had left Sabito's, gone back to their houses and were dragging a few possessions into the bar. Patricia turned away from the sight of the tattered, jumbled objects. Her whole life that's what's been offered, she thought, pushing against the screaming bird inside her, objects that were second-rate, second-hand, a little less than they should be, a poor imitation, an ugly rendition of what's in the magazines or on the television. Trying to raise Beth it seemed like nothing ever fit and nothing worked for more than a month. Objects? They were the things that made you feel duped: they told the world what you wanted and then laughed in your face when you couldn't have it. Finally, she had found an end to that. A steady income, a wife. She bought top-of-the-line now and the appliances worked. Things became what they were, just things, just objects that she controlled. They couldn't humiliate her anymore. Until today. Macy's Catalog Revealed As Sadistic Plot, she thought, laying her head on her arm again.

There had never been enough comfort in the world to make it stop hurting, she thought, looking around the bar, not enough alcohol or drugs or chocolate cake to ease the pain, and so she had given up on using any of them. Closing her eyes, she wanted to curl up somewhere and sleep until the pain was gone. She needed to dream away the sight of young girls who had laughed at her clothes in high school, the sound of her mother banging her chair into the table when her father drove away, the look on Beth's face when the cheap toys broke, the specter of the woman whose eyes rolled back in her head. Always, it seemed to her today, she had the options of soaring away on her anger, clinging blindly to the nest of sleep, or losing herself in the taste of her lover's lips.

Groups of women came back to the bar with stories of looters, men with tarps and canvas sheets that they were filling with other people's goods. Brazen, the women said, but so many of them, and so threatening, that no one on the street even shouted at them as they carried away possessions.

The threat of men looting their homes pushed the group to action. The women pulled fliers off the wall, turned them to their blank backsides and posted them again. One would be a message board, one a list of resources. A patrol was formed to accompany women back to their houses to collect what was most important. A few women designated themselves a scouting party to collect food and utensils. They would all have to be fed, after all, and the dinner hour was coming soon enough. How would they all sleep here?

One woman took up a collection, and women approached, emptying their pockets, suddenly energized and relieved to be focused on a task and the ad-hoc collective being formed. A few couples held hands in the corner, deciding to leave the crowd and save their money, to rebuild on their own.

"Let me see what kind of hook-up you've got to cook this stuff," Patricia said to Louise. "You got a hot-plate or anything? Butane camp stove?"

"You'll have to find it yourself. I'm stayin' behind the bar," Louise said to Patricia. "Always did say it was the safest place." She laughed weakly and folded her arms over her chest.

Patricia looked at her suspiciously, pulled on her beer and jumped off the barstool. That joke isn't funny anymore, she thought. What's the matter with her?

Patricia walked slowly toward the back of the bar. She should be fighting her way through crowds to get to a telephone, she thought. She could set up all the electrical rigs in the world, but what to do about her most precious item, her little Trout? Shit, on a good day it was nearly more faith than Patricia had to send Trout out into the world. Sometimes she'd turned away when Trout left the house and she knew Trout probably thought she didn't care, or was just too damn sleepy to gather her up and kiss her, but it wasn't true, just the opposite. On mornings like that, if she had moved one foot she would have thrown herself in front of the door. There were too many tragedies. Every day Americans read about a new technique for cutting up bodies or raping women, about another form of transportation that tore off your limbs and scattered you from the clouds. She bet people were flocking to the neighborhoods that were destroyed right now, just to take a look. Every person in the country was a goddamn Guiness Book of freak accident information, Patricia thought. They all held the newspaper with their arms wide so the details seeped right into their hearts. Death Fetish Voted National Sport, she thought. Where the hell was Trout? She must be going crazy with worry. And what about Evelyn and Maria? God knew Emeryville and Oakland had to be hit hard. She should try to get to a phone. But what if she didn't get through? Then she'd really worry. What was the alternative? she scolded herself, sit here and do nothing? She could pretend she sat here because she'd be easier to find if she stayed in one place, but she knew better. Woman Without Wife Exposed As Stick Figure.

*L*ynn heard music when she uncovered her ears. Gregorian chant, or was it Latin sung by young girls? She couldn't decipher it, anymore than she could determine which was Chinese, Irish, Jesus, Buddha. Who to call on to carry her out of this mess? She had to make a choice. And if she did not, where was she? Suspended in air with an Irish-American serviceman and a half-Chinese woman? Floating. Could it be unraveled, this Buddha man, Lady with the Baby? Could either comfort a woman under a stone bench with raining glass? If she called them now, if she finally decided, just as she had to choose at the office, would one of them throw her a rope that would carry her out of the park? Buddha, rope and baby, would one of them take her away from a glassless office where Chinese were being 'penetrated'?

She had tried to choose, twice. Tried to make her decision in a church. The light through the honeycomb windows, the vault, the touch of cool water on her forehead. It had been a great dome of a roof, a ceiling that called up loneliness she didn't even know she had, made it well up in her chest. It had seemed so unfair: create a place filled with pain and then parcel out tenderness with flickering candle cups and a few broken bodies. A painstaking and gold-leafed effort at solace. She fell to her knees like a child, but for just an instant, then she had sat, as if at a desk, through all the bowing and the kneeling, not turning to see the stained glass mural of the shaven-headed. She had never gone back. Her father, the big freckled Irishman—you could see the saints in his eyes, and when he walked past the churches she could feel his hand in hers struggling not to cross himself.

"Wouldn't be fair to your mother," he had told her once, then snapped his newspaper in front of his face to end her curiosity.

The second time was at grandmother's altar. Her Buddha, her flowers, oranges in cups, were closed within her bedroom. She caught a glimpse of the old woman bowing once, just before her mother shut the door. Next day her grandmother had pressed a postcard into her hand, barely whispering a few words before she straightened and turned her back on the child to face her own daughter who stood with a unmoving face. It became a secret, a chant, a story her grandmother would tell her when her parents had gone out at night. She sat on her grandmother's lap with her postcard. "The cloak of the Buddha, in the Temple of Ten Thousand Buddhas," the old woman had said. It was the only Chinese thing she knew. Under the stone bench today, Lynn heard the sound of the squeaking prayer wheel. Buddhas lining five flights of balconies, but none as grand as the standing Buddha, my grandmother had said, five stories high, carved from a single tree and dragged from Tibet. "Enter the temple and stand at its calf," her grandmother had said with a whisper that dampened her ear.

Adrift, that's what she was. What was a woman who couldn't bend at the knee or join voices in the ragged little unison, a woman too proud to spin a prayer wheel or press her hands together? She had closed her heart against the starburst ceiling, the smell of bodies perspiring remorse. So who had ever lit a candle for her? When had her name twinkled in a bank of votive cups? Buddha Blue Cloak or Lady with Baby, they hadn't claimed her, they hadn't reached her, and she hadn't bent her head or chosen one. She had no ties that bound, no cord that rang the bell for the call to prayer, no rope that the Bird of Offering could climb to spill the Water of Good Fortune, no golden sash, no Christian, no Buddhist blessing to stop the trembling under this stone bench.

*T*rout stuffed the chinos pants-pockets with any provision she could find or trade (half of the piece of sausage had gotten her work gloves and the work gloves had been traded for a small blanket). She flung her hair backward like a horse's mane, feeling a sense of adventure she hadn't allowed herself in years, like a woman who thinks the sexual part of life is over, only to discover it can be awakened again. She had saved a baby's life, for Christsake, she had escorted a woman and her children through the city, she had the guts to walk away from the junk of her house and the monotony of her life. Patricia was safe; it was just a matter of meeting.

Released from it all now, Trout wanted to stay in the canvas pants and tennis shoes, buy a 4x4 (no, steal a 4x4, she thought, taking a bite of the sausage), become a cowgirl, live without bleached floors, a polished car or pantyhose—those damnable, fucking pantyhose. She wanted to leave the holes in shirts again, drink and sweat like a goddamn hoodlum. It was finished, as if the season had ended and her father had walked through the door to announce his jubilant comradeship with the water fowl: the season was over. There were no more cans to pull out of the water.

The winter of her junior year in high school, Tracy had come home and found her father working with tools in the middle of the house, using tin snips and propane torches. He had been trying to hook the electrical outlet to the ironing board and the iron into the outlet. He had worked at it for hours, but each time Trout would come into the room, he had soldered another item onto the board until the cover was singed around the edges, melted in spots, hung with items from all over the house. Trout had suddenly felt very young and frail, helpless against the threat that had been directed from her father toward the world, and the world toward him, but that had never been from him to his own home. After he went to sleep, she locked up the torch and the wire cutters. She could protect him with paperwork and meals because the rules of the world had a simple order to them, she had learned long before. She had no chance, however, of following the winding path of his mind and anticipating what lethal invention he might create. As the winter continued, his contraptions had no visible purpose, only a lengthy and cumbersome explanation that Trout had listened to with one ear while checking for signs of power sources, plugs, gas connections, or blades. Soon his machines had had no beginning or end, nor a reason that hadn't been babble and disjointed words. The first time Trout called the hospital, she had come home from school and found he had outwitted her: he had clipped the plug and stripped the cord from the washing machine and plugged it in. The wire hung sparking and sizzling against the wall. The ambulance drivers had glanced at it and told her to leave the house immediately.

As pieces of people's lives rolled onto the sidewalk, Trout imagined she saw the world as her father had, as a great adventure strewn with the nonsensical, unconnected jumble of goods and garbage. Why had she agreed to send him away, she thought painfully. Because his contraptions had no purpose? Because junk was junk, inventions were useful, and the lines between them must never be crossed? Today she wasn't so sure. She could have figured out a way to make his creations harmless, to let him build and sculpt. His madness was tolerable if he spent his time doing things that sane people did, but when he turned his insanity into an art form, moved from reciting logical data to creating whimsy, she and the rest of the world locked him up.

Trout turned toward the bright sound of young girls giggling and shrieking. The children were clambering over pieces of cement in what had been a vacant lot, pulling from under pieces of wood a doll, a mask, a crazy hat. They had found a toy store. Trout started toward them to warn them about glass, then walked into the debris as if in a trance, was drawn to their laughter and the items they had found. There was a stick horse with a fabric head, a top that shot sparks, a witch's mask. She looked with amazement at the game pieces and play money that had spilled into the dirt. She pulled out a stuffed tiger and danced it through the air, wrapped her shoulders in a black cape with an orange plastic cat on the front. She sat in the dirt with the girls and they passed each other items, pulling the triggers of guns, yanking on the strings of talking dolls.

'Because the rabbit's ear folded.' Trout thought of a punch line from her childhood. She couldn't remember her father's joke—only the way she had laughed, and the sight of him stumbling down the road to the lake, flailing his arms with delight, doubling over and resting his hands on his knees to laugh at the ground. She had been just a little girl, like these little girls. Her father had been wearing multiple shirts, a plaid over a dotted, over a pattern of chess pieces. The colors of the shirts blended together as he careened down the road several paces ahead of her, throwing his head back to laugh. "The rabbit's ear folded," he shouted to her, his mouth ecstatically open, his eyes wide and bright. Tracy had skipped behind him, laughing, bobbing her head from side to side and throwing her hands up as he had. The tails of his shirts caught the wind and fluttered. The rabbit's ear had folded, and Daddy wore his lemon shirt with his car shirt, his plaid one and the chess pieces. There was sun coming from his eyes and she understood the joke. He had made sense, they were sharing the joke, and there was no one there, just the thick, soft dust that kicked up over their shoes on the road to the lake. The birds hanging on the cattails didn't even fly away.

*U*neasily shifting on their feet, women in Sabito's stepped over the line of fallen brick and pushed the women's territory into the street. People were gathering on the corners, crossing the street to regard their homes from a distance. Who would temper their fear if they sat alone with their frightened children in their apartments? They congregated with a few neighbors or joined the exodus walking toward the rescue center. The women outside Sabito's watched neighbors settle into chairs around the lamp post, a woman hang mattresses over the railings of her stairs, a man drag a crate of canned goods out of a house and sit on it, a group of young girls prop their feet on their television and stereo equipment.

After the balding man left, a woman with mismatched shoes arrived at the corner, cupped her mouth with her hand, and called out instructions on how to turn off the gas valves in the buildings. The woman separated the gathering crowd into groups and equipped each with a single pair of gloves and a wrench. The teams set off down the street with purposeful strides. Women traded jackets for strollers. Couples stormed into the street, furiously shouting with each other over where to go, what to take with them, who they could stay with. Blankets were piled on the stoops and longingly eyed by people passing by. Did you hear Hunter's Point is on fire? they said, describing the clandestine fireworks factory that had exploded, the rotted hotels that went up like Kleenex on a barbecue. The faint smell of burning wood drifted into the Mission and brought a clenching anxiety into their chests. A man with a camper shell on his truck strode into the street like a circus barker and opened bidding.

Patricia joined the women on the other side of the fallen wall as the National Guardsmen tromped through the Mission in groups of four, most dressed in full riot gear, rifles held tensely across their chests. People moved out of their way, then steered around them as the Guards stood motionless on street corners, one on each side of an intersection. Pedestrians stopped for a moment, reconsidered their direction, moved on slowly. People stuffed their goods deeper into their pockets and closed their shopping bags.

"Just what we need," said a man who stopped with a compatriot beside Patricia, "dumb-ass white boys with guns."

Two of the Guardsmen turned suddenly and ran down a side street. The neighborhood flinched. An elderly woman beside Patricia crossed herself and scurried into the church behind them.

"No Guardia in the financial district," the man said. Patricia turned to face him. He leaned toward his companion, dark eyes shouting from beneath a red bandana. "Who needs 'em: go into that neighborhood you get cut to bits."

The man stepped back, looked Patricia up and down.

"*Maricon*," he muttered, "damn dykes."

Patricia sneered, but stepped back, closer to the bar. The men walked away.

They were looking for people with vans, a woman reported as she entered the bar. They needed volunteers to staff the school because there were children whose parents couldn't get to them. They needed people to dispense water. Who has a truck, a jeep? the women asked each other. Can anybody here drive a school bus? Women poured over the list of activities, took a look around Sabito's, and headed through the hole in the wall into the street. When in Doubt, Volunteer, Patricia thought, watching dykes in the crowd raise their hands and follow nuns toward a school yard. A group of women cradled beers that Louise had announced were on the house since everyone had emptied their pockets into the food fund.

*B*eth and K came to a wooded place on the shoulder of Highway 101, a tiny grove of eucalyptus trees that had been hung with big blue tarps and pieces of plastic, glowing with fires. The place looked like a Casaba, Beth thought, looking around at the people selling food out of plastic bags 'til the food was gone, then selling the plastic bags.

People bought anything they could get, anywhere they could break through the crowd to cart off nuts or a block of cheese. Someone said that hours ago a truck from a sporting goods store had driven in and within a matter of minutes the crowd had bought its tents and sleeping bags, beach chairs, purification tablets, metal containers for matches, three legged stools, propane, lanterns, dishes, and cases of dehydrated food. Even inflatable mattresses were bought up as soon as they were held in the air. Now there was nothing for sale but firewood, plastic (most of it used), legumes that had to be soaked for hours, dirty containers for standing on the gray slabs of stone and drawing water from the little inlet behind the Casaba like women at the Ganges.

Men walked through the crowd openly selling things they'd stolen, hawking parts of the cars parked along the route south. Women clung to the outside of the crowd.

Beth and K elbowed their way into the shelter of a set of trees and crouched down. Given enough time, the supplies in the place would dwindle until people would begin bartering for the junk Beth and K had found by the road. Let times get a little tighter, Beth thought, they'd even buy trash. She surveyed the crowd. In the crevice of the tree, a red ball caught her eye, a paddle with the ball attached, probably dropped by some kid here hours before the place turned so mercenary, Beth thought, envisioning some mother grabbing the kid's hand and yanking him away so fast he lost his toy. Beth batted at it, sending the ball out toward the crowd, then out at the fog that had rolled in like a cruel imitation of the fluffy blankets they all sought, like a veil to hide the desperation in their eyes. Beth shot the ball out at the Hotel Ibis, the Days Inn, and the Embassy Suites, where she had heard that officials had pulled guns to keep 'unregistered guests' out of the building, hit the ball out at the fancy black rectangular buildings with neat red trim, buildings where she knew it pointless to even seek shelter.

"You know those boys?" K asked her.

A band of skinheads walked through the crowd, pushing people aside with thrusting fists, then dipped their hands into sacks of food and walked off with it, challenging the sellers to protest.

"Hey, that's the idea, man," K said, "fuck this no money stuff. I'm gonna cut my hair off."

"What the hell for?" Beth said wearily.

"Are you kiddin'? There's only one thing faster than gettin' people to trust you and share," she said, snidely, struggling to stand up, "and that's gettin' people afraid of you and giving up what they got."

"Hey you," she called to one of the skinheads. "You got a blade?"

After she cut her hair with a skin-head's switchblade, she walked around the Casaba. "Haircuts?" she called, brandishing the blade. "Anybody need a haircut?"

Beth watched her pull her collar up, step out of the fog to crouch in front of white men, the blade just underneath their nose.

"You need a haircut, boy?"

"No . . . No I don't." he stammered, his woman suddenly clutching his arm.

"Then gimme five bucks."

"What?"

"Hey, pay your hairdresser 25 to make you look like him. You can pay me 5 so I don't make you look like me."

The man slowly reached in his pocket, without taking his eyes off the punk girl, and handed her a bill. She looked at it, snorted, stuffed it in her pocket and left, calling "Haircuts? Anybody need a haircut?"

Beth turned away, batted the ball. The fog seemed to make distances greater, pulling Beth's vision of people farther away, finally swallowing them altogether until there was nothing but disjointed sound. Beth walked, without destination, past the clumps of eucalyptus trees with their peeling, raw trunks, past groups of people sitting on their haunches like animals ready to spring.

"You seen the Greenpeace boat?" Beth said to anyone who appeared out of the fog. Some just looked at her and moved on.

Beth stumbled against large slabs of concrete, saw little dots of fires on what must be Coyote Point Beach, she thought, moving toward them.

"You seen the Greenpeace boat?" Beth said at each campfire as she surveyed the group for any extra food or sign of welcome.

"Yeah. It's up on the sand at the end. They're taking volunteers and they say they got food," an older man said.

"Thanks," Beth said and hurried down the beach.

*T*oday, Trout slipped on a pair of glasses with bug-eyes on springs, tilted her head to the sun, and laughed. Her father was right: order was simply the wires and tape one used to fasten coat hangers, dolls, hat racks and irons together, all in pursuit of the imagination. Could that have been what her father understood? Trout looked at the little girls sorting through the broken toys. Then imagination it was. Why not? When her careful planning had turned to a pile of junk, why not try the other option, the one her father had chosen? Trout loved Patricia for her sure-footed nature. She could count on her to appreciate the facts, to be focused on the tangible, her mind clamped around reality like starfish on a rock. There was no dislodging her. After growing up with her father, Trout had been thrown onto the shores of Patricia's constancy, her predictability and steadiness, and she had kissed the ground like a new immigrant. But Patricia could use a release from it all too, couldn't she? Why not simply careen around, oblivious to the powers that carried one along, sightless of the life that lay under the bow, of the processes that made one inch the bank and the other the stream? She brushed the cape off her shoulders to hang down her back and laughed until her eyes watered. She wanted to scoop up all the toys she could find, live with them, sleep on them, carry them to every dinner table for the rest of her life. It had all been lifted and there was something else, there was joy and fun and glorious pointlessness. She was like a teenager after her first glass of wine. She wanted fireworks, sparklers. It's independence day, the first glimpse of Oz. She put the bug-eye glasses in her breast pocket, one of the springs dangling the eyeball down her chest. Patricia, she thought: the two of them could run off together. God knew Patricia could use an end to all her endless work as well. She waved goodbye to the girls and kept moving toward Dolores Park.

Red Cross volunteers, and any civilians they could commandeer, were setting up a rescue station. Trout learned from snatches of conversations on the street that every stretch of grass across the city was filling with people. Golden Gate Park had thousands already setting up camp. In Dolores Park, scores of blankets and freeze-dried food bars were being distributed to ever-expanding lines of people. Trout wove among the crowd, climbed the hills surrounding the park and looked slowly, with great concentration, for Patricia and Beth.

With a few provisions in their hands, people managed to tell, with great relief, a few dramatic stories. They recited facts they had learned from the TVs in the appliance store windows and the green grocers: most of the people who died were in Chinatown and a new housing complex in Hunter's Point. The financial district didn't topple like everyone thought it would but had filled to the brim with glass. People were stuck on the bridges. Food was being flown in by helicopters. The only water that was safe anymore was the stuff in your water heater.

Trout looked across the park at the clusters of people, at a make-shift tent lit by a generator. People moved aside for a group of men dragging instrument cases across the grass. With comments to people at their sides, and a bit of ensuing laughter, a band began to set up.

Trout watched the people in Dolores Park grasp at the entertainment with none of the hesitancy of the cluster approached by the mime. They treated the members of this Latin dance band like the new heroes of the city. People gave up their seats in the grass and moved their children to make room for the rag-taggle group now blowing gentle 1940s tunes on the saxophone. With some protests and hanging back from their partners, a few furtive glances, calculating looks, the couples began moving in slow circles. A few people, animated with relief, began staking out their space, putting elbows out and dancing. Others joined them simply for a place to put their bodies. Several women hanging on the edge of the crowd began to cry, finally broken by the strange juxtaposition of a city in ruin still ready to dance. The music drew people off the streets, following the sound, flocking to some semblance of order even if it was simply the structure of tones from a horn, or memories of Saturday nights. The world could not be ending, Trout imagined them thinking, there was still the

rumba. There was a way to grin and bear it, to sit on the
grass of Dolores Park with a precious glass of water and an
Army blanket, and follow the steady beat of the band.

Trout, sitting on the root of a tree, could think of nothing
finer than to dance at a time like this, or anytime for that
matter, she thought. To Trout, dancing had been the best of
romance, something she had talked about with Maggie, the
woman next door, after vacuuming on Saturday. Tracy
would hurry through her chores and change from a t-shirt
into a blouse, run across the lawns buttoning it up. Patricia
contended that Trout was a dedicated femme because it was
something she had studied from afar. In Trout's household
of men's socks and coarse wool shirts, Maggie had been life
in another world, where things were pink, not brown. Maggie
had extra pillows on top of her bedspread and fringed rugs
that weren't there to wipe your feet. She hung pictures of
kittens, not The Fish Species Of Northern Michigan.

As soon as she heard Tracy's knock at the screen door,
Maggie took off the ruffled apron she wore over her slacks.
They kicked off their shoes and pushed Maggie's vacuum
cleaner aside, turned on the record player and slid over the
rug, Maggie in stockings and pedal-pushers, a crewneck
sweater, Tracy in dungarees and a rumpled shirt buttoned
wrong. She and Maggie each held their imaginary dance
partners as Maggie talked of the Dance Club and dressing
up, of stepping out, of men as Dance Partners, and how
infrequently she found one. "Nothin' in the world like a man
with a sense of rhythm," she said conspiratorially, then
lowered her voice, "one who'll move his hips." Tracy
wondered whether her father was capable of remembering
the steps. Out of Maggie's cedar closet every Saturday came
the red Chinese-style silk dress, the one wrapped in plastic,
or the brilliant green polyester brocade, the muskrat stole,
even make-up. Trout lay across Maggie's bed, watching the
woman ready herself for the date, then slipped out the back
door before the man arrived and stationed herself on her
porch. Maggie always made her date regard the water near
Trout's house, knowing the girl was hiding on the porch to
get a look at him.

As a nine-year-old, at Girl Scout day camp, Tracy primped and preened for the Dad's Night Square Dance. Her father had come up from the lake during the height of boat-selling season, just to dance with her. She could finally wear her yellow skirt and blouse, the one Maggie helped her pick out. The camp dining hall, usually smelling of oatmeal or hamburger, was filled with a pine-scented breeze off the lake. Now it was suitable for the magic of low lights and polished floors, for dancing that was not just a joy described by Maggie anymore. Little Tracy twirled and spun and kept up with the alaman lefts. The camp counselors said she was the belle of the ball.

Her father went to the men's room and Tracy slipped out to the screen porch to peek in at the dancers, and at the sight of true love. They made a lacy pattern across the floor with their twirlings and their skirts. She watched for her father, for him to join the web. Her father suddenly burst onto the dance floor, shoving people aside with his exuberance, and began tap dancing, spinning, doing the jig. He grabbed another man around the waist and spun him until the man shoved him away and pulled back into the crowd with a snarl. Tracy watched his feet and thought how happy he must be, then looked around at the reaction of the other men. Everyone was staring at her father. They held their glasses of punch in mid-air, then turned away: there was no music. The night draped itself around her as she stood in the cool, semi-dark, filling with a pain that settled in her joints. He wasn't following the rules.

Tonight, Trout jumped up from where she was sitting and pushed her way into the circle of dancers, stepping with the music, hands on moving hips, raising her arms high into the air, her cape swinging behind her. Vindication for my father, she thought: now we shall celebrate the mess of discordant objects, the whole city dancing in the space where things become disconnected. We are unplugged toasters, bottles without caps, railings with no stairs. I am my father, considering this a fine way to live.

As the hesitant dancers in Dolores Park grew more bold despite lack of drink or even food, Trout slowed her dancing but refused to look at the faces of the crowd. She felt the loneliness of the nine-year-old seeping in again. Where was Patricia? What about Evelyn and Maria in Oakland? Where were the lesbians? All around her were families, groups of young men, but no lesbians. They must be congregating somewhere: dykes always came up with their own systems for themselves. That's at least another place to look for Patricia, she thought, leaving the dance floor and heading toward Sabito's.

*T*he day had not been what San Francisco loyalists called "London weather." ("I quite like the fog, actually. Very English. Gray and all.") But as the unusually warm and clear day turned to evening, the fog rolled into San Francisco. Huge, heavy clouds of it piled around the Golden Gate and across the bridge in strips that moved fast and obscured vision. San Franciscans frequently saw the fog come in rapidly, but rarely this dense. It streamed between buildings, down avenues, enveloping people, catching them in mid-step and taking away their view of the street. The fog crested over the hills and blanketed people as a painter would suddenly draw snow on a landscape. The fog filled the City and held it still.

As Trout coursed through the Mission, people stopped their wanderings, now concerned with where they would sleep. Little bands of people loosely connected now solidified their bond, turned circles in the street looking for a way out of the dampness. Groups of men who were picking through other people's possessions left their endeavors and sought shelters of their own. Families standing in what had been their homes crouched down with their children, groping for something with which to cover themselves. In the density of the fog, people walking down the street appeared to Trout without warning, not just frightening her, but also being frightened by others sitting at the roadside. Trout, after a number of wrong turns, walked into Sabito's as if she had suddenly vaporized into the room.

Patricia held Trout in her arms and cried. The two relayed their stories, touching each other's faces as if meeting after years. Patricia steered Trout into the alley between the buildings and pressed her against the wall, pulling her into her arms with motions of familiarity and hunger. Trout, gleefully, face nuzzling her lover's neck, described the fight to save the baby, the dogs, the dancing in the park. One of Patricia's hands slid into the depth of Trout's hair. Trout flung her arms around Patricia with relief. Beth abandoning her for the ducks, Patricia recounted, as her other hand pressed into the small of Trout back. Her conduit perfectly bent and the horrible sound of the rumble, she said as she cupped Trout's buttocks. The marvelous combinations in the street: a box of cereal, radio parts, Trout said excitedly, venetian blinds twisted around a chair. She bit into Patricia's lips. Patricia turned Trout around, pressed herself into Trout's shoulderblades and slipped her hands inside Trout's bulky shirt. With her arms protectively crossed over Trout's chest, her palms gently on her breasts, Patricia held Trout tighter and told her stories of pain. The way Mark had tumbled down the stairs as they collapsed, the destruction of the truck.

"Baby," Trout said, wiping the tears from her cheeks while smiling, "look at Batman on my shoes!"

A storm door broken by a lamp shade, three cups set on a pillow as if the crown jewels. Patricia couldn't understand why Trout's voice was so bright: it sounded hideous to her. Every item she saw shouted injustice, yet Trout saw comedy. Trout called the debris in the streets in "juxtaposition." Patricia called it junk. How could she tell Trout about the woman's hand waving from between the splintered wood of her stairway, or the way the woman's eyes had tried to jump out of her face onto Patricia? Hear me! Patricia thought, as she removed one of her hands from Trout's blouse and slid it into the ample waist-band of her borrowed trousers. Listen! she pleaded silently as her fingers traversed her lover's mound, and the two inhaled together as Patricia's finger's found Trout's center. Hear me! Patricia thought.

Patricia clutched Trout's hand and led her into the bar. Trout said nothing. It wouldn't be appropriate, even in this

dyke bar. They could kiss, they could even display a
raunchy sexuality, but rarely did the women speak in public
of the intensity of their feelings, and no one ever talked to
others about it. Strange for all of them to be so reticent,
Trout thought. Complaining about one's lover had a
tremendous vocabulary, an unending supply of "She always
has to do it this way" and "She'd kill me if she knew."
People simply didn't want to hear that it was Patricia, her
little face, her graying hair, the way she ran her hand down
Trout's back in a way that Trout could feel through every
vertebra. Trout wanted to decorate Patricia, wrap her up in
something with gold threads. She wondered sometimes if
Patricia really understood how their being together was what
made everything work. And now they had a chance to make
it work in a whole new way, with nothing but their whims
and their desires driving their days.

"Baby, I know this sounds weird but, listen," Trout said,
lowering her voice, "in some ways this earthquake is a
blessing."

"Jesus, Trout," Patricia said, startled.

"No, listen. Now that it's destroyed, everything reverts to
cash value. Do you see what I'm saying? We've got a policy
that pays $40,000 per room in the house for the contents.
Replacement value. Earthquake insurance. Do you see? You
don't remember, but I worked really hard to get this for us.
Years ago. Now, we don't have $40,000 worth of stuff in
every room but there's no way to prove it. Let's go back to
the house and get the insurance papers," Trout said. "Put in
a claim. Do you see what I'm saying? With the money, we
could go anywhere. We're free, finally."

"Free of what?" Patricia regarded her suspiciously. It was
unsettling, these stories of Trout's. This situation was no
goddamn laughing matter. "Half the City's a shambles. The
jobs are gone, do you understand this?" Patricia said.

Trout took a sip of Patricia's beer, as if listening to a
children's story, Patricia thought, as if watching some damn
documentary of a country far away. This wasn't like her.
Patricia looked away for a moment, then looked back at
Trout. Where was her traditional "now Patricia, it won't be so
hard to make this right. . ." or her contention that things

moved in circles—that was one of her great ones ("it's simply a cycle, Patricia, one power rises and then falls. You should read more history")—or even the simple way Trout set her hand against Patricia's cheek as if to say "now now, don't take it too deeply into your heart." Trout was saying nothing.

"I'm telling you," Patricia said, raising both the volume and intensity of her voice, "what about the nuclear reactor built on the fault?"

"We could live for years on the profit if we moved to Greece, or Mexico," Trout said dreamily.

"Earth to Trout," Patricia said. "I don't draw a salary, remember? No truck—you know the truck is destroyed, don't you?—no tools. The tools were in the truck. Hello? Anybody home in your head?"

Patricia slid her arm farther down the bar and leaned her head in her palm, regarding Trout's silent face.

"Do you still have a job, do you suppose?" Patricia asked.

"God, I hope not," Trout said, laughing.

"Your company has no reason to build in San Francisco again, so both of us are out of work. Plain and simple. No money, no home." And the sound of a woman screaming in my head, Patricia thought.

"I don't want to do that again," Trout said quietly.

"Do what?" Patricia said carefully.

"I don't want to do another job like that."

"All right, get a different one, if you can."

"No, I mean I don't want . . . any job."

Patricia laughed. "Yeah, well, you got company all over America, honey, but that's the way it works." Patricia cleared her throat. This wasn't like Trout at all. She must be very frightened, and that made Patricia very frightened.

"No."

Patricia straightened, sat upright.

"No, what?"

"I can't do that again. I . . . don't want to live that way again. All that . . . planning."

"That's what it takes, Trout," Patricia said cautiously, "tiny gain on top of tiny gain. You can't stop. You can't."

"We can move to Mexico. Just live, Patricia."

"You can't escape by running to Mexico," Patricia said incredulously. "For God's sake, girl, only the really rich believe that money comes in, regardless. The rest of us have to plan like sons-of-bitches."

"Now we can leave, don't you understand that? Honeymoon," Trout pleaded. "We can run on the beach like kids. Now really nothing is important but being together."

Being together and being alone? Patricia wondered. What about other women? Trout had made sure they didn't have many friends (why cope with communal decisions? she always said), but Patricia couldn't leave this behind, watching women on the streets, in their cars together, dancing, walking by her with their scents of musk and rosewater, soap, hairspray. She needed them. Sometimes she went to the bars alone (go ahead, Trout would say, I can't stand to see people get sloppy) just to smell them, to watch them walk. Now Trout wanted to pack it in and move to a Mexican beach town, not a lesbian within a hundred miles. Patricia would dry up and die. Not that they spent any time with other people here: 'Why should we have a dinner party?' Trout would exclaim. 'Let's just go to a restaurant. Then we don't have to guess what everyone wants to eat.' But always, alone. Why did she do that? Did Trout really find other people that unmanageable? Fear of Entree Varieties Drives Couple to Forgo Friends. And now to forgo an entire city.

Patricia had to believe it, Trout thought. She had to agree. It was the only plan she could think of, and there had to be a plan didn't there? The plan just didn't have to be as . . . well, as severe as the last one. Didn't Patricia understand that it was over? It wasn't possible to put a machine like that back together. The system had . . . failed. It had only one task left and that was to cash itself out.

And why not, she thought? Her whole life had been consumed by statement due dates and charts of prescriptions. She had owned a goddamn receipt box when she was twelve years old. Wasn't there someplace where she could make . . . sand castles for a change? Isn't that what children did? Couldn't they go where she wouldn't even wonder if it would be a sunny day, where the sunshine was

so plentiful they could close the shutters against the
afternoon? She wanted to live in a place where her most
challenging decision would be whether to ask for mangoes
or papayas with the chicken. Patricia could learn to fish.
Commerce would be reaching across a stall for the reddest
pomegranate, a couple of coins in her palm. Time would be
measured by the slap of waves. Evenings could be
perspiring glasses and the torpid struggle of ceiling fans. In
the mornings they'd check the bathroom walls for lizards
and brew the local coffee. Patricia would lay her head in her
lap as she recited from a dog-eared paperback they'd
already read. Sand would cling to the rounds of their arms
and breasts, falling on the tables and towels, no trouble, no
struggle, it would become part of their decor, their make-up,
the feel of their sheets and the taste of sex. Why couldn't
Patricia understand how beautiful that could be? Even for
just a few years, long enough to lose the tag of *tourist* and
find a couple of kids who would stop by for candy, even that
much would be a relief. She could arrange that. Compared
to the intricate machinery she'd concocted around their life
in San Francisco, life on an island had to be heaven. Put in
for the insurance refund, sell a few stocks to finance them
while they waited for the checks, book a flight, and let the
accountant track the paperwork for them. Couldn't they be
just people who lived their lives for the sheer joy of it? For
the minute-to-minute blessing?

"Hey Louise," Patricia called. "You hear this? Trout wants
to move to Mexico. Whaddaya think of that?"

A woman at the end of the bar, in leather, with
close-cropped orange hair and shaved temples, turned to the
group with a sparkle in her eye. "Mexico? Now there's an
idea."

Louise moved cautiously toward them, crossed her arms
over her chest, watching out of the corner of her eye the
leather-clad woman inching her way toward Trout and
Patricia.

"I say, where the lady goes, I'd follow," Louise said.

Patricia tossed her head back in irritation. "Forever,
Louise. She wants to live there. Never come back. No job,
no work, nothin' but the goddamn beach."

"Forever?" Louise asked.

"Forever," Patricia drove home her point.

"Then I say, buy a gun."

"You see?" Patricia said, gesturing to Louise, "who would want to live in Mexico? You know what the men are like down there? And where are the lesbians? The lesbian bars?"

"I don't care about lesbian bars," Trout said plaintively.

Patricia rubbed her forehead, looked at Trout sternly.

"Any gathering place . . . for safe relaxation," Patricia said pointedly.

Trout turned away. When had she ever lived for the smell of a breeze? When had she ever jumped into the ocean for the feel of the water? Even as a child, she only canoed when she had booby-traps to check, or skated when she feared a problem might be developing with the ice shacks. Always an end result. To everything. They didn't live anymore. They planned for, or protected themselves against, a life that might possibly develop in the future. Couldn't they just eat and sleep and fuck without it leading somewhere, without results all the time, without the calculations and the objectives and the file folders? There had to be life without these God-awful projects, existence without a paper-trail. Patricia would see. It would be marvelous. She'd start on it in the morning.

"We're free, Patricia," Trout said again, hoping it might strike a chord in the woman this time.

"Yeah," the leather-clad carrot-top said. "Mexico. You need a traveling companion?"

Patricia glared at the woman, turned her back to her and stared closely at Trout.

"Mexico, yeah. Only place the dollar's worth anything," carrot-top said. "I'll go with you, blondie. Even pay my own way."

"This is not your conversation," Patricia said, standing tall and taking her hands out of her pockets, "and this absolutely does not concern you."

"See," Trout said, gesturing at the red-head. "It's an idea that appeals."

"And is hinged upon the reaction of an insurance company," Patricia said, trying to point out the contradiction.

"Sweetheart, we have the best insurance money can buy: I researched it for two months. Eastern company, small, very high rate of payments to their insured. Replacement value."

"Lower your voice," Patricia said sternly, shooting a look at the leather-girl who was reaching for a martini olive and snuggling closer to Trout.

"Besides, we have to replace all the stuff first," Patricia said.

"No."

"Show receipts. We'll get lost in the paper shuffle. It'll be years before we see a goddamn dime."

"No receipts. It goes by blue-book, current listing price of items. We're talking," Patricia grabbed Trout's arm and pulled her closer as the carrot-top leaned into them. Trout looked around the room, lowered her voice, "two hundred thousand dollars, easily."

"We have to pay for all that shit first," Patricia said irritably.

"Alright, so $190,000."

"And the truck."

"$175,000, then. Can't you imagine how long we could live on that money? My God, we'd both be retirement age."

"Cabo San Lucas," carrot-top said, moving into the middle of the room and doing the rumba with a beer bottle pressed to her stomach. "Warm sun, white sand beach." She shuffled across the dance floor, pushing backpacks and suitcases out of the way. Women who were curled on the floor with their possessions snarled at her but pulled their goods closer to them.

"Let me get this straight, Trout," Patricia said, feeling the pressure increase in her chest and the tone in her voice become more sarcastic. "This plan works because we'd be living in a goddamn grass hut the rest of our lives?"

*T*he spinning lights of police cars and the miniaturized gestures of cranes made Jacob and Cherice look at each other, aware of how isolated and high above the ground they were. Jacob balanced on one foot, put his hand on Cherice's shoulder.

"We'll be all right," he said. "We'll get out of here."

"I'm in no hurry, Peaches," she said, with false gaiety, throwing her hands up at the city. "Now we really know brandy is in order."

She was never in a hurry to get home, was she? Stopped in at every green grocer as she walked home, didn't even turn on the lights when she got there, just threw her clothes on the floor and went to bed. What was there? The furniture was rented: her memorabilia was in storage (since Monica left you, a voice said but was quickly silenced).

"Maybe we should call someone." He hobbled to the phone, punched every button on the console but couldn't get a line out. Cherice was relieved. Well, why not? Who said you had to live a House-and-Garden existence? She put up the front. Wasn't that all anybody could expect? Nice suits, manicured nails, a good briefcase. Everyone thought she was the picture-perfect type. But it only went so far.

"Just as well," Jacob said, leaning heavily on the desk.

See what I mean? Cherice wanted to shout. It was a free day. The market was suspended, no one was working, nothing was expected of anyone. She'd listen to his troubles, no problem, just don't put us back out there. Don't force us back into context, she thought, then wondered why he should matter so much, this two-bit, beautiful accountant.

"I call home there's bound to be a man answering the phone."

"You live with a man?" Cherice asked.

"No," he said, a little too emphatically for Cherice's taste. "My . . . girlfriend's moving out. He'll be there, sure as hell." Cherice didn't reply.

"Ah, a brilliant bouquet," Cherice said, waving both brandy snifters under her nose. "Here you go, Peaches."

"I hope everything in my apartment broke," he said, taking the brandy from her and tossing back a large swallow.

"She's the type to take everything in sight?"

"Yeah," he said shortly.

Aren't we all, Cherice thought. "Ah, you'll find somebody else, Peaches."

What did she know? he sighed. Shitty job, no relationship. He wasn't competitive. Women flocked to him, all right, and then ran away like chickens in high heels.

"Look, she left me today, OK?" he said. "The whole city's fallen down. My foot hurts. So I'm not in a good mood. This is a crime?"

"Fine, be miserable," Cherice said. "It must be tough being a good-looking white man," she said sarcastically. "Go lay down; put your foot up."

Jacob hobbled to the sofa and stretched out. She didn't know. Men are like the British Empire, he thought mournfully as he settled his foot on a pillow. The old crumbling order. Old men wearing white gloves and morning dress to fetch junk mail. One old guy, one old servant, the whole house screaming, "This used to be something, will you pretend it still is?" That's what white straight men are, didn't she get it? Charade of the glory days. People hated them for it, and rightly so, but what Jacob hadn't expected was that people hoped they would hold up the standards at the same time. To show that they once had had power, had held the reins. Women wanted just enough chivalry to know that the men had once been schooled in how to be dominant, just enough money for the women to fool themselves into believing it was because the men were good at what they did, that they were smart, not because of Oxford shirts, straight blonde hair and a knack for making their bosses feel like members of the fucking Polo Club. Jacob knew it: he was a Jew who looked like a Cherokee, watching the white boys every day of his life. The women flocked to him, that much Cherice was right about, but the men stayed clear. He didn't remind them of the old order.

And he wasn't the old order. He was a radical, and even that they discounted. They slipped his objections to their racist jokes and their sexist sleight of hands into their definition of him as an East Coast liberal Jew, and they assumed he was a good accountant, since "they" are so good with money, after all.

"I don't even know why it fell apart," Jacob said. "She just announced it last night."

Cherice turned away. Here he goes, she thought. Hets just dished up information about themselves, spilling out the details of their marriages, lovers, their kids, the number of abortions they'd had, and where they go dancing. All the details came tumbling out, at the drinking fountains, at the coffee stand. Cherice was always amazed. Their vacation pictures were passed around like so much corporate stationery: pictures of them lying around in each other's arms, kissing on the terrace. What freedom they had! What a privilege their exposure was! Everyone knew the details of the courtship, the wedding, the flowers, the in-laws, the hall and the dress and the goddamn honeymoon. She went to their wedding showers and saw the contents of their cupboards; she went to their baby showers and knew what sheets got wet at night. They bloody well got paid for the time they were gone! Announce that you're marrying another woman and they'd give you something at the office alright, but it sure wouldn't be a party. If this guy wants to spill his guts all over the rug, let him, but he better not expect it in return.

Ten minutes later, Cherice was pacing the rug, hand on her hip. Now she'd really done it, just gone and laid herself wide open, swearing all the way that it wasn't any of his business and she bloody well wasn't going to let him in on it. Why did she have to tell him she was a lesbian, or used to be a lesbian, or was a lesbian in confusion? She couldn't stand it, the way their faces all of a sudden became constricted, as they tried to maintain the same expression while their minds raced around their ideas of what was a lesbian and what wasn't.

"She's got the pink lace bra and the pink lace panties and pink satin on her tennis shoes, can you believe that?" she continued, dancing around the information she had just thrown out like it had been the time of day. Cherice had turned the sound off the television and had settled into a chair near the sofa.

"She's doin' the deodorant spray and the feminine spray and the shoe spray and the hair spray. I swear to you, there are more fluorocarbons comin' off this woman than a GE plant and I think, now *that's* straight. Seriously," she said, leaning forward. "Do you know that straight women can eat an entire meal without the food ever touching their lips?"

"Oh, for God's sake," Jacob said. All he did was bring up Abigail, he wasn't asking for a senatorial debate on the ways of women, let alone this . . . new information. Jesus.

"No, I mean it," she said, as Jacob shifted on the sofa in disagreement. "Have you watched them? Turns out they're trying to avoid their lipstick. It's amazing."

What was she saying? Jacob thought. She's pacing around the room talking about pumps and push-up bras and he's thinking, it's true, it's true for me as well. At last week's meeting the white boys were insufferable. He couldn't say, though God knows he was tempted, 'What! The schmuck owns your gonads? Do something!' but no, you straighten your tie, clear your throat like phlegm gave you authority or something and say 'Clearly, the client, now in arrears on the payment due, is no longer entitled to avail himself of the blah blah.' You don't even know it's your own voice talking.

"They pick up things without using the ends of their fingers, scratch themselves without ever touching skin on skin," she said, going through the motions of a woman rubbing her eye with the long tip of a fingernail. "They never hug you. Not really. They just sort of bend at the waist. 'Oh, it's so good to see you'," she said in a high voice, "'come give me . . . a lean.'"

Jacob chuckled, then feigned seriousness. "That's a sweeping generalization," he said, but thinking, quite surprised, that's right, and I don't wear a yarmulke in the Fillmore. You don't wear it in the Financial District, either, unless you don't mind that everyone assumes you're selling diamonds, can you beat that? There are ways you talk when you're surrounded by Jews that you don't in front of the goyim. You just don't. So she's a lesbian, eh?

"Admittedly, a generalization," Cherice said, throwing her arms out, then growing serious.

Oh this is a good one, Jacob thought, I should call my Aunt Sylvie, say 'Hey, I was talking with this lesbian and she's got a point.' That'd go over big.

Cherice crossed her legs. Jacob regarded her electric blue silk blouse, the raw silk suit, the long legs ending in sheer matching stockings. Very expensive, he thought. Hard to imagine she's a lesbian: she dresses so well. Guess a comment about that wouldn't go over.

"Anyway," she said softly. "Funny how you always have to go through this. You say different things, but every time you meet someone who's straight, whether you say it or just imply it, you have to have this Lesbian Studies 101 discussion."

"Sorry to bore you," Jacob said sarcastically.

"Oh, I'm sorry. I didn't mean it that way. But don't you find that's true?"

Jacob didn't answer. Like inviting Presbyterians to a Seder, he thought. Despite living in San Francisco, he didn't really have any gay friends. A couple gay guys came to parties, but no lesbians. Definitely not lesbians. The friends he did have wouldn't even go into the Castro to restaurants. A neighborhood full of skin flicks, they always said.

"Frankly, I don't even see how men and women get together. It's incredible to me," she said, waving her Scotch glass. "You watch movies, and the things that are said astound me."

"Oh for Christsake, you can't base stuff like that on Hollywood!" he said defensively.

"All right, Peaches, example. He says, 'have dinner with me' and what he means to say is 'commit to something, some liaison. Come out in public where people will assume we have a connection. Better yet, let's go somewhere in my car so you're stranded if you leave me. Listen to my explanation, drink some wine to break down your resolve.' Then she says 'no' and tries to close the door. He sticks his foot in the door. Now, in a man's culture, the guy'd get his goddamn toes blown off, you see what I mean?"

"Yeah, well," Jacob said uneasily.

"But in the courtship rituals of men and women, that's considered pursuit. He pursues even if it means being deceitful," Cherice continued. "So she says 'no,' and you know what he says? He says 'I'll pick you up at eight.' And he closes the door. She hasn't even said yes but that doesn't matter."

"That's overcoming adversity," Jacob said.

"That's deceit," Cherice said vehemently, pointing at him with a lacquered nail.

"That's romance."

"Precisely my point: in your culture, deceit is considered romantic," Cherice said. "Or this one," she said, warming to her topic. "He never says, 'Have a relationship with me,' or even just 'Have pointless sex with me.'"

"Hey now," Jacob warned.

"Whatever, but he says, 'have dinner; you've got to eat anyway,' and describes the menu. Reduce it to logical little pieces, you see it a thousand times, it's incredible. 'Just let me drive you home.' 'Just let me . . . something.' Or he says 'put suntan lotion on my back.' So she says 'no' and he picks up her hand—that's the part I hate the most—puts suntan lotion in it, and lays it on his back," she said, pausing for effect. "Let me tell you, any man picks up a man's hand, it's fighting time. But that kind of action is considered romantic."

Jacob studied his foot, which he imagined was swelling to grotesque proportions as every minute passed. He had to admit that as she described the scenario, he could see it was true. But what was worse, as far as he was concerned, was the nagging suspicion that he was sick of it all, too. Women said he wasn't romantic, he didn't communicate. He didn't sweep them off their feet, they said, and he wondered if they meant he wouldn't act like Cherice's Hollywood movies.

"What is this, all his fault?" he said rhetorically.

"No, of course not," Cherice said, animated now that he had engaged in the conversation. "She says no to dinner at eight, and at seven o'clock, gets dressed. Unbelievable," she said, slapping her hands on her hips. She poured herself another brandy. "I don't know why you people find dishonesty so alluring!"

Jacob sat back against the cushions. "Yeah. I'm pretty sick of it myself."

Y ou'd love it, Patricia," Trout pleaded, following Patricia
as she paced around the bar, bumping into women who
continued to haul bags of groceries and bedding into the bar.
"Live like the leisure class for a change," she whispered.

"No," Patricia said, getting angry. "Don't try to hook me in
with that. I've lived in the middle of nowhere and there's
nothing peaceful about it. And I've also lived in somebody
else's culture, remember? I've left before, and you know
what? All it means is comin' home with your tail even deeper
between yours legs."

"Oh Patricia, don't be so negative."

"Uno mas cervesa, bartender. Who else wants to move to
Mexico?" the carrot-top called as she spun around in the bar.

"I told you," Patricia said, charging across the floor, "this
doesn't fucking concern you."

"Hey, hey. Just buildin' community."

"Well do it for yourself," Patricia said. "I don't need your
assistance."

She turned to Trout. "You remember, that scholarship
money came to my apartment instead of the admissions
office and off I went. First real money ever hit my palm and I
was gone. Big beautiful Europe. You ever met a
working-class girl who jets off to Europe? Neither had I,
that's why I did it. Shipped Beth back to my Mom like
someone returning a stolen watch: give her up, no, keep her,
no, give her up."

Patricia had fussed over the child's shoes, her sweater,
tried to stuff short hairs into a pony-tail. Beth was ten years
old, and Patricia had regarded her with fear: then she was a
child, round-stomached and silly, but soon she would begin
asking tough questions, making up her own mind, and
damned if she wasn't going to demand that Patricia
understand what she, herself, believed. Unmasked her, that's
what she would have done, shown up her own confusion.
Better the kid grow up with the strictness of Meredith, even if
it was all out of proportion to what could be expected in the
world, even if it was couched in headlines. At least it was
unflinching. Better that than see her mother waffle, Patricia
had thought.

"This was my chance to finally see something, to be somebody other than the tree-tall woman from Kentucky, that's what I thought," Patricia said. "I thought this was my chance, like you think, but let me tell you, it hurt. It hurt bad."

When the bus had finally pulled away, taking her daughter back to Kentucky, Patricia had stared for an hour at a puddle of transmission fluid the bus had left behind, then boarded a bus to her apartment, and packed for Europe.

"It's the same everywhere, Trout: you're rich, you live like the rich. You're poor, you live poor. Doesn't matter you can't speak the language, or you don't have the accent right. I wound up in squats, abandoned buildings. Bunch'a Leftist boys pried a cement block from a boarded-up window, delved out the flats to the most God-awful band of people."

"It doesn't have to be that way."

"Hey, I was free, Trout," Patricia said. "Planned my days around the opening of the bar across the street, since it was the only toilet nearby. Now that's planning for the future, don't you think? Spent my time on picket lines, demonstrations. Christ, we took over Westminster Abbey for an afternoon."

"But your time was your own," Trout lamented. "You didn't have to . . . account for everything."

There was no accounting for anything at all, Patricia thought. She had gone to Amsterdam, thinking the problem might be the English, the squats, but it wasn't. One weekend had been enough to tell her, one Friday evening of leaning on a marble bar, one Friday night with a pair of long legs wrapped around her, a Friday midnight of sweat and motion, a daybreak of spent candles, deep sleep. Mystery Legs Weave Night of Wonder.

"Yeah, great," Patricia said sarcastically. "Those times had their price."

Far away from her daughter, thousands of miles from people or a culture she knew, what had she been? Not English, not Dutch, she hadn't even been a mother there. And in the morning, she hadn't been a lover, either. Dripping from the shower, Patricia had returned to an empty room.

No lover, no name, no phone number. Departure of Hypnotic Legs Throws Cold Sheen on Frosty City. There had been no belonging and so no solution, no nothing.

"Patricia," Trout said, looking away, looking back, unable to say anything more.

"You can't leave motherhood behind. All that happened is that I had to come back to a country where I had to start again. That's what I think of your precious freedom."

Trout looked away. Patricia took her hand.

"You can't run away, Trout. It follows you."

When she had come to collect Beth, she had faced a grown woman, it seemed, a woman who had learned the answers to too many questions from someone else, Patricia thought shamefully. Patricia had pretended not to notice that there was something wrong, pretended she was still convinced the poor answers the child had gotten were better than the confusion she had to offer. Beth's face had been closed and hard, as if she had breathed in the smoke of Meredith's anger and it had embittered her, too. Beth had stood with a defiant twist to her foot, her hand shoved into a coat pocket. She had flung her hair out of her face before she spoke and her mouth seemed to curl at one end. Beth had stared at Patricia for quite a while but said nothing, then turned to Meredith, kissed her lightly on the cheek, and climbed into Patricia's car.

For that matter, Patricia wondered, what about Beth now? Who knew if Beth was even safe? How could she have gotten across town? Why would she go? That would be a fine situation: run off to some foreign country while the kid was out of town. What's gotten into Trout? She isn't flaky like this. Sure, she's an optimist, but she always took care of business first. Starting over was going to be hard enough, without postponing it for a few years with some damn vacation. Besides, Trout wasn't even talking about a vacation: she wanted to live in Mexico. Absurd. Waste all their money on island life? Today the kid might be resilient, Patricia thought, but what if she were sleeping alone on a cardboard box like she had seen other people doing? She wanted Beth here. The whole city was in chaos, so her own confusion seemed less noticeable. If she left for Mexico she'd lose another chance to make it right with Beth, she thought, surprised that she even had the desire. It wasn't something she had recognized before. Mother Sweeps Rubble of Life Aside to Bond With Bitter Child. She'd have to explain this to Trout.

Beans were cooking on one of the burners Patricia had constructed, sending great plumes of steam into the air when someone lifted the lid. Patricia squeezed Trout's hand, hoping to wring some gesture of . . . what, Patricia wondered? A returned grasp that told her to hang on, they'd make it? That Patricia's story of Europe had finally gotten through to her? She needed to hold her, to touch that crazy hair of hers, but her hand just sat there framing the beer bottle. Trout wasn't acting like herself.

"Why hadn't you told me this before?" Trout asked.

"I've told you about Europe."

"Yeah, but not this part."

"Well," Patricia said skeptically, "it had never come up."

Because I never asked, Trout thought. I never questioned why she was so determined to build such an ordinary life, she thought as if meeting her for the first time. That's what I built for my father, and that's what I've built her. It was sad. Trout peeled a set of napkins off the pile on the bar and stared at her lap.

Answer Woman Fails Test of Seismic Shock, Patricia thought. This silence had never happened before. You could tell her anything and she'd give you a perspective. One word and Patricia would pull Trout up against her cheek, but Trout wasn't saying it. The desire pushed against the inside of her chest, felt like it was collecting like a rash on the palms of her hands.

"Trout," Patricia said sternly, unsure of whether she was going to mention her concerns for Beth or break down and recount the story of the dead woman. Trout should be able to see it in her face, she always had. Then she'd stop this nonsense. Tonight, Trout broke away and climbed back onto a barstool, folded shapes from cocktail napkins and swung her feet. Patricia glared at her. She's got to see the pain here, she thought.

"Duck," Trout said smiling, holding her paper creation up to Patricia's face.

W e're better we're off here in the hospital, Mrs.
Williamson thought. She looked at her children, counted them again, bent her shoulders lower over the baby with its bandaged leg. When her husband saw what had happened to his house he would be angry, but when Charlie saw the destruction of his project room, his soldering iron, his remote control airplanes, his model boats, well, there'd be hell to pay. And she'd have to pay it.

The neon Schlitz bull was smashed, and his picture of him and his brother on their fishing trip, all the special fly-tying gear, the casting reels, the ornaments for the truck he had bought and hadn't even had time to install; she had seen the fragments when she got that neighbor girl a saw. It hadn't started that way, she thought, looking past her children. He had worked on the house and she only had to come down the basement steps, say "Charlie?" dressed in something new, or with her hair done, and he'd set down his tools and scoop her up. Then the babies arrived, and so did the beer bottles. "Charlie?" she'd say and he wouldn't look up. More packages arrived, more and more babies. More bruises. She'd fought him every step of the way when he brought them home like booty; he'd show her circuitry and joysticks while she screamed about children who needed dental work. Always an impasse, always a bellowing voice and finally his big hand that slammed on the table as warning that one more word and it'd slam into her. And it always did. She'd wind up with bruises where the kids couldn't see, because of a variable speed, miniature dune-buggy. She'd paid the price when each of the damn things arrived, but she knew better than to hang around now that they'd all been lost. Everything, all the replacement parts, the drills and screwdrivers, the glue-guns. She didn't have room for that many bruises. She'd go to San Jose, to her sister's, and when he'd stopped raging over his trinkets enough to think about his children, she'd have moved on to Modesto, or maybe Texas. Charlie Jr. was already developing a taste for electronic trucks and remote controls, the way some boys inherit their father's noses. One boy-toy junkie was enough, she thought, rocking the baby closer to her. One was plenty.

*P*atricia ran her tongue across the back of her teeth. Something's different. Patricia looked at Trout and wondered who she was. She again saw Trout's wide-set, lashless eyes and the way her nose pulled a bit to one side. Trout had those stupid glasses in her pocket. Everybody else is scrambling for a warm shirt and Trout's covered up with a felt witch's cape. Christ. Patricia noticed whole patches of gray in Trout's wild fluff of hair. She's got more wrinkles than I thought. Patricia saw the outline of Trout's body, the air between them, the place where Trout's tennis shoe met the floor. There was something wrong here, she thought.

There were women in Sabito's who claimed they had been prepared, girls who had known it was coming by the weather and the time of year, the ways the birds had acted. They had filled backpacks with provisions. For the rest of them, though, communities had gotten jumbled and alliances built on proximity. Patricia had heard snatches of stories as she wandered through the bar: the jock had thrown her life in with a man who was a real estate lawyer living upstairs; the punk had gotten trapped in a back yard with an old lady with her groceries and a man with his child; a drug addict and a Goddess girl had joined forces against a group of men hawking bad bottled water. Groups of women had joined the voluntary patrols telling people how to get the water from their water heaters, how to use fire extinguishers, the principles of CPR, how and why to go to the rescue centers throughout the city. A few even joined the brave and muscled sorts digging through buildings in Chinatown for survivors. A couple of the clean-and-sobers traded can openers and flashlights with the fervor they had previously reserved for pills, pot, and dope. Everybody chased the religious from the street corner when they tried to draw a connection between the sinful homosexuals of the city and God's wrath.

Patricia put her head in her hands and closed her eyes, working against the fierceness that was distorting her features, turning her hands to claws.

"Not a bad outfit for survival camp, is it?" Trout exclaimed, jumping off her barstool and twirling around in front of Patricia. Patricia regarded her with a disgusted look. Not now, not after five years together. What was this earthquake to Trout: some kind of game, some way to slum it or something? People's lives—hers for one—were going down in flames, and Trout had rosy cheeks. It wasn't like them to be at such cross-purposes: it simply didn't happen to them.

Tonight, though, Patricia turned to her lover and she didn't like what she saw. This wasn't a project, goddamn it, not some business/insurance puzzle to figure out, or a good excuse for a vacation. If Trout bothered to look down, she'd probably see blood on her shoes, Patricia thought.

In Sabito's, the women organized sleeping arrangements, pooling what few jackets there were, distributing the bar towels and aprons for pillows. They carefully worked out who would sleep where. Trout expected the women to circle the floor several times before they curled up, as she imagined the full-bellied dogs to be doing.

"I wanna sleep on the bar," Trout said, smiling. Patricia looked askance and said nothing. "Think of it, sweetie. Finally enough money. Besides, you need a vacation."

Patricia stared at her. "I'm not going back there," she said, and walked away.

Trout followed her like a Border Collie rounding up stray sheep. "What are you talking about? Not going where? To the house? We have to get documentation. You know how they are about policy numbers and triplicates of carbons."

"I'm not going. Can't you understand? It's over. We're ruined, Trout, what's the matter with you?"

"Patricia," Trout said. She lowered her voice, feeling herself at odds with the pinched faces and the survival plans of the lesbians around her. She put her hand on Patricia's and looked her in the eyes.

Patricia held herself back from pulling Trout to her. She's going to say it, Patricia thought, yearning for it more than she realized.

"We don't have to live this way anymore," Trout said quietly. "Now we can sail away, just push off the shore and go."

Patricia closed her eyes as if slapped. She shook her head.

"Hey," Trout said, brightening, "at least it'll be easy to pack."

Patricia gritted her teeth, pulled her hand away, laid her face in her palms. Trout couldn't be serious. She'd settle down; she had to. Woman Taps Last Reserves To Avoid Violent Outburst, Dies In Process. Patricia looked Trout in the eyes.

"If you want us . . . to go to . . . Mexico," Patricia said carefully, "I want you to figure out a way . . . to take Beth."

"Beth? Don't be ridiculous," Trout said, straightening her cape. Patricia stared at her without moving a muscle.

"Look, you know how to do these things," Patricia said through clenched teeth. "You know the agencies, and the officials to ask. That's the only way we're going."

"She'll just say no, Patricia," Trout said incredulously. "Let her go. Let her work with the ducks if that's what she wants. She's never done anything you've asked anyway."

"This is not a question of what she wants, goddamnit," Patricia shouted. The women along the bar turned to stare at her. Patricia set her beer down and looked away. What did Trout think, for Christsake, that motherhood was something you could just decide not to pursue all of a sudden? Something you could abandon?

"Look, I have a sense of responsibility," Patricia said, "and what I can't understand is what's happened to yours."

"Responsibility?!" Trout shrieked. "What am I but responsibility?"

Women in the bar started steering around them to avoid the confrontation. Patricia saw their faces tense as they pretended not to notice the argument. She took Trout by the elbow and led her out the front door of the bar, into the fog.

"My whole life has been spent fulfilling responsibilities," Trout shouted, turning through the dense fog to face Patricia. "And you know what I've discovered? All of a sudden, the machinery I've set up to protect me, owns me."

"Don't be ridiculous," Patricia said.

"It's not ridiculous," Trout pleaded, knowing that she wasn't offering the solace that had always been so automatically given. She couldn't cool Patricia's temper this time. A year ago, if Patricia had wanted something, Trout would have figured out a way to make it happen. Would have presented her facts and figures like presents in bright wrappings. Not now. The straight and narrow hadn't worked, so there was only one other choice. "We set up a machinery to work for us, Patricia, so let it. Let it take care of us for a while."

Trout watched Patricia glaring at her and felt like the child Tracy holding a string of cans. This time, though, she wasn't taking no answer, for an answer. Don't leave it to me this time, she thought to herself, wringing her hands, determined but uneasy with her new tactic.

"Life doesn't work like that," Patricia growled.

"Do you know how much money we've put out to insurance companies over the past five years? It's staggering. We're way over-insured, Patricia, and now there's an advantage to it. Now's our big break."

"Let me set you straight on this, Trout," Patricia said gravely, charging toward her through the fog. "I'm not moving to no fuckin' Mexico."

"Fine. Let's go to Bali. Maybe Greece. We could ask Evelyn and Maria to go with us, be a little community." Trout saw the look on Patricia's face. "I'm not suggesting we take just . . . anybody" she said, nodding her head toward the inside of the bar and the carrot-top. "It's not that far away: we can come back for vacations and stuff."

"I'm not goin' anywhere. I work my ass off for a reason, Tracy. It means something to me that I don't have polyester lace on my windows, don't you see that? I'm one step ahead of that because I have to be."

"What windows?" Trout laughed, gesturing into the fog that swallowed up her movements. "We don't even have any windows, so bag it. Just take the money and run."

"What money, Trout? Are you forgetting that we have to pay for all that stuff first?" Patricia glared at her.

"It's very straightforward," Trout said firmly. "I've got it all worked out. Forty thousand a room, five rooms, Patricia. We get the documents, go to our accountant and let her do the paper shuffling. Cash some stocks to tide us over until the insurance claim comes through. There's more than enough to pay for everything and live a life of leisure. It's a good plan, Patricia. Now I want to consider it seriously."

"So what do you suggest we do, come back when the money's gone and eat cat food when we're 65? If we have money left over, we're buying a house."

"A house?!"

"Yes, a house. You invest money, Trout, you don't piss it away on a harebrained vacation. Brick by brick, you have to build toward some kind of security, for Christssake!"

"Absolutely not! A house? Jesus," Trout said. "This is not a joke, Patricia. This is a well-orchestrated plan. Evelyn and Maria did it. Evelyn even went to Cleveland—and who would want to do that?—when Maria had to go to medical school."

"To come back and be a doctor, for Christssake, Trout. It moved them forward. It wasn't a plan to . . . give up."

"I know this is a switch. . . ."

"I'll say!"

"But . . . on the one hand, all this is. . ." Trout stammered. Patricia watched her with alarm as she struggled for words.

"It's all ruined, our life as it was. . ." Trout said. Tell her what happens when the system fails, Trout, she admonished herself. Tell her the consequences. "But on the other hand . . . the system is working perfectly, don't you see? I set up this procedure to take care of us, so. . ."

"It won't work, Trout!"

"That's it, isn't it? You can't deal with the idea that something good might happen to you! Can't imagine that hard work might pay off. You have no concept of success, Patricia."

"Don't you tell me about success, goddamnit. You want me to bet my life on an insurance company? That's ridiculous. And even if they did come through, wasting your money in the bug-infested tropics is not my idea of success."

"Then what is? Endless, ceaseless, relentless work?" Trout screamed. "When do we get to have fun?"

"Buying a house is fun," Patricia said, though with less force than behind her previous arguments. "You're good at that stuff."

"No!" Trout shouted, putting out her hands. "I won't add another file folder to the pile, Patricia. I won't set up another . . . automatic payment mechanism and . . . and worry about another set of financial . . . variables. I can't do it, Patricia, don't you see that? It's time for me now. Me!"

"You come up with another solution, Trout," Patricia said, pointing at her. "You come up with a compromise."

Patricia couldn't even look at Trout anymore. She had to walk away or she'd start screaming and she was afraid she wouldn't be able to stop. She stormed back into the bar, into Louise's backroom/office and closed the door.

W hy is that woman staring? Louise thought, more crossly than usual. Who sent these femmes to school, anyway? Who taught them all, every fucking one of them, to moon across a bar at a butch with that light in their eyes? Savior is what their eyes said. Rescue me and make it right. Christ. Then they had you. No matter what you did. Stare back like a challenge and they come on. Ignore them and they want you more. Once a femme got that look on her face it was all over. A mess is what you got. Nothin' but a big mess on your hands, sure as shit.

"Excuse me," the young woman said, leaning her whole body against the bar, "don't you own this place?"

Oh God, a real observant one here. "Yeah. That's right. For what it's worth," Louise said.

The woman sat on a barstool, put her chin in her hands and watched Louise.

Just can't figure them out, Louise thought, straightening the bottles behind the bar. Femmes. They dress like straight girls, wave their hands around like faggots, and drive nails like a bulldagger. The ones in lace, they're the ones, all right. Just when you think you're talkin' to a secretary she announces she's a proctologist or some fuckin' thing. They want you to light their cigarettes, but there's hell to pay you leave 'em off the construction crew. And who's this one?

The woman at the bar was mussed, despite the way she occasionally ran her hands through her hair. She was dusty and her face was smudged with dirt. Her eyes were red, with puffy lids. As if she could read Louise's thoughts, she plopped her hands on the bar and announced:

"Bunch of people got crushed where I work."

Louise straightened another couple of bottles, looked sideways to see if the woman were speaking to someone else.

"Trapped just inside the door of the factory," the woman said, her chin starting to quiver and her eyes filling again. "I've been crying for so many hours I've forgotten how to do anything else."

Louise stood in front of her, her face grave and withdrawn. "I'm sorry."

The woman shook her head as if trying to chase the thoughts out of her mind. She wiped a dirty hand over her face, covered her eyes, straightened and looked at Louise with a sorrowful face that made Louise want to back away.

"Now I just don't know what to do," she pleaded. "I gave the police all the information and you know what they said? They said, 'that'll be all now. You better move along.' That'll be all? I said 'all of what?' All of everything? Damn right."

The woman stretched her arms across the bar and laid her head down, eyes tightly closed.

Louise's hands gripped the edge of the bar. There were highlights in the woman's hair, and she lay across the wood so still and forlorn. Louise wanted to slide her arms forward and encircle her, grip her forearms, stand over her like a shield. The rusty, crusty ol' ironworks of Louise Batten. Shit. Have a heart, she admonished herself. She shifted her weight on her tired feet and slowly, shaking (from the hangover, she wondered?) put her wide white hand on the woman's head, slowing moving down to her shoulders. It was a gesture as much related to petting a dog as touching a woman, she reassured herself. Louise watched her hand as if it were a separated part of her body, as if there were someone behind her, putting their arms forward.

All of everything, Louise thought, wondering what that felt like. When she had packed up and moved to California, she had recited to herself, 'You're not everything in the world,' as she drove the freeway. Crossing the third state, her chant had become 'You're not anything at all,' and for once she hadn't been lying to herself. The relationship hadn't been anything. Never has been a relationship that was anything. Everyone assumed there had been a great heartbreak, but there wasn't. It made people uncomfortable to know a woman who had never been in love. It was like meeting a middle-aged woman who was a virgin or something, only the loveless didn't even have the political correctness of virginity. Louise pulled her hand away. The woman rubbed her eyes and turned her head to stare out the broken window beside the door. She didn't look up at Louise. Louise watched her, waiting to see what could happen now that she had broken her rule and caressed a customer. No reaction, Louise thought scornfully. Well, who cares? She didn't need someone in a state like this. God, they flocked to her, she thought, knowing she was overestimating her draw. Forget this woman. Someone else will talk to her, get her to a shelter or something. Louise had a bar to run, and besides, the woman would just turn out to be somebody else. If Louise rescued her from this, the woman would turn around and try to rescue Louise to even the score, and the two would spend months throwing each other from boats to haul one another in again. After she had dried her tears all over Louise's life, she'd turn out to be some Twelve-Step junkie or something. She'd call herself a *co-alcoholic* and throw down her apron. Christ. Fuckin' 'co's.' Sounded like salmon. Swim upstream to get to her, then change their colors and die. She'd watched it happen from her vantage point behind the bar, seen so many relationships come and go through these doors, she should sell her brain to Nancy Friday. Secret Garden my ass, Louise thought.

"You wanna wash up a little?" Louise offered softly, stepping backward. The woman sat up and nodded. Louise pointed toward the bathroom.

"I'll see about some towels," Louise said hesitantly as she felt her eyes meet the other woman's. What am I doing? she asked herself. She looked around at the women dragging sofa cushions and buckets of things into the bar. "I suppose a bunch of us would like showers. I'll . . . look for something."

Sabito's seemed to be moving away from her, the room receding from the edge of the bar, everything behind the stools becoming a blur. Those tables seemed no longer to be hers, the walls belonging to somebody else's place. Women were moving in their God-awful purposeful way, organizing things, asking each other questions and scribbling on the walls. This wasn't her place, just like it wasn't her hand that had stroked the woman's hair. Things happened like that sometimes, she thought. Every year or so a special mood hit the crowd and they created their own stage set, enclosed by the bar but not defined by it. They moved around inside here, driven by their own design, regardless of the way she'd laid out the place. Never like this, though, Louise thought. Now they seemed to have detached the floor from the bar and all their damn gyrations and committee forming were jiggling the room right on down the street. Louise stood with a small stack of clean dish towels in her hand and felt that the long wooden bar that had always separated her from the women was even more important to her now.

"My name's Jennifer," the woman said, reaching out for a towel.

"Louise," she said shortly, handing her one and turning away.

"Thank you," the woman said meekly to Louise's back and headed toward the kitchen.

"See if Patricia. . ." Louise said, gesturing toward the back,
". . . hey Patricia, you know anything about plumbing?"

"What?" Patricia called from inside the kitchen.

"Hook that . . . dishwasher thing . . . the sprayer, hook it
to the wall and let's have a shower in there."

Patricia came out of the kitchen with her tool belt on,
holding a screw-driver. Louise didn't move from behind the
bar.

"Careful of the temperature gauge," Louise said meekly,
knowing she should go into the kitchen herself. "It's set on
high to get the damn lipstick off the glasses."

Patricia leaned against the wall. Louise hadn't moved in
hours, wouldn't even go to her own house. What was she
avoiding?

"Hey you guys with the clipboards," Louise called into the
receding room. "Let's organize some showers here."

The women brightened, cheered, and moved toward the
kitchen until Patricia was pushed back inside. Louise didn't
move.

*T*rout paced up and down through the fog. Numbers,
that's all anybody ever wanted. Numbers and logic. The
plan is a good one, you bitch! she wanted to scream. So the
root of it was the simple statement . . . the rare utterance . . .
'I want it. I want it for me.' Not for logic. Not for profit or
reasonableness. For the . . . joy of it. Patricia wanted a
compromise and that's what wouldn't work. You couldn't
have a little bit of this, a little bit of that. She'd tried that
before, and it was disastrous.

The year Tracy had moved away from the lake her father
had been in the hospital the entire winter, and would not be
back for the summer, either. She had been expected at
college in a week. All his correspondence was being
forwarded to her at her dorm. Still, she sat on the porch,
immobilized, her back flattened against the chair by the
pressure of an enormous chore that was not completed: she
wouldn't be able to pull the booby-traps from the water any

longer. People would descend with their onslaught of paper, the due dates in small boxes in tiny type, she thought, sitting on her suitcases, waiting for a car she had hired to take her to the bus. Whole birds will be cut to a pulp and the blood will leech into the water because she wasn't there, because she couldn't protect him anymore. Welcome to the University of Michigan: A New World of Opportunity, said the brochure on her lap. She looked down at her packed suitcases in the empty house: he was safe in the hospital now, but what if he got out? They'd spin her father in circles in traffic intersections and sneer when he fell down, she had thought. They'd leave him reciting bird names in the drugstore until he collapsed and people stepped over him. They'd beat the smile from his face.

During her sophomore year of college, her father's voice came across the phone lines late at night, a thin wiry voice in the thinnest hour of the day.

"They're picking on me, again," he had said quietly.

Trout felt a grip in her stomach. This medication was not working, either.

Growing up with a man like her father was not a simple question of asking "are you drinking again?" Trout tried to explain to her college friends. This was not an empty bottle you could discover in the kitchen cabinet or a pint unearthed in the laundry room. You had to listen carefully for clues. Was that a rational response? Had he said anything about machines? Every time they talked, Trout had a portion of her ear tuned to the precision of his words and the linearity of his thinking. Was this combination of pills going to do the trick? If he wasn't in the hospital, he was home with her carefully constructed system: as long as the bills were being forwarded to her dormitory, the cleaning service came weekly, and the meal service delivered the standing order, things were relatively secure.

She had been home for Thanksgiving during her junior year, having a real conversation, and she was reminding herself to check on exactly which pills he was on. The phone rang.

"Is this Mrs. Giovanni?"

"Yes," Trout said, which had always been an easier response than explaining.

"I'm calling regarding your Visa bill," said the woman on the phone. "We show a current overdue balance of $6,000."

Trout discovered not just hordes of unopened packages stashed in the garage, but the receipts for plane tickets that he had purchased to stand at the airport and watch the flights depart, as if awe-struck by a Ferris wheel at the circus.

That was a compromise, she thought, staring out at the fog as if she could actually see something. She had gone to college, and look what had happened. You build a machine to work for you. You don't leave it a little bit on, a little bit off. That's what she had done with her father.

*P*atricia felt as alone as if a wind had poured through her shirt. She pounded her hand against the wall. She was as cold and furious as the day she and her mother had sat inside a shed behind the Catholic school in Kentucky, looking at cardboard boxes filled with moldy books and decades-old encyclopedias. Her mother had muttered between clenched teeth, "They want me to make a library out of this? Take a look at this stuff, honey: this is what the rich call donations." Settle for less, be contended with junk, she heard ringing in her ears again. No one stood beside her telling her that the basketball hoops and faucets in the street, the water draining from shop floors didn't mean what she knew it meant. And there was no one to hear the story of the woman with the scream and how the others just trundled off down the street (herself included, she thought guiltily). She opened the door from the back room to the alley.

In the corner by the entrance, a figure crouched, shivering.

"Who's there?" Patricia said cautiously.

"Patricia?" the woman said.

"Who is it?" she said, drawing closer, bending to see.

"Me."

"Lynn?" Patricia said, incredulously.

"I can't stop the trembling, Patricia, can't stop."

"Come inside, Lynn," Patricia said, trying to reach for her hand.

"The paper's blowing out the windows," Lynn said.

Patricia got on her knees, tried to see Lynn's eyes.

"You're at Sabito's, Lynn," Patricia said, tenderly. "Come inside and eat. None of it matters now."

"No, the glass."

"You're not at work anymore, Lynn. C'mon now. How did you get out of the financial district: I heard it was chin-deep in glass?"

"Beam truck lifted me over the glass."

"Boom truck," Patricia corrected, then rubbed her eyes.

"I screamed and hollered until they turned the ladder to me," Lynn said. "See, the sky is paper now."

"It's over, OK?" Patricia said grasping her arms. "What's the matter with you, Lynn? Get a grip, for Christsake."

"The competition's in Illinois. The computer's destroyed. Can you understand that, Patricia? My corner office with all the windows, the glass that no one wanted to see through, to see the Chinese girl with blonde hair? 'What would they want for presents,' the manager said, 'another painted fan?' The guy said 'No, Charles, just a good haircut.'"

"Listen, Lynn," Patricia said, not understanding her growing irritation, "It's been over for hours. You can't do this. You can't talk like this. Come inside and settle down."

"The grocer put up a handwritten sign, 'cash only.'" Lynn said. "He knows: no offices, no plastic. A bankrupt crowd in linen suits. Don't you know, Patricia?" her voice low and conspiratorial, "They'll proffer their Gucci watches for a box of rye toast. I need a rope. I need watches, Patricia."

"Lynn!" Patricia pulled the woman to her feet, shook her hard, her fingers tight around the flesh of her arms. "You can't!"

Lynn stopped talking and pushed the hair away from her face with cupped hands. She stared into Patricia's eyes and, with her hands still on her head, moved forward, leaning first her hips into Patricia, then her chest. Patricia's eyes darted around Lynn's face. The woman's totally disoriented and now she comes on to me, after all these years. Lynn laid her palms on Patricia's biceps, slid her hands to her armpits so

her forearms pressed against Patricia's breasts. Patricia knew
she should pull away but couldn't. Maybe it was the only
anchor the woman had. If she just put her arms around
Lynn's waist she might settle down. She could certainly use
a little comfort herself, and Lynn was warm and searching.
Well why not? The earthquake had broken more than
bric-a-brac and water mains. All around Sabito's, Patricia had
seen tough girls leaning on the shoulders of friends, throwing
their arms around strangers. Without traffic lights, walls, or
the freeway system, who the hell was to say what a gesture
meant? Everything had developed leaks, including women's
desires. Catastrophe Drives Monogamous to Seek Other's
Lips and Skin. Why would Patricia put her arms around
Lynn, a woman who was her lover's ex-? On a day like this,
why not? The fucking world is ruined, what's a little hug
between friends? Patricia slid her hands over Lynn's waist,
around to the small of her back. Like the rest of the day, it
was a jolt to a place in the mind she hadn't known was so
settled. This was clearly not Trout; this was a voluptuous
body, round and soft, not the thin angularity of her wife.
Come back here, Lynn, she thought, and at the same time,
she felt some kinship, as if her arms held a woman who
understood that the earth had cracked open and swallowed
her life whole. Lynn was the blithering hysteric Patricia felt
herself to be, and there was comfort here, in the breasts
pressed against her, in the thighs that touched her own.
There was some possibility in the rounding small of her back.

"You could stop the trembling," Lynn whispered into
Patricia's ear, "cover me in your bright Blue Cloak to slow
the flight of my courage."

Patricia leaned her head back and breathed deeply.

"The cloak of the Buddha, in the Temple of Ten Thousand
Buddhas," Lynn said, murmuring into Patricia's dark hair
and her strong neck. "I would stand at its calf," Lynn said,
unbuttoning Patricia's shirt. She met Patricia's resistant
hands.

"I'd stand at your calf, Blessed One, kneel at your
ankle. . ." she said, sliding down the front of Patricia and
grasping the buttons of her pants.

"Lynn, don't."

"Not even try to look up at your smiling face or meet your eyes. Just drape the edge of your cloak around me."

"Lynn, we . . . can't do this." Patricia bent and pulled her to her feet again, put her hand deep into Lynn's tangled hair and kissed her, pressed into the woman's lips the whole day of sadness, of the fear of bloodied hands under debris, of the terror of seeing Trout wander away, of the disgust and concern for her daughter. Lynn gasped for breath, her eyes looking even more wild than when she first appeared. She pushed her hair from her face, ran her hand down Patricia's cheek, and backed down the alley into the fog again.

Women weren't any good at it at all, this romance stuff, Cherice thought uneasily, afraid to sip from the snifter for fear she'd spill the rest of her story. Women talk about it, incessantly, all of it, analyzing every little topic until they could outline the structure of their entire gray matter and present computer printouts to each other instead of making love. This is what I think, this is what I feel, this is where my mother's influence gives way to nine years of psychotherapy. Unresolved issues printed here in bold include paternal abandonment and a fear of spiders. Wanna cigarette now? There was no great divide to reach across, no enormous longing to bridge with their bodies. Fifty-fifty, until there was no one to stride across a room and envelope her with overriding, undeniable passion. Boycotts and judgmentalism, the great lesbian sports. She could recite the contraband list: you don't eat grapes, Nestle products, Coors beer or coffee from El Salvador. No tuna, no Stouffers. No Shell oil, Exxon gas, perfumes, products from South Africa, or GE. By the time Monica left her, the hot topic was whether keeping a pet was slavery, for Christsake. Not that she didn't support all that—she did, she agreed with all of it—it's just that it was all so . . . brittle, and non-sensual. Well, fuck them, fuck the whole thing, with their insipid women's music and insipid women's lit and their dorky goddamn clothing.

Why shouldn't she want something different? Why not get good service in restaurants for a change, be seated in the window instead of a dark corner table by the kitchen? Why not take a present to the gift wrap counter and when the girl says "is this for a man or a woman" not feel like your privacy was in jeopardy? Shouldn't she be able to come into the office and describe her Saturday night instead of being afraid to reveal the name of the dance club? Why not be with someone who would take your face in their hands and kiss you without asking for consensus? Why not be able to hold hands on any street, in any town, goddamn it? Why not?

She wasn't going to say it, wasn't going to tell him that after a few years of entwining their lives, she and Monica had just stopped having sex. Couldn't find any more romance in their relationship because romance was mystery, wasn't it, and when she's got the same body and the same clothes and the same friends, where was the mystery? More than that, they were so into that insipid equality that no one would take the initiative. Like two people both trying to follow on the dance floor. You go nowhere. She couldn't take it anymore. Maybe with men at least whatever it was that made them think about sex all the time would keep it going. She'd started watching too many Hollywood movies, imagined being pressed against the wall by a broad-chested someone. Jesus, Cherice, stop it, she thought, just because he's sitting there and he's gorgeous . . . no, it wouldn't do.

After Monica had left her, she had gone to Paris, on a whim, without luggage. Black skirt, black stockings, black silk blouse and a pair of flats. She wandered Paris buying bracelets and earrings she wore out of the store, then a raincoat, sat in cafes watching the saucers pile up under her wine glass. She let the hairdresser and the shop clerk define the way she looked, a mannequin being draped as they festooned her as a straight woman. The more she shopped, the more men gravitated to the park bench she rested on, the edge of the fountain where she paused. The men were so easy, she had thought. They asked so little. They insisted, it seemed to her, that they not know her, that the lines between them were clearly drawn, that no woman would enter their deepest feelings, that is, if they, themselves, even entered their deepest feelings. They were an endless source of sweat and hollow compliments, their bodies pressed into her and their minds pressed into themselves. She, in her costume, smiled a little and revealed nothing at all. There were no second dates; there couldn't be. Outside of bed, her mind began working again, her former self rearing up as he ordered her a plate of food after she insisted she wouldn't eat, after he filled her glass when she said she'd had enough, as he talked to his soccer friends in the corner of the bar leaving her at the table like a prized antelope head in his den. She dumped the plate of food he had ordered for her onto his own, and walked out. But each time she was drawn back to the sex. The shape of a man's body defined her own: his breadth accented her lines, his hair revealed her hairlessness, his muscled chest made voluptuous the mounds of her breasts. If Monica had been intimacy, then intimacy was not what she wanted, she had thought. Each time, as he pounded into her, she chanted 'don't ask me to care, don't ask me to analyze, don't ask me to serve up my past and my feelings on a platter to dissect.' They never did. Cherice and her men each performed their mysterious ritual of washing and dressing, of make-up and short socks, their customs so different that they did not illuminate each other nor comment on each other, and each of them was safe within the walls of their uniqueness.

She had taken a train to Amsterdam, also on a whim, this time with two small suitcases full of dresses. She walked through the cobbled streets of the old section of town, stopping for coffee without premeditation, one minute walking, the next minute sitting. She bought things to eat along the way without considering what she was gathering and stayed in hotels that happened to be in her path at dusk. By the end of the week, Cherice started getting nervous, noticing she was walking down the same streets that she had the day before, the familiarity making her uneasy. She thought about buying a map to expand her wanderings, considered asking for directions or taking a bus, but was more afraid of having a course of action than of seeing the same bakery. She continued to walk, trying to look inside the windows to glimpse things she hadn't seen before and wouldn't again.

That's when she saw the dark-haired woman, leaning against a marble bar, raising a beer to her lips as if she meant to kiss the foam rather than drink the liquid. Cherice stood outside the red velvet curtains, the brass railings, the yellow circle of light spilling onto the uneven street, and felt herself brush against the now-moist lips of the woman in the bar. Dropping her sandwich roll into the gutter without seeing it fall, she went into the bar and leaned beside the woman.

That night, it was there again, that feeling of falling toward someone, tumbling together without breaks, without walls or safeguards. No broader chest or longer arms cutting a space that didn't exist for the other, there was nothing to distinguish them from each other except the knowledge of the heat that could be felt inside but not outside. There was no shock of difference, of separation as there had been with the men in Paris, where every movement had said 'you aren't me, go away.' The sex was not an act of definition: it was throwing shirts to the floor, soft hands against soft necks, skin on skin and knowing. It was the same rhythm, and hands that fit inside, it was moistened palms, narcotic sex. They fucked until the garbage men rolled their small green trolley down the street, they fucked until the street lamps went out, they sweated and moved until the communal shower was no longer in demand, until the maid knocked on the door. The dark-haired woman fetched breakfast, and they fucked while they ate fruit and Nutella. The sheets were nowhere to be found, the pillows across the room, the candles little puddles on the table. The air was a drug of heat and sweat and pussy. While the woman was in the shower, Cherice put her clothes on and ran down the street, took the first plane back to America.

"You have no idea what it's like," Cherice said gravely to Jacob, "to spend six years without being able to hold your lover's hand in public.

"Hey, Peaches," she said, turning back to him, "I've got a joke for you." Jacob smiled sadly and pushed his long hair from his face.

"Why do we know conclusively that God is not a woman?" she said.

"Oh Jesus," Jacob said, running his big hand over his forehead. "Why?"

"Because if God were a woman, men's dicks would be on their chins."

When Patricia returned to her barstool and didn't look in her lover's direction, Trout did a double-take. There was something in the way Patricia looked, Trout thought, as if in possession of some odd piece of information. She had seen it on Patricia so many times: three days after it appeared and then seemed to abate, Patricia would tell her the story of seeing a girl nearly hit by a car, or a stabbing in the street, something deplorable at work, and Trout would remember the face of the previous days that said 'I know something I wish I didn't know.' What had she seen? Trout closed her eyes.

Patricia leaned against the bar. Maybe Lynn was just confused. A little lost. Lynn couldn't be ruined, too. Not Lynn, Patricia thought. She expected it from others, expected the world to do it to others, but not to Lynn. To choose to go crazy, throw herself at me and then rush back into the fog, when she possessed the kind of money and security everyone else wanted, why would she allow herself to lose her mind? What sense did it make? She should be concerned about Lynn, she told herself as she wrapped her black hair behind her ears and leaned on the bar, but she was angry. At both Lynn and herself. She couldn't rush into the fog to find her: her marriage might be on the skids, but that would ruin it for sure because Patricia knew she was too unsteady to resist the woman's haunting advances. Patricia turned to lean her elbows behind her on the bar, daring to show her face for a moment. Trout was sitting there not even noticing the guilt that must be oozing from her skin. She wasn't asking what was wrong, not like usual when she reached out a hand to cover Patricia's knuckles and fingers. The cardinal sin of their relationship, and Trout sat there with that little grin. That was it, now. Earthquake my ass— everything had collapsed, every little morsel of what she had known was gone. After all these years, my girl turns out to be a foolish indulgent. Christ, there's no point in a relationship like that.

"Trout," Patricia said, pulling away from the bar. "It was Lynn."

"Where is she?"

"She's gone. Ran away."

"On the end of whose leash?" Trout said, readjusting the glasses in her pocket and taking a sip of a beer.

"That's not funny. Where's your compassion, for God's sake? She's your ex-lover, and she's cracked," Patricia said softly, hopelessly. And I've cracked too, Trout, Patricia thought. I could have fallen onto the ground and made love to her right that moment. Passionately. We don't allow those kinds of things.

I don't have any responsibility to her, Trout thought crossly.

Trout slid off her stool and dug into her pockets as she crossed the room. Fuck Lynn, she thought. I'm not taking care of her anymore. She stood in front of the jukebox lifting her cape from side to side and dumped a mass of quarters into the slot. She punched the buttons with vehement dive-bombs of her fingers.

"Shake it up baby, twist and shout," Trout sang at the top of her lungs, bouncing up and down on the balls of her Batman tennis shoes. The women organizing the Security Team stopped their conference because of the volume of the music. Others turned at the sudden movement of the floor, expecting another quake. Trout spun around on the dance floor, her arms out like windmills.

"Com'on com'on baby now, work it on out," she screamed, throwing back her head and closing her eyes. The women in the bar turned to her with their mouths open. A few clambered off the floor to join her, relieved.

Patricia rushed across the dance floor and threw her arms around Trout's chest, trapping Trout's arms at her side.

"Stop it!" Patricia screamed, clenching her teeth, her face inches from Trout's. Trout squirmed in Patricia's grip but couldn't break free. Wide-eyed with surprise, she looked at Patricia. "Stop it," Patricia growled, then averted her eyes shamefully and let her go.

Trout pushed wisps of her curls from her forehead. Patricia bent and pulled the jukebox plug from the wall.

*J*acob rubbed his face with his hands as he laughed, then folded his hands across his chest and shivered.

"I think the Valium and brandy is wearing off," Jacob said.

"You need a shirt, or a sweater," Cherice said. She went into the closets that lined the way to the bedroom, pulled out a yellow silk shirt, a cashmere jacket, another undershirt for a new binding. "Paydirt!" she shouted, holding the clothing high in the air.

Jacob slipped into the shirt with a skeptical eye on Cherice.

"Neck size is wrong."

"But surprisingly close," she said, holding out the jacket. She returned to the closet, pulling out a couple of sweaters, a raw silk jacket.

"I can't take these, Cherice," he said, as she turned and went back into the bedroom.

"Don't be silly, of course you can," she said as she covered him with a down comforter.

The phone rang and both of them started, turned to look at the desk. Jacob tried to lift himself off the couch, but Cherice pushed him down. The answering machine picked up the call, and Cherice rushed to the desk, increased the volume.

"It's Tokyo," she said, surprised, yanking open a drawer and rummaging for a pen and paper. She scribbled down the information, beaming at Jacob.

"Yes!" she said, clenching her fist as the call rang off. "Oh, this is beautiful. Beautiful. Now the question is, where are the computers? Stock tips, Peaches," she said, as she opened drawers in the desk. "Oh, of course, only the best." She reached into a bottom cabinet in the desk, and the computer began to whir, a monitor threw a grayish light onto her face from a glass panel in the desk. "Their stock tips, my money. Ah, it bodes well for us, my man."

"If the phone is working, let's call someone and get out of here," Jacob said incredulously. Cherice looked up from the terminal, then looked down again.

"I'm not leaving."

"Jesus Christ, woman. Call this number: 564-8182. Call it!" he shouted.

Cherice picked up the phone. "The line's dead. Incoming calls only it must be."

"I don't believe you."

"Look, I'll dial it, and then we can just hit last number re-dial, OK? And we'll keep trying."

"We can't stay here! What the hell are you doing?"

"I'm making money and having a party, my two favorite activities. You want to go? Go."

"You know I can't do that with a busted foot."

"Well what am I, the Angel of Mercy? I can't fly us across fourteen blocks of glass. Besides, who could ask for more? Great brandy, good, if relatively uninteresting food, and a chance to cash in on someone else's information."

"You cannot live in a fantasy, Cherice," Jacob said, holding himself nearly off the couch in his anger.

She scowled at him. "Why not!"

"You cannot just steal what isn't yours!"

"Do you know what this man does for a living, Jacob? He bets against the farmers, OK? His biggest account is with Adolph Coors."

"Have you no scruples at all?"

"Spoken like a true. . ." she stopped herself, picked up her brandy glass, "never mind."

"No, go ahead, say it, spoken like a man."

"Spoken like a white man. You really believe the world is set up for justice? That only the cream rises to the top? You're the one in fantasy, Peaches."

"Hey, I'm a Jew, goddamnit, I know there's no justice."

"You ever lived in the closet?" she said, challenging him.

"Yeah, yeah," he said, as if it were a new idea to him. "I don't talk about bar mitzvahs at the office, or my nephew's breis. And you know what happens if you complain about your mother? They're all thinking . . . well, you know what they're thinking."

Cherice raised her glass to him, more as a challenge than an acknowledgment.

"You know what I'd like to do, for a living I mean? Be a forest ranger."

"Really?" she said with genuine interest. "Well, do it!"

"Yeah, well it sounds nice, doesn't it? You ever seen the fine people of the state of Georgia give a Jew a gun and send him into the woods to arrest white boys? That's where I grew up, Georgia. You catch on fast about Jews, in Georgia."

"So why all the Boy Scout stuff?"

"What do you think Cherice, that identity is just a . . . a statement? A simple affirmation? You say 'this is what I am' and that's it? Find the right identity and then all the answers are easy and they're things you can trot into the broad daylight all the time? I'm tellin' you: you watch too much Hollywood."

Cherice looked down at the keyboard, punched in a set of numbers, then stopped.

"So what are you saying, Jacob," she said softly, "that it's tough all over?"

"No, just that everybody's . . . mutable," he said, struggling with the concept. "Sometimes you show one part of yourself and hide a few for safety's sake, and sometimes you show more. I don't know. You . . . you uncover what's been hidden in certain company and uncover other things later. If you're lucky, you discover things you didn't even know were hidden," he said. "But it's just not a question of . . . trying to be chairman of the brokerage firm when you're not. Identity isn't someone else's cashmere jacket you can walk off with. Steal from the wicked, yes, but, I don't know Cherice, you're doing something else."

Cherice turned away, looked out the window. She didn't have to tell him about the men in Paris, he knew. Maybe not about the men, but about the confusion.

"And the girls say you don't communicate," she said, trying to sound flippant. "You date bimbos?"

"What is that, a compliment?" Jacob said.

"All right. We make just a little bit of money," she said conspiratorially, "and then we go."

"All right, so buy, sell," Jacob said with a sly smile, waving her back to her work.

Cherice and Jacob stuffed their pockets with the information on their stock transactions and a bottle of VSOP, and prepared for departure.

They tied Jacob to a secretary's chair, fixed the chair to the credenza with a long expanse of sheet and tied a mop in his hands. They opened the door, and against the suction of the wind, pushed the furniture until it wedged in the door frame. The mop pulled against Jacob's arms like it would snap his wrists off. Cherice, tied with more sheet to his waist, clambered onto the credenza and straddled him from behind, wedging her bare feet against the door frame and clamping her hands around his wrists. With the mop whipping around like a mad conductor's baton, they slapped at the marble wall and finally struck the elevator button. Jacob shouted to Cherice, though his words were lost in the tangle of his hair and the wind. Like a man sliding into third base, he threw himself toward the slowly opening door. Cherice landed like a rag doll on his back, grabbing the edges of the elevator and pushing him inward, ass first, with her knees. The wind pressed them against the sides of the elevator and Cherice slammed the door-close button.

"We lost the VSOP," Cherice said, rolling to a sitting position and leaning her head against the elevator wall.

Jacob, his chest heaving with the effort to breathe, lifted his foot a few inches and collapsed against the floor, exhausted.

"I think . . . " he said between gasps, ". . . that you've broken my rib cage."

Wasn't my fault, Cherice thought angrily: they could be partying in the penthouse except for his desire to chase after a woman who's already left him. Cherice looked over at him, his hands still taped to the mop.

"Sorry," she said. "I guess I've racked you up pretty badly."

Jacob turned onto his back. "Untie me, unstrap me, untape me."

Cherice and Jacob rode to the lobby and wedged the door open with the mop. Jacob remained lying on the floor as Cherice walked through the lobby, frightened by the silence, turning in circles and looking over her shoulder. The light outside the lobby windows was very dark, shot through with streaks of light like the sudden glow of undersea creatures in the ocean depths. As Cherice neared the revolving doors, she stopped; her mouth dropped open. The door was wedged closed by broken glass piled higher than her head, and as she turned, she realized that outside the lobby, the building was submerged in glass. She ran back to the elevator and quickly pressed a button to a higher floor. Jacob looked at her, and seeing the panic on her face, covered his eyes with one of his hands and said nothing.

On the second floor, Cherice braced herself against the wall and carefully peered out. The windows had blown out as they had on the 36th floor but the wind was no more than a stiff breeze. She paced to one end of the hall, then the other, leaning out the window. Jacob could hear her shouting, imagined her waving like a damsel in a tower. She walked past the elevator. He heard a door open, then saw her pushing a secretary's chair down the hall. An enormous crash resounded from outside the window.

"Cherice!" he shouted.

She called from the window. "Well, I wasn't going to wave all night."

Jacob heard the whine of machinery. "Your chauffeur, sir," Cherice shouted. When Jacob didn't immediately appear, Cherice returned to the elevator and helped him up, draped his arm around her shoulder.

"The ribs, watch the ribs," Jacob said.

The bucket on the end of a boom truck maneuvered into place. Cherice smiled. "Faye Rae and Peaches make a daring escape," she said softly, and Jacob smiled at her. He stepped out of the window, carefully lifting his hurt foot over the tall side of the bucket and clambering in. Cherice attempted to climb in after him, but her skirt restrained her. She looked up at Jacob with embarrassment, then laid her palms on her thighs.

"Don't look," she said fiercely. Jacob held his hand out to her.

Cherice lifted her skirt to her waist, exposing sheer stockings and lacy French-cut panties. Jacob watched her climb into the lift, the round of her ass exposed to the lamplight. He inhaled until it hurt his ribs. Cherice straightened her skirt and the bucket lurched downward, throwing them off balance. Cherice put her arm around his waist to steady him while he stood on one foot, and Jacob felt a wave of sadness running around his damaged chest. It can't just be that she's made it clear she's off limits, can it? he thought, suspicious of himself. On the other hand, when he headed home to the absence of Abigail it would be nice to have her stride in ahead of him and break up the atmosphere. One snide comment would do it. One joke.

Cherice stood back as firefighters helped Jacob out of the bucket and motioned for him to go in a van to the hospital.

"Cherice," he called. She strode to the van, but stopped two feet away from the door.

"So, Jacob. . ." she said, averting her eyes. "Um, thanks. And . . . good luck with your girlfriend."

"Wait a minute, you're just going to . . . Couldn't we. . ." he said, holding his hands, palms up as if ready to grasp at anything. "You gotta eat, right?" he said.

Cherice smiled. "Stock broker, remember? Not even house plants."

L ouise folded her arms over her big chest. Pity about Trout and Patricia. Can't stand to see a couple'a girls that right for each other goin' at it. Poor Trout. Any monkey with a frontal lobe could see the woman had had it. And why not? Christ, if Trout asked *her* to move to Mexico the only question would be, "when do we leave?" What did Patricia think—that she wasn't in exile here? An illegal electrician who had just lost everything? How did that loyalty make any sense? She knew, she could tell Patricia, you live like a stranger in a strange land most times anyway, why not do it on the beach? Jesus, they could always come back and start over: why not wait 'til somebody else had cleared the rubble away. When you have nothin' in the world there's always time to start from scratch. But how many chances did she have for a beautiful woman to look up and say "Baby, take me away from here!" Christ, Trout wasn't even that demanding: in Trout's case it was "Let me take you away." Lucky butch. What she wouldn't give.

And Trout deserved it. Every Friday in here with the corporate drag and the fifty-pound briefcase. So she wants to leave town without a plan of action. Lay me out on a beach under thatchy umbrella, a rum-filled pineapple in my hand. That's the kind of plan she could go for. Take her, take her. It had been all she could do to stop herself from hissing the command into Patricia's ear. Shit. What's all the repetitive industry going to get her here: a couple pieces of furniture and a spot at the same old bar? It was a wasteland now, and it had always been a wasteland. Patricia wasn't goin' anywhere. If she left town, she'd just miss a couple plug installations, couple rewiring jobs. Half the things said and done around her had no impact on Patricia's life anyway. The rich ran the country for themselves, so what was the difference? That she couldn't understand the language? What a blessing! Patricia knew the Spanish for *dyke* and *whore* and that's all the English she ever heard on the street anyway. Wasn't that being in exile? Wasn't this a foreign country, with the cops sweeping through the neighborhood and the courts not seeing a family as it stood right in front of them? Jesus, they brought tour buses through the Castro for a reason. Let Trout relax, Louise thought crossly as she grabbed a glass, iced it, filled it with water and drank. Let Trout set down that briefcase and get a goddamn tan. Life became ordinary plenty soon enough.

D espite Patricia's conviction that heavy covers and an open window were as close to orgasm as you could get at an eight-hour stretch, she couldn't sleep. Her pillow had always been her life buoy. All around her, women were snoring, drooling into their knapsacks turned to pillows, spooning into the legs and butts of their girlfriends or friends who would soon be girlfriends, or curled into the fetal for lack of blankets, but not Patricia. Jolt of Earth and Marriage Turns Somnambulist to Insomnia. She sat up, let her back rest against the wall, pulled her knees up to her chest. She didn't look over at Trout, defying the woman to continue sleeping in her witch's cape with her bug-eye glasses at her side. A couple of hard-cores sat on bar stools, while Louise stood behind the bar, looking past her arms folded over her chest, into their silent and mournful faces. There was a cowgirl with long blonde hair, a UPS worker, a couple of leather-jacket girls with junk hangin' off their lapels, and at the end of the bar, by herself, an ash-blonde in an electric blue suit—obviously high-dollar—with long, gorgeous legs.

Patricia watched The Blue Suit sip from a large martini glass that seemed to defy gravity by remaining upright as she held it loosely in her fingers. There was something in the way the woman re-crossed her legs, she thought. Patricia suddenly sat forward, stealthily got up from the floor.

"Amsterdam, right?" Cherice said when Patricia stood at her elbow.

"That's right," Patricia said, as if it were a challenge.

Cherice took another sip of her martini as if she didn't notice Patricia were there any longer, as if the subject were closed.

"So what happened to you?" Patricia said with hostility.

Cherice set her glass down and cleared her throat nervously.

"I suppose I owe you a drink."

"I'd settle for an explanation," Patricia said.

"It was so many years ago, sweetie. Let's start with a drink."

Patricia leaned one elbow on the bar and put a hand into her pants pocket.

"I was watching you sleep, just now, or trying to sleep," Cherice said, the closeness of Patricia starting to make her uncomfortable. She remembered how Patricia had stood in the cafe in Amsterdam, how she had leaned just like this, her black hair glinting and her eyes ready to slide all over Cherice's body. Cherice could feel beads of sweat gathering in her cleavage. "Are you having trouble at home?"

Patricia turned away and shook her head at the woman's boldness.

"She wants to give up and move to Mexico," Patricia said as if it were a challenge to Cherice.

"Oh, sounds wonderful," Cherice said.

Patricia snorted. "Yeah. I'd expect you to think so."

Cherice shifted uncomfortably on her stool.

Patricia looked around at the women in the bar. "Some of these girls are doubting your credentials."

Cherice turned on the barstool, pulled her skirt up and stuck her leg out, pursed her lips.

"Is that hostility or the way you come on these days?" Patricia said.

"Look, we had a little roll around a room. It was very nice. The best, if you want to know the truth," Cherice said cautiously, "but. . ."

"But what?" Patricia said, challenging, trying to hide her own interest in the curve of the woman's blouse, the movement of her long legs.

"But nothing," Cherice said pointedly. "I'm not in the market for relationships, not future ones, and certainly not past ones."

Patricia felt her teeth clenching.

"I'm sorry," Cherice said, smiling, "sit down, and tell me what you've been up to since I saw you in that moment of glory."

Patricia leaned into her face. "Not until you tell me. Why did you leave, Cherice? Why did you run away like that?"

"What is this, the hour of reckoning, or something?"

"Why?" Patricia growled.

"You scared me, all right?" Cherice said. "You scared the unholy piss out of me. I could see us three years from that very night: no sex, at least not like it was, lots of little arguments that never got really settled, a whole bunch of bickering in public and correcting each other in front of our friends. Nothing but . . . entanglement."

"Entanglement?" Patricia said scornfully. "Funniest word for love I've ever heard."

"Yeah, well it happens. Maybe in your own house?"

"Not in my house," Patricia said defensively, but without conviction.

"Oh, I see. Sit down. What did we call you? Raven? Let me buy you a drink, my lovely."

Patricia didn't move.

"What?" Cherice said, "a woman tells you you're the best sex she's ever had and she can't buy you a drink? What code of ethics is that?"

Patricia reluctantly took her hand out of her pocket and settled onto the barstool. She thought sadly of the night in Amsterdam, of Cherice's beautiful legs.

Louise, driven by her own sense of timing, paced to their end of the bar and looked at Patricia.

"Just . . . I don't know, a beer, if you would, Louise."

Patricia recounted her marriage, at first as a defense, then with genuine appreciation. Something in her tone, though, she thought, made it sound like the past tense.

"I prefer stock options and real estate deals," Cherice said, explaining her lack of relationships. "The climax is more predictable."

Patricia remembered Cherice with her hair dampening the pillow, her lips closing around short bursts of air.

"Now in your case, I don't really see the problem," Cherice said. "If you don't want to go to Mexico, don't go."

"And end it all?" Patricia said incredulously.

"Well certainly. Unless you're into phone sex."

"Don't get disgusting about my marriage," Patricia said pointedly.

"Look, you've reached an impasse, so let her go."

*P*atricia wanted to jump off the barstool and shake the woman by the shoulders, wanted to drag her over to Trout's bed and say 'Look, Trout, this is what you'll become, do you understand that? A woman who runs every time there's something at stake.' Instead, she stared at Cherice, frightened to the pit of her stomach. Trout had already become just such a woman. Wife Becomes Free-Floater When Demands Mount. Trout was a fly-by-night, dumping excess parts of her life like chipped drinking glasses. Stones under the truck tires, Patricia thought. A blue-black color tinted everything she saw, like the veil of exhaust. Not just a man had driven away this time, an entire city had given up on its promise. The flat they had rented had turned into a sham. Now, even Trout had abandoned her, skipping through the rubble while Patricia stood as if watching her father tear up the driveway in fear of her.

They had worked too hard to give it up now. Hell, in the beginning they had fought over things that turned out to be the stuff of different class backgrounds. Quips, jokes, methods of spending money, grammar, table manners, the relative importance of automobiles and savings accounts: Subterranean Language and Mythology Discovered in Cross-Cultural Marriage. Then, two years into their relationship, the phrase "in my culture, we. . ." came into the conversation. They knew the secret codes now. They discussed their pasts as if describing a landscape. What did your family buy at Penny's? What was considered a vacation? Were there books in your house? Did you collect S&H Green or Blue Chip Stamps and what did you buy with them: art or appliances? See how far they had come, Patricia wanted to tell the women at Sabito's: they now understood the difference between a family that played Bingo and one that played Bridge.

But fine, then, just fine, if she wants to give up on all that work. Let her run away like Cherice. Five years of her life invested in the goddamn thing, and it folds like a cardboard shack. Well fuck it. Who needs the woman anyway with her damn frizzy hair and her way of insisting that the forks go at right angles? she thought without conviction. Obsessive compulsive, that's what she was. Five years she'd dated her and danced her and believed that when the woman paid the bills it was an act of love, Patricia thought, hoping that in some way, it was still true. That was what Trout had always said. And now, when the chips were down, she showed her true colors. When the world exposed its really ugly side, the one that Patricia had known was there all along, the woman just dressed up and went to the circus. Was that love? No way.

Love was bringing a wash cloth to her mother's forehead when the woman had gotten stiffed for a raise again; it was sitting quietly in the corner while she ranted and raved. It wasn't taking the opportunity, when something bad hit, to run off and play like a goddamn child. Or act like Cherice, who had thrown clothes onto a body covered with sex-sweat and run down the street. Trout was a fake. A goddamn fake. All these years, all her so-called protection. It was nothing. What did she understand? There were things you counted on in the world, you had a right to believe in. What was a marriage but two people who relied on each other? Patricia knew she was a good woman. She was worthy of that kind of dedication, wasn't she? Trout obviously didn't think so. Trout didn't want to live in the real world, where bad things happened and you had to pick yourself up. Jesus Christ, what was life but the ability to pick yourself up after the shit hit? What could Trout be thinking? That the world was all sunshine and beach-life? Maybe Trout grew up where the money stockpiled by itself, arrived in little brown envelopes from her mother's insurance policy, but that wasn't her life and she'd be damned if she was going to throw in the towel and move to some Mexican beach-town because suddenly reality shook them up a bit. She had a daughter to make amends with, and she couldn't do it from south of the border.

Cherice noticed the stiffening muscles in Patricia's back, the way her neck was growing sinewy as the conversation continued. I'm everything Patricia hates, she thought, but couldn't help noticing that her silk blouse was now sticking to her cleavage. She thought about asking her to slip into the alley for a re-enactment, but from the sound of her dripping, clinging relationship, there seemed little point. Besides, a part of Cherice wanted to run into the fog and preserve her memories of the evening, not face the woman who had created such intense excitement and then turned out to demand the high price of marriage in return for her sexual skills. That could be her on the floor over there, marooned from their joint apartment, their consensus management, their communal sock drawer. Their child, God forbid. From all she could tell, they even believed in joint bank accounts.

Patricia finished her beer and set the bottle down ceremoniously. What was the point of continuing the conversation? The spectacular sex was now cheap and painful.

"I need to get some sleep," she said quietly, more tired than she had been in years. She could never sleep away the devastation caused by their meeting. Her memories of Amsterdam had been destroyed, her belief in Lynn had been shattered, and she was shocked that her own dedication to monogamy was not as solid as she had thought. "I have a lot to do in the morning. There's a shower in the kitchen, though I doubt there's any dry towels at this point. Floor space you have to find for yourself."

Cherice nodded, chewed the inside of her lip and re-crossed her legs.

Patricia took one last look at her, slid off the barstool and went back to Trout. Cherice watched her from the corner of her eye as Patricia curled herself on the floor beside Trout, carefully picked up the woman's hand, and held it to her cheek as if the gesture were a plea. Cherice turned away. Idiots, she thought, and yet the gesture tied a knot in her stomach.

*I*n the morning, Patricia and Trout woke early and lay on the floor not speaking. Patricia looked around cautiously, but Cherice was gone. Some of the women passed around a single cigarette, appearing not to have slept at all. Trout headed toward the line of women at the bathroom. Before entering, each one looked up at the ceiling, peered at the junction of the walls for signs of cracks, hesitant to go into such a small, enclosed space. Could be an aftershock any minute, their faces said, and no one wanted to be trapped. The woman next to Trout leaned against the wall, clutching her stomach.

When Trout suggested they head back to the house to look for the safe full of insurance papers, and find breakfast on the way, Patricia looked at her skeptically, considered the hazards of leaving the security of Sabito's. Let her take a look at her candlesticks, Patricia thought, she'll change her mind about Mexico. Control Freak, Driven Mad By Chaos, Relents. She followed silently, fearful of what she might say if she woke up enough to speak.

As they walked to the flat, occasionally looking from side to side, Patricia refused to peer too deeply into people's homes. The city was swollen with people, not the small, cosmopolitan town of San Francisco, but Manhattan during rush hour or the way she figured China must be. All those commuters had been trapped inside the city, she had heard, tripling the population and these people wandered around without even a pile of junk to sort through. Damned if the city wasn't quiet, though. No roar of traffic and people just quietly moved down the street.

Trout studied the gardens along the way: those not festooned with garbage seemed more beautiful than ever. The flowers had taken on a brighter hue, as one does when the adrenalin of truth brings a blush to the face, she thought. People pushed anything capable of moving: carts were made of boxes nailed to skateboards, tables on casters held tottering loads of goods. Trout and Patricia bought a cup of coffee from a curbside stand made of a sawhorse, a door, an extension cord, and a percolator. Further down the street they ate mushy fruit ice and Mexican pastries. A man slept on sofa cushions next to a bird cage, four children slept on a mattress next to their mother whose hand gripped the edge of the bed as if it might float away. Trout stepped over buckets filled with kitchen goods and cassette tapes. A young man had curled up on a blanket next to a pile of new truck tires.

The two of them stood shoulder-to-shoulder at the base of their street and stared. Demolition Scene Promises Great Jewels, Patricia thought sardonically, tears starting to collect in her eyes.

Trout strode through the rubble as if she were jumping stones in a brook. Patricia stood at the edge of the street, sickened by the sight. She moved to the back of the house, avoiding the area being combed by Trout. They picked through their house, looking for the safe that contained the insurance papers, proof of ownership of the car, and searching for, but not mentioning, the power of attorney papers and the wills.

Patricia bent over the slabs of torn concrete, her forehead tight with a frown that seemed to tear her face downward. She wasn't going to open her mouth, wasn't going to say a word. After these many years, you had to step around a fight like this or it would blow you apart. She kicked at the debris with her boot. Clipboard, pipe, dust, spatula. Lover in the Clouds, Daughter with Ducks. It was like smelling that black wind back home that ran on the back of the creek and brought the ugly season. You smelled that wind it either meant winter or someone was going to die. Alarmist Lost In Black Hole of Own Mind, she thought.

Trout grabbed at objects and exclaimed. She filled a box with books, then dragged it across the cement shards of the living room wall. After more than an hour of poking through debris, Patricia wandered off to find water and returned with another crate for their goods. She tossed it furiously next to Trout.

"There are some . . . shoes in there," Patricia said angrily, not mentioning the shirts and pants she couldn't bring herself to pull from the dust. That wasn't the sort of thing she would ever wear, she thought to herself. Newly Poor Shop Saks Fifth Avenue in Self-Defense, she thought.

"I feel like a terrier after a mouse," Trout said brightly, masking the tension she felt over the argument that could erupt if she wasn't careful. They couldn't be in that much trouble, she reasoned. Last night it seemed as if they had reached an impasse. Maybe if they kept it all on the practical level they could find some reason to continue.

"Jesus!" Patricia shouted, turning on her heel and striding over to Trout. "Can't you stop with that dog stuff, that goddamn canine babble? City Tumbles Down, Woman Turns into Basset Hound," she said, throwing her hands up in the air. "What should I do for you, Trout, tell you our lives are ruined and set out a bowl of kibble? In Time of Crisis, Lover Puts Faith in Kal-Can?"

"Well you're not much help," Trout said pointedly, "you and your goddamn headlines."

"Oh, and you off actin' like Indiana Jones and her Wonder Dog all in one woman!"

"I only wanted to be Harrison Ford for one minute and you'll never let me forget it," Trout said.

"Yeah, well it's pretty weird if you ask me," Patricia said.

"What's weird? His outfit was nice."

"Bullshit!" Patricia shouted, stumbling over cement pieces and heading into the house.

"Why are you fighting me so hard on this?" Trout yelled at her. "It's a perfectly reasonable plan. We can . . . we can even get one of those mail-in courses so you can get your contractor's license, for Christsake."

"Great," Patricia said scornfully. "Buy a couple Mexican pipe-benders, I'm all set."

"What's the alternative here, Patricia? Buy another egg beater?" Trout hollered, picking a battered one from the rubble and throwing it down, "get another skillet, set the books in alphabetical order again? Another chart for the oil, tire, filter changes? Are we going to vacuum the carpet for another thousand Saturdays after working another thousand weeks in an office? Is that your idea of the good life: endless loads of laundry, more pantyhose, and another two-week vacation? What for?"

"You'll feel differently when you own your own home."

"Buy a house? And what are you going to do? Pull my chair out for me when I sit down to slog through the paperwork? Why is it always me? Some butch you are! I can't believe I've spent all these years pampering you like this."

"Pampering me!" Patricia screamed. And why not? she wanted to shout. Life is hard enough. She'd put up with plenty. You love someone, you take care of them, for Christsake. She'd spent enough of her time with her hands clenched like claws; she didn't think she had to do it at home. How could this be coming out of Trout's mouth?

"Pretend you hadn't noticed, Patricia. Who does the paperwork in this household? Not you! Who keeps the bills in order? Not our fearless butch. Everything is set up so you don't have to dirty your hands with reality. Can't have that, Patricia might get angry, and that wouldn't do, would it? Do you know when the oil has to be changed in the truck? I do. Do you know exactly when your teeth are to be cleaned or. . ."

"What do I care, Trout?" Patricia said, leaning into her face to make a point. "Do you think it matters to me if the truck's oil is changed at 3001 miles instead of exactly 3000? No. It matters to you."

"Oh that's easy to say. It just seems that way to you because you never have to make any decisions about it. You sit there like a goddamn king and I do it! I do all the work. I've done such a great job you can't even see what I've done. That's how insulated you are."

"And why is that, Tracy," Patricia sneered, "because you love me?" If she was going to threaten their relationship like this, she was going to hear it, full volume, all the music.

Yes, Trout wanted to scream. Because I love you down to my fucking bones.

"No," Patricia said pointedly. "Not because you love me. Because that's the way you think someone's life ought to be lived. And now that it can't be lived that way, you're giving up. It's not love to you, Trout, it's just . . . efficiency." The words cut into Patricia's chest as she realized they were true. Trout didn't pick up the broken cups of Patricia's anger because she loved her: she just didn't like the clutter.

"Fuck you!" Trout screamed.

"I hate to break it you, Trout," Patricia said, glaring at her, "but this is not the time to play. You're not a child anymore."

"What do you mean, anymore? I never was a child. I deserve that chance, Patricia."

"Look, I'm sorry you didn't get a childhood, but it's over. Those days are over, Trout, and I'm not paying for the crimes of your goddamn lunatic father."

"You shut up about my father."

"Just be sad, Trout," Patricia said. "Just be sad that it didn't happen for you, but don't try to distort our life because of it. It doesn't work that way."

"You're a drone, Patricia."

"Fuck you. I'm not runnin' away, Trout. My father did, and I ran away from my daughter for a while, but not now."

"Oh, so now you're going to play the model mother, right?" Trout shouted at her. "As long as you can get me to figure it out for you. She doesn't want to live with you, Patricia. Talk about 'over,' honey, those are the days that are over. You growl at her and send her away. You fight with her and off she goes. What kind of a bond is that? Surprise, Patricia, but repetitive hostility does not count as mothering!"

"Don't you dare talk about my mothering, you middle-class whore!" Patricia screamed, charging back and forth over the jagged cement.

"My buying her a ticket to Mexico won't make you a mother. And quite frankly, all those goddamn checks you slip her don't make you a mother, either."

Patricia stopped her pacing and pushed her hands into her pockets.

"Oh I know, I know all about them. You think you do it behind my back but I know. We get a goddamn postcard and suddenly there's no money for the new coffee table. Or the vacation. Or for you to join me for that business trip in New York, and you knew it was important to me. You're so sly about it—straight out of the savings account so I don't find the check. And now," she said, her voice shrill and grating, "now you want me to stay in the rubble and set up another paperwork system, tote another fucking briefcase so you can include your mean-spirited daughter in the bills-to-be-paid. You want to be a mother . . ." she screamed, then turned away. Then take her in your arms, she thought, like was never done for me. Hold her. Kiss her. Talk to her about schoolwork or her love problems, reach your hand across a table. The tears poured down her cheeks. Not a single time. Not once did little Tracy have that chance.

"What do you know about being nineteen with responsibility for a child?" Patricia screamed.

"What do I know!" Trout shouted back. "Oh, I know all right. I know all about it! Only thing I don't know about mothering is diapers! I've spent my entire life taking care of people."

"Oh, don't give me that," Patricia growled. "You didn't do all that shit for your father."

"What?!"

"It wasn't for him and you know it. It was for you, Trout. For some cock-eyed notion of your own."

Trout spun around as if the words were too much to take head-on.

"Why didn't you let someone help you? Huh?" Patricia shouted, struggling over the cement to face her. "Your relatives all trooped in one by one, but would you go somewhere where you could have a childhood? Where someone would mother you? No. You had to prove something, didn't you?"

"Shut up!"

"No, no I won't."

"If that's what you thought, why didn't you say so a long time ago?"

"Your pain is your own, Trout. It's yours to work out, but just quit talkin' like you were . . . the valiant commander of a goddamn . . . paternal rescue team," Patricia shouted, but wondered to herself why, as Trout said, she hadn't mentioned it before.

Trout started crying, gritting her teeth. Ask for an inch, you're shoved against the wall again.

We're a perfect pair, Patricia thought, this time not with the love and pride she usually felt, but with shame and disgust. I'm convinced the world's already shit on me, and she's so afraid it's going to she's building a bomb shelter. Christ.

"Let's come up with a compromise," Patricia said cautiously.

"No!" Trout screamed. "There is no compromise. There's one way or the other. We've done it your way for years. It's always been compromise with me. You want to hear about settling for less?" She turned back to the rubble, as the memory of her father flooded over her. Compromise: the road to tragedy. She'd tell her about compromise, about settling for less than the real thing. A million stories and any one of them would curl a normal person's hair. Her name, for Christsake. Let her tell just that one and watch her weep.

"Luke," Maggie had said, pulling Tracy in front of her to face her father's back as he rocked in the old leather chair, "I want you to say you're glad she's going away to college. You stand right here Tracy Lynn. Luke, tell her that."

"Large mouth bass require special flies, tied counterclockwise."

"Tell your daughter you're glad she's going to college, that you're proud of her, pursuing her life like she should be."

"Maggie, don't," Tracy said, twisting under her grip.

"Quiet. Any father ought to, and this man is your father, goddamnit."

No, don't make him, Tracy had thought, starting to cry. He won't say it. He shouldn't have to. Her father bounced back and forth in his chair on the porch, the light beside him spotlighting his immobilized arm. She wanted to reach out and rock the back of the chair for him, to wrap her arms around the chair's breadth and hold him. She saw herself slip under the chair's base and become the springs, the struts that steadied his rocking. Maggie clutched her firmly by the shoulders.

"Luke!" Maggie shouted. "You lily-ass bastard, you've been running this girl ragged. Now get over here and give her your blessing."

Luke stood up and held the back of his chair, appearing to Tracy a tiny man in the puddle of yellow light, moving unsteadily as his chair continued to rock without him.

"You're my Trout. The finest of fish," he said forlornly. "Trout, little darling, you're the smart one. The craftiest survivor."

He had turned his back and crossed the porch to the door, slipped into the blackness of the evening.

"My name, Patricia," Trout growled through her tears. "My goddamn name is a compromise. Settling for less? That's as close to love as he could come: the name of a goddamn fish! I can't do it anymore."

"It's all or nothing with you, isn't it?" Patricia said, horrified, grasping at anything to shake Trout out of this state. "Oh, you're happy for a while, as long as you're building something, buying something, protecting yourself against the fear that things might fall apart. But give us a chance to just live a normal life, just an average, reasonable life, and you're the thing that falls to pieces. You don't know how to be normal, Tracy."

"I've tried normal, Patricia, and it doesn't work," she hissed. "It doesn't even exist. I tried normal with my father. You'll never meet anyone who tried normal harder than I have! And this is what we got," Trout said, choking on her anger and her tears as she held her arms out at the destruction around her.

"I don't know what we're gonna do," Patricia wailed, turning away.

"Well I do!" Trout shouted, pacing after her. "Let me do this one last thing for us."

"Right. Here's one of your good pumps," Patricia said, throwing the shoe savagely into the crate. "And Harrison Ford looked like a dirt bag. You want to go to Mexico, you're goin' by yourself."

Patricia stormed into the house and threw pieces of cement at the remaining pillars, then returned.

"All right, all right," Patricia said, trying to calm herself by breathing deeply and looking down at her boots. "Let's look at this again. Are you telling me . . . that we are no longer compatible with each other's lifestyles?"

Trout closed her eyes. She hadn't thought the problem would be unresolvable, something that would generate real incompatibility, but she was wrong. There was no moving

Patricia on this, and she couldn't back down. She was exhausted, drained of whatever it took to make their relationship work as it had. She thought of how many of their friends had been together for years, then abandoned their relationships when one had to move to Pittsburgh for a job or decided to have children. Incompatible. It couldn't happen to them. But it had.

"I'm telling you. . ." Trout said with clenched teeth, "that I'm no longer compatible . . . with my own lifestyle."

Why had she asked? Patricia moaned to herself. Couldn't they have left it unspoken for a while? Now that it was said there was no turning back. No way to pretend that they hadn't drawn a line down the middle of their life together and refused to cross it. She was the woman under the porch steps now; the blood on her boots was her own. Life without Trout? She felt the sky go black. She took a deep breath. Trout had made her stand. Patricia crossed her arms over her chest. There was nothing left to do but to make her own stand. Let Trout wander through this so-called playground by herself, then, if that's what she thought of all this. Maybe I'll look for Lynn, Patricia considered.

"I think we should split up," Patricia said.

"What?" Trout said. Goddamnit. One request. One simple request. Two tickets to Mexico. It wasn't even that complicated, but, oh no, there was no room for her. Not for her desires. And after five years.

Patricia put her hands out to stop her from speaking.

"Wait. We'll just do different things for a while. License or no license, they need electricians. And I have to start working. We've got bills to pay: just because we can't find them doesn't mean we don't have to pay them. Besides, I can't just sit around Sabito's all day, I'll turn into a drunk."

Trout put her hands on her hips and shook her head. That was it, then, Trout thought. Once again, the equation had been shown to her: put yourself first, you put yourself out there alone. Patricia could change her mind, right this minute, but Trout knew their relationship would never be the same, if it would be a relationship at all.

"Let me do this for us, Patricia," Trout pleaded. "It's a perfect plan. I've been working this for years without even knowing it. Don't you see, I thought what I was doing was protecting us from ruin, and it has! What's more ruinous than this?" she said, gesturing at the space that used to be their apartment, "and we're fine. We're better than fine. For this first time, we're free! Don't you see what that means?"

"Beth's place will be our base camp," Patricia said gravely. "You go ahead and put in the insurance claim if that's what you think is important. I'll . . . meet you there at night."

"And Trout," Patricia added, "I'm sorry I grabbed you in the bar. You know I don't like that kind of stuff."

*T*rout saw Patricia moving toward the house as if she were watching a dream. Split up? It was inconceivable. A couple of fish floundering on the sand, that's what they were, each of them helpless to do anything for the other. Trout saw Patricia squirming with pain, but knew she was too far up the shore herself to do anything.

Trout had to admit that despite her jovial attitude, it was much worse to be here in the flat and find little items that had meant something to them. Looked at as a whole, Trout didn't mind losing everything and starting from scratch. Now, faced with the feelings she had embedded in these objects, confronted by the crack on the glass that she had tried for years to prevent, the smashed tea set she had polished to protect from tarnish, the torn and filthy white chairs, the vase that did, finally, fall off the mantle, Trout went through the pain of a thousand little accidents all at once. It had been better when she had just faced the devastated building and called everything a loss, written off thousands of dollars of furniture and possessions, calculated the insurance refund. To sort through it all, to hold the pieces, was too much pain.

The flat had been very important to her. A new domesticity had blossomed in her: not the everyday pick-up and put-away feeling she had had living with her father. There was a precision and a gentleness in the way she went about her chores each evening after coming home, as if even her muscles now knew that she had a spouse, a few nice things worth coveting, a peace that came when she stacked clean glass bowls inside one another and slid them across a wooden shelf. Had her mother smoothed a table cloth and straightened a knife beside a plate with a feeling that the exactitude of her motions brought solace, serenity? It was hard for Trout to imagine. There was only one picture of her mother, kept on the bureau in the kitchen, and by the time she was old enough to ask for stories of the woman, her father had already slipped into his private world of canoeing and building strange contraptions. The girl didn't ask, fearing that the stories she would hear would turn out to be as disjointed as the found objects that her father called inventions.

Tracy had been left to discover the world of womanhood on her own, and while she emulated the girls at school, she never forgot that behind the science of which lipstick to use and how to highlight the bridge of the nose lay a culture filled with ceremonies and folklore that she would never know. To walk through her flat as an adult, preparing dinner or polishing their wooden furniture, she participated in a found culture.

What had happened to the homemaker? Since the earthquake, she had swung from a maniacal housekeeper to someone convinced she preferred to live in a tent. Trout held her forehead. She had pushed Patricia to the brink, that was clear, and despite their dirt-streaked and tired faces, despite the shock of the way their flat looked, the new shapes created by their twisted floor lamps and the patterns of their clothing thrown into heaps, each of them wore a familiar look on her face. Too familiar, Trout thought, as if she saw her own face reflected in Patricia's eyes. Trout looked down and reluctantly pulled a potato peeler from the box of books at her feet. Trout sighed and walked, head bent, to find the box for the kitchen utensils. She should separate all the objects by room and purpose, she knew that. She turned toward Patricia, then looked away. The trip to Mexico made no sense without Patricia.

Patricia wanted Trout to make the situation better, and she had tried to. This was her plan. She didn't want it without Patricia. She just wanted something different, with her. But she knew the look on Patricia's face. Trout's actions told Patricia that she was leaving her alone in the world to work it out or piece it together the best she could. How could she have offered Patricia that option when she herself had always railed against any kind of isolation? Trout shunned people who spoke in a language she didn't understand. She avoided women who whispered in public. She became enraged when dental or medical students used Latin terms in conversation. It terrified her. She immediately saw images of her father, spending his evenings muttering to the blow torch or the soldering iron. Now, here she was with Patricia, absent while present, bronco-busting in a ruined city while her lover stood in front of her with a frightened face, wondering how to survive. She would have to talk to Patricia about it; she would have to find a way to tell her she was sorry for leaving her in that horrid place she herself knew so well. The question now was how to tell Patricia that she was right.

"Trout!" Patricia called from deep inside the house. "I found the safe."

Trout's shoulders dropped, and she sighed for the things in her life and the payments they demanded. Faced with the crumbled, looted, and filthy pile that was her house, tired after hours of resurrecting little pieces of their life, scraping her hands and forearms, the cement brick biting into her ankles, she wondered what would happen to her joy in a life without jobs and possessions if she had to have that life without Patricia.

Trout moved toward the street where they had set their little beer bottle of water, hidden where the front steps had been so a passer-by wouldn't steal it. Trout bent to pick at the pieces of the VCR stand, looted of its contents. She had sailed off into the netherworld like her father. How could Patricia forgive her when she had never been able to forgive him?

A rumbling began that first sounded like a large truck going by, and Trout turned in the hopes that it was bringing food and water, or that it somehow meant that the streets were cleared, though she knew they weren't. The sound grew louder in an instant, and people began screaming, running toward what they thought was the street, running in circles,

with no home to flee and no idea where to go. Some
dropped to their knees. Trout, still clutching the beer bottle
of water, turned to Patricia, her eyes wide. Her heart
suddenly stopped. As the ground began to vibrate, Patricia
struggled to clamber out of the house. Trout fell to her knees
from the shaking and screamed as the blocks of cement cut
into her skin. The glasses fell out of her pocket. She looked
up to see a pipe fall from the building and hit Patricia across
the back of the shoulders. She saw her fall. Trout heard
screaming, coming from an unknown place inside herself,
felt her body struggle to get up and then fall again as the
shaking continued. In the distance, the sound of explosions
and parts of buildings falling mingled with the internal sound
of Trout's screaming.

She didn't know when the shaking stopped. Over and
over, she saw the pipe come down, saw the moment when it
knocked Patricia to the ground, saw Patricia disappear from
view. Time and again, as she clambered over the concrete
like a child up her first flight of stairs, Trout wondered where
the screaming was coming from.

Two men on the street with a canvas stretcher, Army
surplus (from where Trout didn't bother to question), helped
Trout begin to carry Patricia, unconscious, across the
Mission toward General Hospital. Unlike the sure-footed
journey with Mrs. Williamson, Trout staggered down the
street, frantic over the slow progress. Trout tore off her black
cape and threw it on the sidewalk. A Muni bus, equipped as
an ambulance, stopped for the entourage and took Patricia
and Trout slowly through the crowded streets. She hadn't
said it, Trout thought, there hadn't been time. It was my
hare-brained idea to go to the house. The medics pushed
Trout aside to tend to Patricia, and when they zipped her
into an inflatable bag to immobilize her spine, Trout put her
face in her hands and cried.

*B*eth tossed another dead, oil-soaked bird onto the hard ground, grimacing as its neck and head flopped beside its body. The birds were piling up, and every time Beth carried a bunch, in a bag, in her arms, she wanted to throw them. Slam them against the ground. It was all she could do to keep from kicking them, but that wouldn't go over big with the organizers. She didn't know why she wanted to take it out on the birds. Wasn't their fault. They looked like a coal tipple near Grandma Meredith's. Maybe that was it. Toxins.

Her whole life rumblin' around in toxins. And nowhere near your mother's home, a voice inside her said. Ah, who cared about her mother? 'Course she hadn't even asked about Patricia's house, or Trout, she thought. First mention of the roof falling in on Patricia and she had turned and run. Run as far as she could. That was the way it was with them. She'd get this urge to be a little girl, curl up on Patricia's lap, and so she'd pack a bag. That was the safest. Send a postcard. Somethin' glossy with the sun shining on some busted-up Nebraska stadium, or a card of a giant ice cream cone that was really a hot dog stand. 'Merry Christmas. Bah Humbug. Me and roaches do great party—B.' Got an irate phone call and a little money out of that one. Never told her she had Christmas dinner at the St. Anthony Shelter. 'Happy Belated Birthday, Ma. Don't get mellow. Ha.—Your Best Bet(h).' She could go back to San Francisco. Find Patricia, try to pal around. But it was pointless. They'd get in a fight and what good would that do? She'd never say . . . she was scared. Postcards were better. 'Birds dying. Thinking of you—B'

At the hospital, a doctor strode into the room, looked at Trout holding Patricia's hand and stopped.

"Relatives only," he said curtly.

"I beg your pardon?"

"Only those people directly responsible for the patient can be admitted to these rooms," he said, moving to Patricia's side and taking her pulse, lifting Patricia's eyelids as if Trout were no longer in the room.

"I'm her . . . I'm directly responsible for her."

The man straightened, put his hands in his pockets with an authoritarian, yet dismissive stance.

"This hospital is filled to the rafters with people, young lady. Only those. . ." he said slowly, with a sneer, "who are blood relatives, those who can authorize treatment in other words, are allowed in the rooms. I can't have neighbors and friends giving the go-ahead for operations. Or we'll all wind up in court for the rest of our lives."

"I hold power of attorney over this woman and I intend to stay here."

"Not without proof you won't," he said. "What are you . . . her sister?"

Trout didn't answer, only glared at him, biting back her desire to scream at him.

"I hold power of attorney and you want to see a lawsuit, just try to bar me from this room."

"Without your paperwork, you'll have to leave," the doctor said dismissively. "Guard!" the man shouted. "Have this woman removed!"

"There's nothing to do but be patient," the nurse told her as she stormed out of the room, one step ahead of the National Guardsman. "She has a concussion and has slipped into a coma. Some pull out quite nicely, but . . . others don't. There's just no telling. It's up to her now."

"Up to whom?"

"The patient."

"There's got to be something you can do, for God's sake!" Trout shrieked, turning and trying to walk around the nurse, back into the room.

The nurse grabbed her by the arm, spoke secretively. "Get your paperwork. The Guard is being very strict. Coma patients need two things: oxygen and constant stimulus. I'll work on trying to find a tank of oxygen somewhere. You get back here and talk to her. None of us want brain damage here."

"Brain damage!"

"Please, do you know how many people are injured? Just go."

How could she explain it to them? The proof she had was not something that could be contained on paper. Fuck paperwork, she wanted to scream. She's my wife. I sit on a little stool beside the tub every night and hand her a wine glass, shampoo, her precious little loufa sponge. That's a marriage, get it? I used to circle the good news in the newspaper with a yellow highlighting pen to help her keep her chin up. Pretty soon I didn't have to circle them anymore, do you understand? What's marriage but that? There's no one in the world who thinks her life and her body more precious than I, not even her mother—any mother, who has seen her fall and get up again, who has watched her burn herself after being told not to touch and thinks to herself I told her so. I don't ever think that, do you get it?

Waiting outside the intensive care unit, Trout stood in a blinding rage. How could it be like this, worlds without order or structure and her desiring less so in her own life but now, needing her file folders, her ordered paperwork? How could they just put her out of here? she screamed silently to herself, and why on earth did she make Patricia go back to the house? It was her fault. She had given up and it had happened again, like the canoe in the river. She had said she wouldn't do it anymore, and the world had opened up and swallowed her love again. She hadn't had a chance to apologize.

When Luke had returned from the hospital, the doctor had said he had been stabilized by a new medication and Tracy, home on spring break, was surprised by how complete their conversations were. If he stays on his pills, we may have this thing licked, the doctor had told Tracy. Luke had taken the canoe from its rack on the side of the house, and Tracy had fought her first reaction to take it away like a sharp knife from a child. He was bright-eyed and clear, Trout remembered. Luke had maps, he had water and trail mix and suddenly looked like a father again, someone who knew that the gear had to be strapped just in front of the bow seat, someone who could actually navigate water. He gripped the gunwale of the boat for her like a man who could be counted on to steady the craft for her step. Tracy sat in the stern seat and let him paddle (but insisted they stay close to the shore), jubilantly listening to him talk about current events and instruct her in the proper way to tack against the wind.

Later that summer when she got the call from the sheriff, she knew the scenario before he described it. Her father had drowned, the sheriff said, but she knew he had finally just sailed away. The meals had continued to arrive and the house to be cleaned, but he had slipped through the net she had built. She saw him paddling in circles, sitting backward in the boat, endlessly sliding the lake that became a river, turned into creeks, broke open into estuaries, water that constantly traveled and took her father with it, pointlessly, endlessly, out of control and chartless, a man in a boat not capable of seeing where he was going or why he should come ashore, a man sitting cross-legged in a canoe reciting its parts: "stern thwart, bow, sheer line, freeboard, keel, stern thwart, bow," as the sun baked his head until it balded and tore, and the water made his feet as black and cracked as those of bag ladies on the street. He had finally become completely lost, rocking back and forth, in a canoe tumbling down a river, the only sign of life visible from the shore her father's hands gripping the gunwale.

Trout replayed in her mind the sight of her father sailing away and knew that she was the one who had pushed him off the shore. She had collected the bills, packed his checkbook, torn up the Visa card, but had taken the bus back to college. What was the medication? She hadn't asked. She hadn't set up a system for him to take his pills. She had wanted to live a life like other people, and she had made him vulnerable as a result. She had watched him take the canoe down from its rack, knowing she had had nothing left to give.

Today, in the panicked city of San Francisco, she was the young girl Tracy, hoping there was a controlled and logical underpinning to the world, a way to put things in order again. Her hands were his as he died, helplessly clutching a paddle in water he didn't know.

She paced up and down the hall, trying to push her flossy hair into a bun, past beds filled with people who looked as though they had been here since before the earthquake, those whose ailments were diseases that couldn't be seen, perhaps weren't even known. Jesus, that would be torture, Trout thought. To watch one's life go down the tubes, victim to something that couldn't be viewed, couldn't even be understood. At least she knew what had happened: a secured pipe became unsecured, it gave way, a coma. She understood, but she was left nonetheless, standing passively, hands behind her back, leaning against the wall of the hospital corridor. Passive. Not something she ever expected herself to be during a crisis, worse than any other crisis she could imagine. Houses could fall down, jobs lost, but there were always others. The doctors couldn't simply put a cast on Patricia, do an operation, cut her open, sew her up.

Patricia lying there silently, eyes closed, unresponsive, with tubes being put into both arms, nurses strapping monitors to her chest and her forehead. Patricia was going to do something that would make the difference? Trout pushed herself off the wall and paced into the waiting room, stepping over people who sat on the floor.

As she rounded the corner, Trout's breath caught in her throat at the sight of all the people. The clutching need for each of them to find a solution, the necessity to have something fixed, to have it put back into order, not stone and brick, not just a bank statement or even a green card, but something fixed that perhaps would never mend, could not heal, would not change. She was in the middle of it, just like them. It caught in her throat as if it were all the rubble of her house, and drove her into the street.

*T*rout stood perfectly still in the middle of Portrero
Avenue. The pink had drained out of the sky. The color
had been sapped from everything: the brick buildings were
gray, people's faces pale white, clothing nothing but ash
hanging from bodies. How had this happened, she thought?
She knew how the pipe had come down, relived it again
when the doctor was talking, when she walked down the
flights of stairs, pushed her way through people on the
street, over and over, the pipe fell and Patricia's
expressionless face fell forward, never hitting the ground,
disappearing from Trout's view and so continuing to fall.

Trout's body was thin now, with hair of gruesome brillo,
covered by skin that had died before. She was a single skein
of gristle standing in shreds of clothing that were as
inadequate protection as a dishrag trying to cover a house.
Patricia was in a coma. It wasn't possible.

She should have expected the doctor's response: surely
she understood that people in power were only gracious
when they thought they had something to spare, when they
mistook social responsibility for some sort of generosity.
Trout spit on the ground. She should have known it; earlier
in the day she had seen the Fire Department handing out
rubber gloves to the people clustered outside the hospital,
explaining that they should put them on if they suspected
someone bleeding of having AIDS. Within minutes people
had looped the gloves over their belts and were eyeing each
other suspiciously, and Trout knew they were asking
themselves, "who looks gay," "who looks like a drug
addict?" The sight had chilled her.

Trout walked slowly through the crowd, people glancing at
her with fear, moving out of her way. She would get her
power of attorney papers, goddamn it. There wasn't going to
be another Sharon Kowalski here, not one woman helpless
in the hospital and another helpless to get to her.

She crossed blocks of the city with a wide and furious
stride. Damn doctors, she thought, knowing that her anger
was larger than that. She was furious with Patricia. She didn't
trust Patricia to pull out of it on her own. Patricia was the
one who called all lost. Where would she find the faith in life
to pull through this, where would she find belief in the beauty

of things? What was it that would make her decide she could turn around in the dark tunnel of her coma and come back? Was it the sound of birds, the smell of flowers, something she left undone, some remembrance of Beth in a backyard somewhere? Could Trout hope for something like her own love as the enticement for life on earth? Wasn't that what they said, that jetting on toward that beautiful light at the end of the tunnel you are suddenly called back by a woman's voice saying "we need you here," and you turn around, wake up to happy faces, grateful tears?

Not Patricia. Patricia was her loving cynic, the woman who could look at a rose garden and talk about pesticides, the woman whose belief in doom and gloom and nuclear destruction was unabating, not in a rhetorical way, not in a stilted, Leftist-Party sort of banter, but in a true lament, the genuine wail of a woman who had seen so much pain, who understood the wretched connections between things, who saw the secret, insidious way that money and class and race and food, school, art, clothing, sunshine, resources, men and women together, all fit into an oppressive grip on the world. Patricia saw it clearly, like a single gray, gruesome crack that could be traced from the top of a mosaic through the labyrinth to the bottom. Trout thought Patricia's viewpoint was insightful, astute, the fine machinations of the woman's mind. Sometimes, though, Trout found Patricia's politics debilitating, a defense at best. Today, wondering where Patricia was going to summon the hope to come back to a world she considered imperfect beyond repair, Trout cursed the woman's attitude as the final injustice, a potentially fatal flaw.

That left the saving up to her, she thought. Sit and be patient? As difficult for her as being optimistic is impossible for Patricia, she thought, as she stuffed her hands into her chinos and pushed her way, elbows out, through the crowds. She thought of herself as the type who could, in fact, heal herself from a major disease, could survive on lifeboats, in downed planes. She read the books about survivors whenever they hit the stands. Put the rotting corpses outside the plane in the snow, distill piss through cloth, don't ever put water on your lips: she remembered these bits of survival trivia, it was important to her. Though she told her friends she was simply interested, she knew it was, in fact, because she wanted to be prepared, because she insisted on having every single bit of information possible, just in case. She wanted every advantage, every conceivable option for life and freedom and longevity.

Why couldn't it have been her in the coma? She would pull through. She would be the type of patient the doctors would leave in the recovery room and, pulling off their operating masks, say to the waiting lover, "That Tracy has a tremendous will to live." Why couldn't it have been her? She couldn't let Patricia do this alone, she couldn't sit still, "patiently" as the nurse said, and let her decide . . . my God, whether to live or not. No. There would be no autonomy here. Trout began crying, pushing faster and faster through the crowd. Here she was, a survival junky, in love with a tragic doomsayer.

She didn't trust her. She had thought they were a team, two people with different strengths, but they weren't. Trout didn't trust her. That's why she did everything. Because there wasn't any reason to leave paperwork to Patricia: she couldn't do it as well. She didn't do it right. That was the truth that she couldn't speak. She wanted to move to Mexico because she couldn't face rebuilding their life, and she wasn't prepared to let Patricia build it for them. At least in Mexico Trout's burden would be simplified, even if she shouldered it herself. She didn't trust her.

Was this it, then, Trout wondered? Was it death, Patricia deserting her, Patricia no longer in the world, let alone at her side? The pain wasn't even pain as she knew it, wasn't sharp or cutting, but a feeling that everything inside her skin had been dug out, her insides suddenly aching with the draining of her substance, the way the sky and the faces around her appeared. This was not being afraid, she thought, this was being scorched. The city of San Francisco seemed to fade from her, to wheel away on a dolly until even those in the crowd whose breath she could feel against her cheeks seemed yards away, tiny little figures on a long street.

ertain she was making her way toward the house but not sure that she was moving, Trout saw a long line of men—the first time she had seen men standing dutifully in line, not crowding forward or shouting, not reaching long arms out to grab. These men looked down, looked away, would not meet the gaze of women walking by. As Trout neared them she saw the liquor store behind the crowd of people. Its sign had fallen off the front, but its wired glass windows, shattered, still held the row of bottles. One by one the men were let into the building.

She went to Beth's house, her body tired. She saw her pain fill the room. It was the dust on the mantle, the dirt on the sill. It was the cloud that rose from the chair as her palms flopped on the overstuffed arms. She rose and walked back to join the crowd at the liquor store.

Walking down the street, Trout drank out of the Scotch bottle with such hunger that the bitter stuff ran down the sides of her mouth and onto the front of her shirt. This will simply not happen. That's all there was to it. It just couldn't, she thought, as she passed a narrow alley between two doorways and heard mutterings.

"I need a rope. Your rope, Buddha," the woman said, her voice rising in volume with every word. Trout stopped, clutching the bottle by the neck, listening to the sound of the voice.

"Lynn? Is that you?"

"The rope I clutch when they say, 'the Chinese are good businessmen, if only they'd skip the tea.'"

Trout knelt down beside Lynn, who was crouched on the cement with a little pile of sticks between her knees as if ready to build a tiny fire. Lynn looked at Trout, then drew her tongue over her lips in a slow, deliberate movement.

"The rope you send me, hay-colored," Lynn said, softer, "that I clutch, my thread of life, the force of my clutching calming me tightly."

"Are you . . . praying?" Trout said, looking intently at her.

Lynn poked at the little sticks but did not look over at Trout. She pushed her straggled hair to one side.

"I never even went back to the office. I left them there," she said softly.

"There wasn't anything you could do, Lynn. You can't get up fifteen stories during an earthquake."

"That was the first," Lynn said, even softer looking back at her little pile of sticks. "Then soon you grew to wrap me in it, winding my body with the rope and I felt covered, comforted, bound and gagged and motionless, a good feeling."

"Lynn, Patricia's been hurt. She's in the hospital in a coma."

"Give it to me, here in my cement home, alone with the hair my mother adores." Lynn turned to Trout.

"Lynn, stop it. Come with me. You're raving, do you know that?" Trout asked weakly, beginning to feel drawn into the monologue. Trout considered for a moment, then knelt with Lynn, nose touching the points of her fingers. She could pray for a moment. Goddess knew she needed the help.

"Or the net you gave me later," Lynn continued, "teaching me that the rope that binds can also be flung outward. The cords of a fishing net tossed to gather are connected and secure, yet venturing. Can you throw me outward from this place?"

Trout looked ahead at the brick wall of the alley, then closed her eyes. Trout's knees got cold, then stiff. She sat silently, listening to the chanting of this woman.

"Lynn," Trout said softly, "why all this stuff with the Buddha?" Trout had never heard her talk about anything Chinese in all the years she had known her. Her race was something that one forced oneself to remember, like recalling a friend's home town, relevant but not apparent.

"Ask me now and I'll kneel, not lie here like a fish, the sun on the side of my face like a hoax, like the sun in my grandmother's garden warming the stones and me, listening to the hollowness of the wind chimes, tapping my foot on the cement walk way, my foot in little ballet shoes, tapping as if it were a part of Grandma's prayer. Pink tights and a tutu, like a white girl on a music box. I threw one of my grandmother's embroidered jackets over my shoulders; it stuck out to cover the tutu. Then my mother and grandmother came running into the garden, my mother pulling off the jacket and my grandmother grabbing the tutu, each trying to pull off me the things that they were that they weren't."

"Lynn," Trout said, touching her arm, "come with me now, or go to Sabito's. Do you remember where that is? You need to calm down."

Lynn pulled back, stood, and walked away.

"I need your help, goddamnit!" Trout shouted after her. Lynn kept walking, ran both hands along the cement wall of a building, looking up, sweeping her hands along the surface as if toward the sun, as if feeling it for the first time. She turned the corner.

Wasn't there anyone left who was willing to do anything? Determined to make something happen? Trout thought, furious as she watched the woman disappear around the corner. Goddamnit, if she had to save Patricia herself, then that's what she would do. She turned and marched toward her house.

Trout put the Scotch bottle behind a slab of cement at her house and started in toward the room that would have held the safe.

"Hold it right there," a voice called out behind her. A man (she assumed it was a man, hidden under a big rubber suit, a huge hat) strode over to her. "No entrance to any building."

"This is my . . . was my house," Trout said, gesturing at the half-constructed box behind her.

"All destroyed property falls under the jurisdiction of the Fire Department," the man said sternly. "There's no admittance under any condition."

"This is a goddamn case of life or death," Trout said, clenching her teeth.

"Not under any circumstances."

"Look," Trout said, putting her hands on her hips. She hoped he couldn't smell the Scotch on her breath. "There are some critical documents inside that I need. My . . . friend is in the hospital, and I need documents for her treatment."

"Look, lady, you go in there something could happen."

"Something already has happened, for Christsake!" Trout shouted.

"You harrass me I'm authorized to arrest you, on the spot."

"This is my house, goddamnit, and I need those papers, now!"

"I don't know this is your house," he said.

How could she possibly prove that? she thought indignantly. No social security number on her. No credit cards or letters or driver's license. She couldn't describe the layout of the building, or distinguishing marks like a mole on a dog. When you have nothing on you, she thought, how do you prove one stack of lathe and plaster is any more yours than others?

What could she say? She couldn't tell him that if she were a man she would be at her lover's side right this minute, admitted to the room by a simple, "I'm her husband." All over the city, she could imagine it, gay people scrambled for little slips of paper that they hoped would protect them, snippets of white in the chaos of the city, to wave in the faces of people who couldn't possibly care, who, even in this time when an extra body to tend for someone should be so welcome, balked at arrangements and marriages less repetitive than their own. Tell this man you're a lesbian and you'll be damned if anyone is going to keep you away from your lover, she thought. Tell him, right to his goddamn face, that the woman in the hospital was everything you'd built your life on and if necessary you'd tear through seven houses of concrete to find the papers to nurse her to health. Scream it in his fucking face, she thought, her cheeks getting red. Doesn't he know that sometimes devotion isn't something that sits in the mind like an abstract thought, or rings the heart like decoration? It's solidity itself, it's the sole of the foot and the palm of the hand, the place the flesh first meets the rest of the world, it's dedication that is the disk and spine and cord of the woman? What the hell is the matter with this man? A fireman. She had heard in Sabito's last night that the entire city had been turned over to the Fire Department, according to the Mayor's Emergency Plan. The department that had been indicted for painting swastikas on the lockers of black firefighters, for refusing to hire women and Latinos, was now in charge of the entire city.

"You see," Trout said softly, drawing close to the man and assuming a refined voice she hoped didn't sound drunk.

"My . . . husband has a very rare allergy to medications and I have to find the paperwork that documents this. As I'm sure you can imagine," she said, warming to her story, "the hospital is stuffed full of people and it's very difficult for them to take the time to discover these things. But . . . it's critical. It's a matter of life and death that . . . he not be given these medications. Perhaps you could help me look?"

Trout could see the man ticking off the words that might fit his agenda. It's the executive training, she thought through the Scotch: give them the key words and they'll forget the rest.

"No one is allowed in their homes, Ma'am."

Ah, it's working, Trout thought. I've gone from "lady" to "Ma'am."

"Have you ever seen someone . . . in chemical shock?" she said gravely. "I'm just going to look over here, where the safe is," she said, moving back into the rubble. "It's right over here. I'll bet you we find it in a minute."

At the sight of this strangely-dressed woman walking away from him, the fireman pushed up his hat and resumed his official stance.

"Outa there. Now!"

"I'll just look over . . . here," she said, stumbling over the concrete.

"Right. That's it. You're under arrest." He moved quickly over the cement blocks, faster in his steel-shanked boots than Trout could in a child's tennis shoes. He grabbed her by the arm and dragged her toward the street.

"The Fire Department has absolute jurisdiction here and you're trespassing," he said, as if reading it off a card. "You're under arrest. This area is full of looters, and we're under strict orders, lady. If the Captain comes by here and sees you, it won't matter what your story is, both of us will be in trouble. Now let's move. And no lip."

Trout was taken to the end of the street and loaded into a flat-bed truck with slatted sides, the kind used for herding cattle. The truck was filled with young men, a couple of middle-aged women, even one with children. Trout snorted. The back of the truck wasn't even locked, just latched with a bolt too complicated for cattle.

"Where are we going?" she asked one of the young men.

"Cow Palace." The young man looked down, kicked the side of the truck. Did they think the Fire Department had enough power to keep them, even without locks? she wondered. Did these people sitting quietly in the truck think at least they would be fed where they were going?

Nothing was going to keep her from the hospital. Not the Fire Department, not slabs of lathe and plaster, not little slips of gay paper. If they were going to book her for a criminal, she would act like a criminal, she thought and with one quick stride, bolted for the back of the truck, yanked off the latch and jumped into the street. She heard the sound of boots behind her and didn't look back to see if it was Fire Department or the other 'criminals' from the truck. She darted down an alley, pressed herself into a doorway as she had seen in the movies.

Night fell quickly, and again the fog made the city air denser than underwater life. Tonight, women on the streets in Trout's neighborhood began to moan at the first sight of the fog, fearful of another night spent crouching in tiny enclosures, no longer able to be strong for their children. Trout wove among the crowds and headed back to her house.

When she got to her house, covered now with the blanket of fog, she could see shadowy figures moving through the rubble, lifting dense articles and carting them away. She crouched among the blocks of cement, found the Scotch bottle, stuffed it awkwardly into her pocket. The living room was to the right of the entrance, the closet in the back of the room. Here is where Patricia was . . . hurt . . . she thought, reliving it again, stopping in her tracks, then moving forward. She avoided the hallway with its hung posters and photos of Beth as a child. She would find the safe. She would get to her lover, get her what she needed, find the cash to build their life again. She could make it right, she could. If she could do anything in her life, she could do this. She had to. A right turn behind this pillar. It had to be here.

Pulling at the plaster, tossing pieces of woodwork aside, Trout found a leather bag, a stone bookend, Patricia's work gloves which she immediately pulled onto her scraped and bruised hands. Protected by the gloves, Trout dug through the boards to the back of her closet and pulled out a dusty leather jacket. She looked around to see if the looters might consider her an encroacher, if they were moving toward her, ready to take what she had discovered. A sound made her turn toward the street. It was the sound of water, of slow, flat pounding, like hands on tables. Peering through the fog, Trout saw boots, shoes moving in unison. Trout saw men marching through the street as if in a parade, as if in war. The National Guard and the Sixth U.S. Army Division had moved into the city, not just in the hospital or the Mission now, but patrolling the streets as well. Trout crouched deeper into a pile of canceled checks and wrapping paper. Now, the costs of her renegade desires, her thrill over being an outlaw, came home to sit on her chest. She had always known there was a price to things, and what foolishness had convinced her that she could simply move around the city like the lawless without the penalties? Now more than ever she had to be careful not to be caught (in her own house, she thought). Now more than ever she had to get the papers, because a scene at the hospital could mean being turned over to the Guards. At least the Fire Department had been schooled in rescue: these paramilitary folks, they lived for wars, and because they had none Trout was sure they would gladly wage one against her.

She crawled among the wreckage like a dog expecting to be hit. There was the safe, dusty, chipped, but intact. Trout threw herself on it, held it in her arms, then seeing that the key was not in the lock, picked it up with one furious motion and threw it against the cement slabs.

"This far, goddamnit," she growled, "and even you against me!" She would pry it open. She would hurl it against walls, the papers were in there and she bloody well would . . . Trout knelt on the ground.

She could see the contents of the safe without having to open it. Now, just like her lover, all that was important was caught up and held away, not protected but removed, the kind of inaccessibility that others called safety. Her lover was "safely" in the hospital where she couldn't see her or hold her; the papers that controlled their destiny "safely" in the box. She knew how the bureaucracy worked: if she wasn't one of the first several thousand filing insurance claims she would wait for years, while she and Patricia were without jobs, renting some flat that had managed to stay standing, not-so-slowly going broke. It all required fast action, she thought wearily.

*T*rout shuffled chair bottoms and pieces of sheetrock to find a sandy place to sleep, looking furtively to the street to avoid the National Guard. She had found a blanket and the drapes from the bedroom. She held them close to her body as she moved toward her spot. Laying on the ground, she stared into the night at the spot where Patricia had been hurt, then tried to discern the safe in the front room. She heard a sound in the house and strained to see in the dark. Was it looters, or the National Guard? Either way it meant trouble. She lay there, wondering if it were safer to blend into the dark, or get up and take action. Trout crawled out of her covers and crouched beside the blankets. She heard repeated lifting and setting of cement pieces clanking against each other, murmuring, then what she thought was muffled crying. As she listened, the crying became louder, until it was nearly a wail. She stumbled forward until she hit her shin and stood still.

"Who's there!" she shouted.

The crying stopped. A figure stood up, then tried to dart behind one of the pillars that held up the second floor.

"Who's there, goddamnit!" Trout growled in what she hoped was her most aggressive voice.

"Trout?" the answer came furtively. "It's Henry," he whispered loudly. "Henry."

"Oh my God." Trout stumbled through the debris. "I'm over here. Where's Jack?"

Henry came through the dark, fell once, picked his way over to her. When he arrived, he wrung his hands, then sat on the slab of cement Trout was using to break the wind above her blankets.

"Thank God it's you. Thank God," Henry said.

"Henry, are you all right? Are you hurt?"

"Oh God, aren't we all," he said, putting his face in his hands. "Jack . . . is dead."

"Oh Jesus," Trout wailed, shaking her head back and forth. "Oh Henry. I'm so sorry."

"He was so sick. And so sick and tired of it all. When the earthquake came he just couldn't hold on anymore. You know what I mean? And I don't . . . I don't blame him," he said, starting to cry.

Trout sat down beside him, put her arm around his shoulders.

"Where is he?" Trout asked quietly. "In the hospital?"

Henry doubled over crying. "Oh God," he said, sitting up and slapping his legs. "I can't stand it. You were his friend. . . ."

"And I'm your friend," Trout said, drawing close.

"Well . . . he's over there, where his apartment . . . was."

"What?"

"I put him there. Trout, swear you won't tell anyone," he wailed, stomping the ground. "I loved that man," he said, clenching his fists to the night sky. "I loved him so much, I would do anything for him."

"Henry, what has happened?" Trout said deliberately.

"Promise you won't tell. My life . . . is at stake," he said, pulling at the front of his shirt. "Jesus I'm filthy. I must stink. Who would have thought the whole city would fall down? Did you have any idea?"

"Of course not. It's unbelievable," Trout said, looking around. "Patricia's in the hospital."

"Oh, God. What happened?"

"Pipe gave way. And the fuckers won't let me in to take care of her. 'Blood family only' they say."

"Don't the assholes rule the earth, I swear," Henry said, wiping his face in disgust.

The two sat in silence, staring into the darkness.

"God, it's nice to have someone I know here," Trout said. "Thank you for being here. I've been gettin' a little crazy. Oh," she said, suddenly jumping up and searching in the covers. "I have a bottle of Scotch," she said, putting her hand on his knee. "Here it is."

"Thank the . . . ah, Goddess!" Henry said.

"The Goddess, eh?"

"Well, isn't that the appropriate gesture for you lesbos?"

"Drink, drink. Patricia's in a coma. They say she might not . . . snap out of it."

"Oh, a tough bulldagger like that, don't you worry sweetheart," he said, suddenly all dish and limp wrist. "I know, I know, what is there to do with yourself but worry? At least she's got a chance."

"Yeah, but how can I make her take the chance?"

Henry was quiet. They passed the bottle.

"You think it's fucked up to drink when your lover's in the hospital?" she asked.

"Jesus, bars would have gone out of business if that was the rule."

It might have been the Scotch, but she began to relax. She and Henry could talk about clothes, gossip in an uppity tone. They conversed with the hand gestures that dykes never did between themselves and straight women didn't even know: the little slap on the bicep that said "oh you bad little thing, I love it." Trout found herself leaning into him with delicious conspiracy, bringing a poised hand to her chest in a way that said "I'm of course shocked by this but do tell. . ."

"I have to tell somebody," he said in a whisper. "I just can't face it by myself."

Trout turned to him. "Henry."

"Jack died earlier today," he said in a whisper. "I buried him under the rubble, so it would look like a fatality, the earthquake, you know. His mother's Catholic, what can I say? This," he said, gesturing to the destruction, "he dies a hero. He was so sick, do you understand, Trout? He was much more depressed than he let on. Smelled terrible, I can't believe I can say that . . . but he was dying," Henry said, starting to cry again. "The lesions were getting so bad he was all bandages. When they put the tube in his neck for the drugs—have you ever seen that? They just graft a tube right into his body to make it easier for the drugs—well, that's when he said all he wanted to do was die. Researched how to do it for weeks."

Trout stared into the fallen house, frightened suddenly knowing there was a dead body beneath all the concrete. She was very quiet.

"When the earthquake came he begged me," Henry said, turning away. "I wouldn't agree to do any of it, and I'm not going to tell you how. I don't know, and you don't want to either. He arranged it all. But I agreed to bury him here and . . . discover him tomorrow. My poor little boy. God, I loved that man."

"I'm . . . proud of you Henry."

He turned to her, clutching the Scotch bottle.

"That must have been a very difficult thing to do . . . and . . . I'm proud of you," she said, her eyes filling with tears.

"It's not wrong, can you understand that?" he said, his voice rising. "I can't believe I've risked my fuckin' life for his mother. Last time she was in town she took me aside she says 'Henny!' that's what she calls me. 'Henny, you're not feeding my boy enough. You spend more of your time in kitchen you hear me?' Right Mrs. Ponski, there is no AIDS, just Henry's bad cooking!" Henry eased the bottle from Trout's hands and took a long swallow.

"He should have had a beautiful death," Henry said softly, suddenly tired and beaten. "A gorgeous old man with scores of the adoring at his bedside, I swear. He deserved it. We would have had a wake to put Burbank to shame. Just to shame," he said, leaning into Trout. "Oh well, Jack, no telling how things work out."

"Well," Trout said, drinking long from the Scotch bottle and wiping her mouth with her hand. "We'll just have to have one of those after all."

Henry turned to her.

"Yeah," she said. "When all this is cleaned up, we'll throw a big wake for him, just like you said. I'll even wear my black dress, that one slit down the back."

"Put the queens in their place, now, girl."

"I will, I will," she said. "Let's get some sleep. You have to help me open a safe in the morning, and that's going to take all the strength you have ever pretended to have."

She curled onto the ground and passed Henry the Scotch bottle and the drapes. Tomorrow she would make it right, but tonight, Trout was shaken to the bone with Henry's story. They had given up, the two of them. It was nearly incomprehensible to Trout, to find the place inside to let go, to say goodbye. It was something she had never considered before. The Scotch ran through her head and she wished the stones and bricks would cover her, show her to be a small bug huddled in fear. She clenched her fists against the desire to scramble over the rubble, drag him out and blow life into his mouth again. Helpless in the face of life. Trout shuddered, and tried to sleep.

In the morning, Trout woke and immediately clambered into the front of the building for the safe. The blank envelopes, the box of rubber bands, the paper clips and supplies from the closet were there, but where was the safe? Trout looked around. The postage stamps were gone, the slide projector was missing. Looters had stolen the safe. No, tell me it isn't true, she thought.

"Fucking idiots!" she screamed at the street. "It's just a bunch of papers!" She charged across the broken sheet rock, out toward the street and back again, stopping to pick up boards, look under them, hurl them away.

Henry came to her side with a grim face.

"Now what am I going to do?" she wailed. Henry put his hands in his pockets.

"C'mon Trout. Let's go nurse our hangovers. We'll think of something. We will."

"I have to find Beth," she said resolutely, with frightened eyes. "She's next of kin and the only one they'll allow in the hospital. I don't know what else to do, Henry."

*T*he duck-cleaning was set up like an outdoor assembly line. It seemed more orderly than the rest of the city, Trout thought, certainly more organized than the standing-room-only ferries that had taken her this far, boats that had ridden low in the water from being overloaded.

"Where is Beth Hanson?" Trout asked. She asked her question again and the man in front of her, bearded, clothing covered with black oil, simply pointed toward the clusters of people moving with a tired purposefulness around wooden troughs and barrels.

"Beth!" she called.

Trout barely recognized her when Beth pushed through the group. Beth's hair was completely covered by a red bandanna, her bright lipstick and dark eyeliner gone. The cigarette she held pinched in her teeth was smudged with black. Trout thought she looked like she'd been crying.

"Tracy. What are 'ya doin' here?"

"I've come to get you. Your mother's been hurt."

"Hurt?"

"You have to come with me. I can't get into the hospital. We were in the house. A pipe fell on her. She's . . . had a concussion and . . . she's in a coma. You're the only one they'll let in the hospital to help her."

Beth looked away. "Help her do what . . . get mad?"

Trout's mouth dropped open.

"I said . . . your mother has been hurt and needs you," Trout said pointedly, glaring at her.

"I can't go back there," Beth said, furiously kicking her toes into the oily sand. "Everything is shit back there."

Trout yanked her hair out of her face and bit her lip. Lynn goes crazy and Beth trots out the cynicism she ordinarily wears on her boot-heels, in her shoelaces, on the ends of the cigarettes she throws into the street.

"Let me tell you this again," Trout said, brushing the dirt off her forearms. "Your mother is in a coma and could die, do you understand that? She needs someone there, and that someone is you."

"Yeah, well they need me here, too."

"You're the only chance I have, young lady, and I intend to bring you back. You may not have noticed, but I love that woman, and there are things in this world worth loving."

"Fuck you," Beth said under her breath, looking down at the ducks that spread out in front of them, dead and rotting in the afternoon sun.

"No, fuck you!" Trout shouted, as if aiming her words at the sky, the city, the flat that had broken the finest woman she knew. "Say goodbye to these people and get moving."

"I'm not going."

"You are unbelievable. Most people would be on their knees over the idea that their mother is hurt, but not you! What's the matter, it isn't cool?"

"Executive asshole . . . you two think you've got the perfect set-up. You don't need me." Beth growled.

Trout spun around, clenched her fists.

"What makes you think you're so great that the world isn't good enough for you?" Trout shouted, knowing she was out of control. "Precious you! Thumb your nose at everybody and everything. Jesus Christ, Beth, what sets you apart from the rest of us except . . . black lipstick? You . . . existentialist."

"What would you know about fashion, you and your dreckie suits," Beth screamed. "Goddamn dyke!" she muttered.

"Oh and what, you've got it better?" Trout shouted, flailing her arms. "What nameless faceless dick did you fuck this weekend, huh?"

"Shut up! Shut up!" Beth ran toward her, put her head down and butted Trout in the stomach. Trout fell to the ground and slapped Beth. Beth jumped up and punched Trout in the side of the head.

"My mother's too goddamn good for you . . . you execu-troid. That's what you are," she shouted, starting to cry. "Why should I do something for you? What the fuck do you know about me? Do you even know when my birthday is? Look at this!" Beth shouted, red-faced. Trout stood still, shocked over the look on Beth's face. "Look at these little things," she screamed, crying now, picking up a dead bird and throwing it at Trout, pulling more off the ground by their necks and pushing them into her chest. "What about these? What about the feelings of these little things?"

The man with the beard ran toward them, raising his hands in the air.

"Hey man, no violence," he said. "This is a peaceful encampment."

"Oh shut the fuck up," both Beth and Trout said at once, turning away from him and setting the birds on the ground.

"God, I hate hippies," Trout growled and laughed under her breath as the man backed away. Beth put her hands on her hips and pretended not to smile. She bit the side of her cheek as the tears started coming to her eyes. She wiped them away with her dirty hand and sniffed. Trout smoothed her hair back. She turned to Beth, looked away, took a deep breath.

"It must be very painful seeing all these birds die," Trout said softly. Beth nodded. "I'm sorry I yelled. I'm just beside myself. The city's a mess," she said, twisting her hair in her hands and starting to cry, "and ah . . . I don't know what to do for your mother. Somebody stole the paperwork out of the house, so they won't let me into the hospital to see her. You're all I've got Beth, and I . . . need you."

Trout was silent, focusing only on the face of the child who had finally managed a full sentence in her direction, who had, for what seemed the first time, had an opinion short of "what the fuck," and a desire more concrete than "who cares?" Well, what about the kid's birthday, Trout wondered? She didn't know when it was; that was true.

"This is the first time I've ever heard you say your mother was good for anything," Trout said softly, trying not to look down at the dead, oil-soaked birds on the ground.

"Well, I lied," Beth said half-heartedly.

"Oh, did you?" Trout said, nodding. "Shall we go?"

"I gotta get my jacket."

Beth and Trout walked to the freeway, then joined the slow-moving procession heading west.

"You're a crack-up, Trout," the girl said, throwing her jacket over her shoulder. "When you say 'fuck,' you sound like a school teacher saying 'pimple.'"

Trout looked at her sideways and smiled to herself.

"She doesn't know when my birthday is, either," Beth said, without much conviction.

"She certainly does, too," Trout said. "She loves you very much."

"Well, she's got a shitty way of showing it."

Trout sighed. Perhaps that was true. The two seemed so backed into their own corners neither seemed to know how to step forward anymore. Their conversations were pointed and short: do this, no I won't, do this, fuck you.

"But she wants to show it," Trout said.

"She had her chance and she blew it. Years ago. Do you know how long she was gone? Two years. That's a long time to have to live with a dreck like my grandmother."

"I've never met Meredith," Trout said with curiosity.

"There's nothin' to do in that town. And Meredith acts like workin' in that church is a high-class post at the country club."

"One chance? Is that all anybody gets in your book?"

"She fuckin' left me. Don't you understand that?" Beth said. "She left me with that lunatic."

Trout looked at her and shook her head.

"Your grandma Meredith is not a lunatic: she's a little dogmatic, but believe me, I know lunatics and she is not crazy. Besides, that's the first and only time anyone's said goodbye? Every goddamn day you do that to someone. You turn on your ratty old boot-heels—all right, all right," she said as Beth turned to glare, "they're not ratty."

"They're hip," Beth said.

"You're right, they're very hip. But you leave, Beth. You leave people even when you're there!"

"You don't know me. Like my name's Bet, not Beth. You know, like a bad bet, or a sure bet."

"Well . . . what about your snide little comments and the way you never, ever say you like something or you think something's nice. That's the same thing."

"Bullshit."

"It is, it is," Trout said, gesturing as she walked. "It's the same because it's saying 'I don't care enough about you to be warm. You can't have my heart. I don't belong here with you.' Isn't that what you're saying? Your mother may have left you with Meredith, but you leave her every goddamn day, Beth. Bet. You leave her standing there wishing for something more from you, some warmth, a sign that you're part of the family."

"What family?" Beth said with a sneer, looking Trout up and down like a man would evaluate a buxom woman.

Trout stopped and dropped her arms to her side in exasperation. There it is again, she thought, show the kid some sense that you want to include her in what you think and she tells you you're not even talking. She wove among people on the bridge, mindless of whether Beth was following. The kid knew how to cut to the quick. What family: two words and Beth had plunged in the knife. Patricia was the wound and Beth the salt that was poured into it. Perhaps the only power Beth knows, the only belonging Beth understands, is to be the thumb pressing into her mother's pain. Beth was grisly and loathsome because she bled all the time, oozing into the street and the sidewalk, the park benches, the bar stools. The girl was blood under a black jacket. Beth's strength was as a caustic substance on another person's flesh, and so she had no self, no self-definition. Trout saw today that Beth herself smarted from her choices more than anyone else, even her mother.

Yet in the duck-cleaning venture her face had seemed softened, Trout thought, taking off her brown leather jacket and looking sideways at Beth. Something was going on here. Was it work? Trout couldn't remember a time when Beth had ever seemed to work at anything. She had seen the girl walk off job sites, heard stories of not returning after lunch, of simply refusing to get out of bed to show up. She had never heard tales of the girl turning from something to go back to work.

"You know what Grandma Meredith said when I left?" Beth asked. "Cocktail Weenie Wraps Self in Plastic to Wander the Streets Forever."

Trout laughed. "Your grandma called you . . . a cocktail weenie?"

"Yeah. Well, I had dyed my hair orange in the middle and brown around the edges, you know? She thought it looked like one of those hot dogs with the cheese inside."

Trout covered her face and laughed, looked at Beth and slapped her leg laughing.

"It's not funny," Beth said, but started to laugh anyway.

"I couldn't afford leather so I bought this black plastic jacket," she snorted.

"Looked a little . . . ah, dreckie, did you?" Trout teased.

"Yeah, I guess," Beth laughed. "But the woman's touched, I'm tellin' ya."

"Look," Trout said. "It's getting late. We can't make it back tonight, and I don't like walking in the dark. People have gotten really weird. Let's get to the bridge and rest."

Beth stopped and looked at her for a long moment, without speaking. Trout continued walking as people pushed past Beth. Trout turned around.

"Is she hurt bad?" Beth asked. Trout nodded. "Fuck."

*T*he boom truck had flung itself out to her and she still hadn't known, was it blue cloak or bloodied hand that was coming for her? Lynn sat up in the park sandbox where she had slept, stretching her sore back and rubbing her arms against the cold. She had wrapped herself around Patricia, but Patricia had not been the rope, either. Lynn had been praying for two days for something that would bind her, tie her to either one or the other and make her choice. Wouldn't that give her the answers to why the world was brittle and sharp, New Year's firecrackers, tram-handrail mornings, elevator days, why time was a clock not a song?

She had been asking and got nothing but more choices. Life is a cardboard cutout, dust to dust and nothing more. It's what her parents had taught her but not been raised on themselves. The back of her father's head had stories of saints and their deaths, sinners and their fun. Her mother had an embroidered past of lotus and incense; she had kneeled with her own mother and set oranges in plates. But

she, the blonde with barely Asian eyes, had a large desk, a
glass office, a world with no more depth or continuum than
yesterday's newspaper. Now, with no glass, no paper, what
had been the point in struggling to get home? Struggling for
anything? All she had or was had been built on glass and
paper, and she had shunned her grandmother, pretended her
father had never owned beads. She struggled to her feet. No
ropes even here: the swing-set had fallen over. She rubbed
her forearms against the damp, brushed the sand from her
legs. But a net. There was her net, a sturdy rope canopy of a
child's redwood jungle-gym. She climbed the iron rungs slick
with morning fog. Crouching on the top rung, pressing her
hands together, she bent her head, and fell forward into the
net. Which rope was it that held her? Did the ropes weave
back upon themselves, intersecting, the threads of each
entwined to make a new strand?

*T*rout sat on the San Mateo Bridge, back against the
siderail, legs stretched toward the cars that were parked,
end to end. The people on the bridge had established their
own order, walking on the right side of the cars, sitting on
the left. As the night began falling, groups of people
squatted down and pulled their jackets around them, women
huddled together in their traveling groups.

Above the water, hemmed in on all sides, Trout leaned her
head against the wall and closed her eyes. Now that her
desire to dance in the streets had proved so foolish, Trout
felt overwhelmed with the clutching need to grasp something
and shake it. Inside her mind, her hands reached for a
screwdriver, a wrench, a notebook, anything to set in a
straight line, to tighten down or construct. Like the city that
seemed to spin on the horizon, farther and farther away from
her, despite her heading toward it, Patricia and the chance
for the life they had led seemed like an elusive orb,
impossible to stop with bare hands or the movement that
arms can make. There had to be something to hang onto.
The crumpled ideas of steel beams and mortgages made her

long for even a flimsy redwood trellis, a roof for a vine-patch, not even to touch but just to see, to breathe in the sight of its right angles and the fulfillment of its expectation and purpose, a structure that did what it promised.

Helicopters littered the horizon, on both sides of the bridge, turning Trout's perception of the freeway from something that ran along the earth to something that moved through the sky. They shunted back and forth with huge woven sacks beneath them swinging very slowly through the air, or metal containers hanging from their claws, sometimes flying over Twin Peaks and seeming to drop out of time, others settling on the roof of General Hospital.

Trout crouched on the ground, hungry, beaten by the day's heat and her long journey across San Francisco to the ferry, then from the ferry to the duck-washing area. Beth was off trying to find food or simply moving around.

The curfew sirens wailed simultaneously from Oakland, San Francisco, and Richmond, filling the air with noise until the sky seemed to be something mechanical, and therefore something that could fall down around them, the night crumbling itself into the debris of the streets.

"Hey, take a look," Beth said, crouching down beside Trout and pulling her hands out of her pockets. "Potatoes!"

"Baked potatoes, here?" Trout said, opening her eyes, glad for something to wrap her hands around.

"Yeah. Carburetor potatoes. These days I don't ask questions," Beth said, "I just buy what I can find."

"You know what phrase I hate?" Trout said to Beth, wiping the potato from her lips. "'Shit Happens.' Christ I can't stand that philosophy. You make things happen."

"Everything?" Beth asked with a smile. Trout, looking at the girl's face, knew what was now a smile would have previously been a sneer.

"Well," Trout considered, "there are . . . unforeseen exigencies."

"That'd make a great bumper sticker, Trout," Beth said grinning, "'There are Unforeseen Exigencies.' Shit, only a Mercedes Benz would have a bumper long enough for it."

Trout looked askance, then laughed.

"Which is appropriate, I suppose," Beth said, and laughed.

Trout wondered why suddenly it should matter to Beth what she thought. Beth had never asked before, but then, she had never taken a step toward the daughter of her lover, either. She had met Patricia when Beth was already grown. Beth was a woman who wrote cryptic postcards from Cincinnati and the areas in South Dakota Trout was certain must be desert. Beth had moved back to San Francisco two years ago, and the relationship between her and her mother was more baffling to Trout than before. She could only imagine what made Patricia do things for Beth. How could she know the feelings a mother had? Mostly, Trout saw Patricia's pain over leaving her child. The phrase itself had a deadly ring to it, she thought. She couldn't comprehend the thinking that drove a mother either to give or to give up. Patricia had done it because she had to, Trout had always reasoned, not even understanding what the phrase meant. Trout was convinced that whenever Patricia reached into her wallet and doled out money to Beth, Patricia must be envisioning some scene of a child in a little miniature outfit. What else would drive her to do it? It must be an automatic reaction, built on years of habitual giving. The only emotion Patricia ever explained to Trout was guilt, an emotion that was sour and rancid from sitting inside Patricia for so long, a pain that seemed to Trout to be so unjust. Every time Patricia spoke of the guilt of the past, Trout's anger rose up inside her, fury and tenderness both at once, wanting to cut away the guilt as if it were a growth that could be removed. She resented Beth for it, and for the way Beth walked through their house as if the walls themselves were evidence of some grand and gruesome crime. Bourgeois, foolish, trendy: Trout had seen these words across the forehead of her lover's daughter as plain as if the girl were a digital billboard. By the time Beth left, loaded up with dinner and money and advice, Trout would be furious with the judgment, and with Patricia's acceptance of the sentence. On the other hand, she had viewed her lover's relationship with her daughter from afar, obviously from farther away than she should have. It had seemed so final, so ruined. Perhaps she had turned away from it because it was negative. There wasn't anything she could do, she had reasoned, and so she chose not to involve herself at all.

"My dog's gone," Beth said, finally.

"God, I hadn't even thought of her," Trout said, looking away. "I'm sorry."

Beth shrugged her shoulders, twisted her mouth. "She's happier."

Trout snorted. "Happier in a city without food and no one to care for her? Jesus," she said, then wished she had been softer in her pronouncement. She had championed the dogs' cause herself a short day ago.

Beth kicked the heel of her boot against the pavement.

"I saw her on the way down," Beth said, softly, turning to look into Trout's eyes as if to discover whether she were listening. "She was with a big pack of dogs, and she didn't want anything to do with me."

Trout looked intently at Beth.

"I saw packs of dogs like that in the city. They're very frightening," Trout said softly. "Some sort of justice, though."

"The dogs had gone wild, gotten mean. My dog actually growled at me, stalked me like an enemy." Beth turned away. "Teeth showing, you know what I mean," she said, with a sudden energy.

Trout stared straight ahead, without looking at Beth. She sighed. Takes a lot of hope to be young, Trout thought, a lot of teeth-gritting dedication to the idea that there is something to grow to. Raised by her mother who chose to believe that there are few possibilities and huge obstacles, Beth had decided that it simply wasn't worth the effort. Better to call the game stupid than to recognize that the cards might somehow be stacked against you. Beth had chosen disengagement, separation. Looking at the girl in the dim light of the bridge markers, Trout wondered if Beth was even a combination of her mother and Trout, despite her absence from their life. Her mother's pessimism drove her to consider that all is lost, and Trout supposed that her example had made it easy for Beth to simply remove herself, to be in tight control of her heart's ability to reach out or latch on.

Trout closed her eyes. What the hell made her sure she was right? Trout had clung and clutched and built and worked, and it had been effective for a while. They had money, they had some facade of security, but what security? Patricia lay in a coma, beyond anyone's reach. The papers that would save them financially and bring them together again were still in the safe, in someone else's possession, far from the claims office and the hospital where they belonged. The women munched on their potatoes.

Trout suddenly felt weak, leaned her head against the railing. Beth's dog was one of the only things that Trout and the girl shared. On Saturdays, the two would take the silver and black animal for long runs over the hills of Point Reyes and the Marin headlands, walking together, the punk-rocker and the executive. Trout was convinced that these were the only times Beth got into the wild. They rarely talked during their little treks, and tonight Trout wondered why. Every time they went on these walks, Trout was overcome with a terrible fear, an uncertainty she had convinced herself was because she was spending time alone with this silent and resigned person she tried to consider a family member. Perhaps it was because it was the only time Trout saw dogs outside of the fenced-in park. Rather than talking, though, Trout watched Beth's Australian Cattle dog dive through the bushes, forging ahead on legs that were both anxious and strong. Her eyes followed the dog's movements with anxiety and appreciation. Trout wanted to be beside the dog, head bent, heedless of the thorns and brambles, paws digging through the moist earth. She wanted her own nose covered with fragrant peat, ears filled with the rustle of weed-heads. Beth let the animal run ahead and push up the hillside, on each walk allowing the dog a little more leeway, first to crest the hill without her, next time to dart into a grove of trees and then return. It was flirting with danger, Trout knew that. Beth toyed with keeping the dog on the edge of the invisible line where the animal could hear a cautious "stay close, girl" and the other side of sound where the dog would run alone, lost, trotting wherever her sense of smell would take her.

Trout knew someday the dog might run ahead so far she would simply disappear, and each time they went out, Beth gave the dog another chance to do so.

"That's why I could never have a dog," Trout said softly. "It's too frightening. Not the part about going wild. The loss, I don't think I could take it. You know they're going to run away, or get hit by a car or something. I just can't love something like that, waiting for everything to fall apart, knowing it will happen."

"Jesus, Trout," Beth said. "Why have you got to have the sure bet all the time? Dogs are like that. They live with you, then they go. What's the difference? You don't have them later, but why not have them now? I think you're weird."

Trout looked away, tried not to cry. My God, it wasn't just her lover she didn't trust. Life was something that needed to be kept in check, that's what she really thought, wasn't it? Henry and Jack, she couldn't imagine it, and a dog that could run—all things that could not be nailed down or filed away brought potential disaster.

"Why did you go to the ducks?" Trout asked.

"You know, it's funny," Beth said. "When you think of a dog goin' back to the wild, you think how happy it will be, no rules, no leashes, that kinda' shit. But you don't think that without those things, maybe it might begin to see danger everywhere. I wasn't sure why I went to the ducks. I just kept walking, but the more I saw, the more people looked like those dogs. Without their stuff, they were so vicious, and they turned, you know, like a dog. Even my friends." Beth looked at Trout. "I don't want to see danger everywhere, you know?"

Trout smiled, thought about reaching out to hold Beth, to just touch her cheek. Perhaps the earthquake had shown Beth that even tossed about and scrambled, the pieces are the same, the demands are still there, and people act in essentially the same way, bad and good, wishing for little more than to hold their children, to be with people who love them, to make some kind of difference in the world. Wouldn't it be wonderful, Trout thought, for Beth to finally understand, even in the midst of the chaos, that the call to commit is very strong.

"Hey," Beth said, breaking from Trout's gaze, "look what I got." She smiled, unzipped her jacket and pulled out a blanket.

Trout laughed a little, as Beth wrapped both their shoulders in the scratchy wool.

"I gotta tell you, Bet, you're good at this."

"Yeah. So, what's this deal about papers?" Beth asked.

"I hold something called Power of Attorney over your mother, which means that when she's hurt I have the legal ability to finance and authorize her care, see," Trout said. Beth raised her eyebrows and shook her head. "You have to have these things when you're gay. Otherwise, the only people who can do those things are a legally sanctioned spouse, or next of kin," she said, gesturing to Beth.

"So what's the problem?"

"The safe was stolen with the papers inside, and the National Guard is at the hospital keeping people out. It's a madhouse. You can't imagine it."

"Well, it's just paper, right?"

"Yeah."

"It's not got shit like microchips or passwords on it or stuff?"

"No. It's just a document. We drew it up ourselves and had it notarized."

"So what's the fuckin' problem? Just draw up another one," Beth said, lowering her voice.

"You can't do that!" Trout said. "It has to have your mother's signature on it, be notarized."

"What were you . . . born in a suit? I'll sign it."

Trout looked around her, laughed at herself. "Yeah, I was born in a suit. Peter Pan collar, the whole bit."

"Oh man, Meredith tried to put me in one of those: I tore it off."

"See, I should have. Just draw one up, huh? We need to find someone with paper. Better yet," Trout said, the two of them standing, scrutinizing the crowd, "someone with a computer."

"Out here?"

"Are you kiddin'? Look at the BMWs, there'll be a laptop out here and I'll bet you they're doing business," Trout said. Wait. I don't have any money."

Beth looked at her with disgust and pulled on her collar.

"All right, all right," Trout said.

"Let's go," Beth said, nudging her with her elbow. "Hey, hey, don't forget the blanket."

Trout and Beth gave up their sleeping places and started walking the line of cars, one on each side, as Beth advised. Trout kept her eye out for expensive sedans, Porsches. A car with a mobile telephone had lines of people around it and a man gathering bills into his palm. He had no computer, but suggested the Mercedes about half a mile up.

"Good evening, sir," Trout said in her executive tone, when they reached the Mercedes. Beth was nowhere in sight. "I'm looking for someone who might have a laptop computer they would be interested in . . . shall we say . . . renting for a moment."

The man got out of his car and looked at her as if she had just given him a good stock tip.

"What do you need it for?" he said suspiciously.

"Simply to create and print a document, then erase it from your hard drive of course. I'm not intent on cluttering your data," Trout said. "Needless to say I'm willing to compensate you for the use of your machinery."

"Cash," the man said.

"Depending on the price," Trout retorted.

The man looked at her, narrowing his eyes. "One hundred dollars," he pronounced.

Trout pretended to be shocked. No sum was too great if the scheme worked. "Seventy-five, in a check. Believe me, I have more credit cards than I could ever use."

"All right." The man opened his trunk and set the computer up with its battery pack on the carpet-covered spare tire. He hovered at her shoulder.

"WordStar?" Trout asked.

"Indeed." The man didn't leave.

"My will. Seems like an opportune moment to redraft, wouldn't you say?"

"Um," the man nodded, "and I imagine there's a number of people who could use this service," he said half to himself, looking around at the crowd.

"Oh, undoubtedly," Trout said, as the man stepped back slightly to give her the privacy for her will. She typed rapidly, leaving the lines for the signatures of the nonexistent parties.

"Control Q-P, is that correct?" Trout said formally.

"It is."

Trout watched the document print, hoping she had used the proper language. She deleted the document from the computer. Just as the paper was being ejected from the machine, a hand from a black leather cuff reached into the trunk and yanked the paper away.

"Hey!" Trout screamed. The man turned to see a black-clad punk run through the crowd and Trout ran after her. She's brilliant, she thought. "Come back here!" she shouted, running away from the man without paying and being swallowed up in the crowd.

Half a mile later, when Trout was exhausted and leaning against the railing, Beth appeared at her side. Trout looked around to see if anyone understood the situation.

"Not bad, eh?" Beth said, beaming.

"What if he'd caught you?"

"Him? And leave his car to be stripped? He wasn't movin' and especially not for you. Here's your paper."

"What about the seal?" Trout said thoughtfully.

"Ah, seals, they're my specialty," Beth said. She took the paper from Trout with a flourish, walked over to the railing of the bridge and pushed the circle of a post into the paper, then walked to a car and rubbed the imprint of a Peugeot emblem inside the circle.

"Nice job, Beth," Trout said admiringly. "Really nice fuckin' job."

"Hey schoolteacher, not so precise," Beth said, "you gotta say fuckin' with it right in the front of your mouth."

"Fuckin'" Trout practiced.

"F-fuckin" Beth corrected, "like you're gonna spit."

Trout chuckled and Beth smiled. "C'mon you," Trout said, throwing her arm over Beth's shoulder and leading her forward, "let's find a place to sleep. I hear there's trucks running up 101 as far as the Army Street ramp, but you've got to be there early before the crowd gets into gridlock."

A t the hospital, Trout and Beth walked up to the National Guardsman who held the clipboard and announced themselves, shook hands when they both made it through the checkpoint.

More beds had been moved into Patricia's ward until curtains between them had been dismantled or thrown over the curtainrods. Trout cautiously walked along the foot of the beds while Beth stood at the door. Patricia's bed was not where it had been, and Trout turned in circles, becoming more frantic as she searched for her lover. What had happened? No, she didn't die. Please, no. There were things to be done. Where was she? Goddess, where?

A nurse came into the room looking haggard, holding a tray that she regarded with fear and confusion, its metal surface heaped with medications and little paper cups of pills that were unmarked and clearly had lost their meaning to her.

"Where is Patricia Hanson?" Trout said, almost crying.

"Who?"

"Where have you moved Patricia Hanson?"

The nurse looked around the room, then back at Trout, without answering.

"She's in a coma," Trout said.

"Comatose patients are down the hall."

"Down the hall where?" Trout said irritably.

"All the way, into the waiting room. Who are you? No visitors of any kind allowed."

"I'm not a goddamn visitor," Trout said through clenched teeth, pulling her papers out of her jacket pocket and unfurled it in the woman's face, then turned and marched out of the room, grabbing Beth by the elbow.

Trout turned the corner and stopped. The beds and gurneys lined the entire length of the hall, head to toe, sometimes two abreast, some taken by people who didn't move, others who moaned and thrashed against their makeshift wrist restraints, people connected to tubes on stands, some of them sharing stands for their IV bottles, the wires stretching like ugly Maypole ribbons. Why were they here? Trout screamed to herself, put out into the hallway to not take up space? Stuffed into the hallways as if they were going somewhere, the staff waiting for them to die and so pushing them a little closer to the door? Men stood at the feet of carts, clutching the railings with resignation, women with fear lacing their foreheads crouched with rosaries in their hands. It was like a morgue in here, and Trout silently started calling to Patricia, 'be here, be alive still. Don't have given up while I was drunk in the rubble with Henry or off fetching Beth. I'm sorry we went back to the house. Please be alive. I had to get the papers. Be here, baby.'

Patricia lay on a gurney, the sheets not even wrinkled from nights that should have been filled with tumultuous dreams. Anything but passivity, Trout wanted to scream. She wanted to shake her, to slap her. Panting suddenly from the emotions running through her, Trout pulled up a little folding chair next to the bed and sat down, looked up at Beth. She rested her hand wearily on Patricia's arm, then closed her fist around Patricia as if to hold her in place. Trout bit her lip and looked around the hall, expecting someone in a dirty green coat to walk up behind her, grab Patricia's cart and wheel her off, to snatch her away and finally allow life to laugh in Trout's face: 'you couldn't do anything. There was so much to be done and you couldn't do it. You can't make anything better.'

"How long as she been like this?" Beth said softly.

"Since the aftershock," Trout said, yanking her hair into a severe pony tail, and then standing, letting her hair flop around her face. "Maybe you shouldn't be here."

"I'm all right," Beth said quietly.

"No. This isn't right. Besides, we'll need to take turns, work in shifts. You go on to your house and try to get some food in there. Sleep. Come back about midnight so I can eat and get some sleep. You take the night shift. You're better at those hours than I."

Beth nodded and walked slowly away. She turned around
to look at Trout, ran a hand through her hair with a nervous
gesture and nodded. She turned again and left.

"It'll be all right now, baby," she said. She hung her head
for a moment, then stood up. "Well, let's get started. Now,"
she cleared her throat, licked her lips. She rubbed her hands
together. "Let's start with your arms." Picking up Patricia's
arm, Trout was taken aback by how heavy it was, daunted
by the needles and tubes. She gently rubbed Patricia's arms,
then started kneading and massaging the muscles. Trout bit
her lip. What to say, when everything on her mind was an
image of destruction and disappointment: what could she
say that would make the woman want to come back? that
the Fire Department was landlord of the city and had called
in the National Guard? that Henry had allowed Jack to die
and could go to prison for it? that she had run into Lynn and
she was, just as Patricia thought, completely out of her
mind? that the house was looted and she had slept there
wrapped in the living room curtains? or that Beth was
changed by the sight of thousands of dead birds stretched
out in the sun? that she was constantly plagued with visions
of her father, and the feeling that it was her fault that Patricia
lay in this bed?

"You can come out, now, baby." Trout looked around the
hall to see if anyone else was listening. It didn't matter, she
thought as she threw her shoulders back. "It's Tracy,
sweetheart. Trout. I'm here now. Everything's OK. I found
the safe." She looked away. She saw the pipe falling again,
the color draining out of the sky. That wasn't the right thing
to say, either.

"You're going to get well, you are. Think about your head.
Think about . . . opening your eyes. Think about . . . how
much I love you," she said, her voice starting to crack.
"Com'on back here and be in love again, Patricia."

When she was close to Patricia, Trout thought, had been
the only time everything seemed in its place, when the bolts
were on the doors, all possible sources of fire or disaster or
violence closed away, put to bed. Trout stood and paced the
floor, biting her lip. When she thought of something to say,
she pounced on the bed, sitting on the edge and leaning

close to Patricia's face. Soon she just sat and stroked
Patricia's cheeks, her forehead, her hair. "I swear," Trout
said, "they didn't even wash your face. You stay here, I'll be
right back," she said, then shook her head. Trout went into
the bathroom at the end of the hall. There was nothing but
paper towels and she soaked a few, brought them back to
tenderly wash Patricia's face. Neither the woman's mouth
nor her eyes moved, and Trout was tempted to bat at her
nose just to see if there was a reaction. She drew very near
to Patricia's face.

"Excuse me," a nurse behind her said. "No one admitted
to the floor except. . ."

"I'm well aware of that and I have proof of Power of
Attorney right here," Trout said defiantly, pulling the papers
out of her jacket but refusing to let the nurse hold them.
"And furthermore, I want a thorough accounting of
everything that's been done to this patient, and a discussion
with the doctors, immediately, about the future course of
action, is this understood?"

"You don't have to get huffy," the nurse said, "you want to
see the doctor you'll have to find him yourself in this mess. I
have too much work to do." She let go of the paper,
mopped her forehead.

Trout softened. "I understand. I just had a terrible time
getting in here . . . and I'm not leaving again."

The nurse looked Trout in the eyes, then turned away and
left.

Trout sat for hours until her back ached and her palms
were burning from the friction of rubbing arms, face, legs,
pulling up the sheets and massaging feet.

Trout lay her head on Patricia's chest and cried, sobbing
as if the house had crumbled into a cavity of her body and
was tumbling out, piece by piece. Exhausted, Trout lay with
her cheek on Patricia, feeling more than ever the chasm that
lay between Patricia's immobility and the wrenching energy
of her pain, her pounding anxiety, the nagging, clawing
demand inside her to grab the situation and straighten it,
marshal things in order, breathe movement into this woman.

"Do you remember," she said softly, tentatively,
"remember . . . our vacation at the lake, when you fell out of

the boat into mud up to your waist and you kept screaming 'Quicksand!' Remember how that dog wouldn't stop barking, and followed us all the way home? Who could blame her, I still say: you smelled terrible. It was beautiful there, the poplars waving their leaves over the deck. The water was so cold. Remember that great barbecue you made? Even Beth liked it.

"What about the trip to Mexico, remember that one? Walking that stretch of stone to the pyramid, the House of the Sun or something. Think about it, Patricia," Trout said, warming to her subject, sitting on the chair and putting her chin on the edge of the bed. "It was hot, all the sand and the desert on all sides of us. Feel that heat, Patricia. And how good the fruit-juice tasted afterward? But remember the walk? We felt like tiny little creatures in slow motion, until we got to the top. You kept saying you were in mid-air. The next day we went to the beach and laid under the banana trees . . . until we found it had spiders."

Trout talked Patricia through the hotel, the margaritas, and the night they had lain spread-eagle on the bed, completely still and silent under the fan and the mosquito netting, feeling as if they were making love without moving.

The heart monitor at the end of the bed bleeped. Trout sat upright. The monitor recorded a surge in Patricia's heart rate, then flattened again.

"Nurse!" Trout shouted, jumping up and running down the hallway. She grabbed the arm of a woman in green walking by the door. The two looked at the monitor.

"It's inconclusive," the woman said irritably. "If it bleeps continuously, come and get someone, or . . . if it suddenly dives and makes a constant alarm." The nurse looked at Trout. Trout stepped back. You mean if she dies, Trout thought, and glared at the woman as if she were willing Patricia away.

"What about oxygen. This patient's nurse was getting oxygen. Can you see to that?"

"We're overloaded but I'll look."

"All right," she said, suddenly, turning back to Patricia as the woman hurried down the hall. "I'll read to you . . . " She got up and took an old magazine off a vacant folding chair.

"*Ladies Home Journal*, great. Our favorite, huh baby? 'Low-Cal Desserts To Beat The Heat. You, too, can conjure up magnificent desserts for your family, without your kitchen becoming a desert wasteland. Add one cup Jell-O' . . . why do these things always involve Jell-O? You think Jell-O Corp. owns these magazines, baby? What are the politics behind that I'd like to know?"

Trout read 'Getting Stains Out of Linen Napkins,' and '10 Days to Better Thighs.' In the middle of a short story about a sea captain and an orphan girl, Trout slapped her leg with the magazine.

"Maybe this isn't good for you—pretty depressing, eh? But you've got to work at this, Patricia," she said, throwing a fist forward as if talking to a baseball player.

*B*eth arrived at 11 p.m., her jacket slung over her shoulder and a grim look on her face.

"There's stuff in the house. You better go home, Tracy."

"You'll be all right here?"

"Yeah. But what do I do?"

"I don't know. Talk to her. They say you have to keep talking."

Beth looked at her as if she had suggested the girl hang from the ceiling by the soles of her shoes. Then she nodded, but didn't move until Trout was out of sight.

Beth lowered herself into the folding chair, put her hands on her knees and scowled.

"You look like a postcard," she said, then turned away. "So what town are you visiting? Got any cheap eats up there?" Beth put her face in her hands.

"Oh shit," she said, bouncing back against the chair seat, the tears rolling down her face. "How come you're always gone?" she said vehemently. "How come?!" She stood up and wiped her face on her shirt sleeve. "I can't talk to you. Jesus, what am I doin' here?" She turned, bumped into people moving down the halls toward the other gurneys. Beth sat down again.

"So the ducks are dying. The oil's just spilling out of the pipes into the Bay, and you know what's really sick? The Chevron workers, they're just standin' there, lookin' out at the water, watchin' it turn black as night. I'm tellin' you, Mom, we're workin' our tails off and they're standin' there. But the ducks aren't any smarter, Christ, they swim right into it.

"You look like a postcard, Mom," Beth said softly. "You always have."

*T*rout made her way through the fog and fell into Beth's bed as if from a great height. She slept crushed into the pillows, then woke and hurried back to the hospital. Beth was sleeping with her head on her arms, and woke with a jolt. She agreed to go home, desperate for sleep.

The day rushed past Trout. She talked until she was hoarse, then massaged Patricia's arms, her temples. She grabbed the arm of every nurse that went by, asking for oxygen. None available, she was told. Not necessary, they scolded her. If there was no medicine, Trout thought nearly delirious, there must be something holistic, some bit of witchcraft or spiritual power.

Trout grew more frantic and exhausted. "All right, now, with me, breathe deeply, concentrate, you're coming to the surface, a little at a time, you're swimming, that's right, you're swimming to the top."

At times when her throat started feeling as if the sides would stick together from lack of water, she pushed her way into the halls and queued up at the vending machine, always watching for something to read to Patricia, then for something that was colorful, a piece of shiny plastic, a bit of cloth in the trash.

Trout could no longer be cheery in her descriptions and banter, but could only place things lovingly, then flee down the hall again. Nothing was working. You had to come out of a coma to avoid brain damage, right? she thought, wringing her hands and pacing.

The doctors hadn't been by since she arrived. No one seemed concerned about the woman in the coma, six carts from the end of a long row of the comatose, a number of them now being watched over by relatives, people capable of simply pulling out a driver's license to prove the same last name. Energy, she thought, anything that could throw off some energy to Patricia. Stones, the glass door knobs she loves so much. Trout paced through the hospital, then went onto the streets, possessed by her idea, her head bent, speechless when she bumped into people, muttering only the names of objects, eyes searching the pavement and the side of the road. She found an old orange, it was healing, perhaps fragrant, she thought. She pulled dusty flowers from bushes, gathered things from the road, a bit of colored glass, a strip of brass, shards of plates and pottery, and slipped her gems into the front tails of her shirt like the looters who had scoured her house.

Trout looked up from her booty. A short, stout woman in a flowered dress pushed an old flat-bed dolly loaded with children. She struggled to maneuver the littered streets.

"Mrs. Williamson!" Trout shouted, gathering her shirt together and moving toward her.

The woman turned her head slightly but didn't see Trout, and bent to push the cart of children with greater urgency. She tapped one of the boys on the head, and he leapt from the cart to join her in pushing. Mr. Williamson was not with them. A breeze ruffled the end of Mrs. Williamson's dress as she and the boy strained forward, the woman throwing furtive glances down alleyways and side streets. Trout had heard Mr. Williamson shouting at his wife as he stormed out the door late at night, had heard him barking at his children in the backyard. Slipping away before he came home, Trout thought, enough guts to pack up her children and look for something better. And this was the woman who had walked two paces behind her.

What was it Patricia needed? she wondered, returning to the hospital without looking for food for herself. She sat at Patricia's bedside, clutching her shirt full of dirty objects.

Maybe she should go back to the house, get pictures of Patricia's mother, little things that she would know from the touch (her rabbit slippers? Trout wondered).

*T*he halls filled again as soon as the National Guardsmen cleared them. The hospital administered food to some while a spontaneous market grew in the halls, appearing to Trout like World War II scenes of women carrying shopping bags and discreetly making transactions. Nylons for cigarettes, cigarettes for chocolate, chocolate for eggs. Now not only were the comatose put into the halls but those with superficial injuries as well, those confined to gurneys who required relatives to go into the streets and gather food to feed them. Dirty and sweaty, Trout didn't know if she had energy to get through the crowd to the drinking fountain, where a Guardsman kept people from filling containers and the plastic bottles they had found. One pint per person was the rule, the Guardsman said, shoving people away from the water and keeping them all in a straight line.

When Beth arrived for her shift, Trout insisted she return home immediately.

"I can't leave," Trout said. "Go, rest. Please, I have to stay."

Beth started to cry and stiffly put herself in Trout's arms. Trout held her, comforting herself as well. Beth pulled up abruptly and roughly smeared the tears from her cheeks, pushed her hands into her pockets, and left.

As the night descended on the hospital and people crowded into the lobby to get out of the blinding fog, Trout moved like a driven woman, heedless of her fear of crowds, gathering magazine pictures of beautiful places, a little barrette that had fallen out of someone's hair, a piece of string to twist into a version of Lynn's sacred rope. Trout laid her booty on Patricia's chest, hung it on the IV bottle-stand, wrapped Patricia's hands around it in the hopes something would seep into that dark place where this woman lay considering death. As the lights in the hall were dimmed, Trout stood back from Patricia's gurney.

The prospect of another funeral, of another loss, love that talks big and departs early, could not be gone through, she thought, standing at Patricia's bedside. At her father's funeral, the relatives cast furtive glances at her, and when across the room, talked openly among themselves about the "poor girl." At 25, she wasn't a child to be taken in hand, and yet not a middle-aged woman who had said goodbye to him each time she had noticed a new wrinkle or the appearance of a walking stick. He had died a madman, he had been crazy for years of her life, and that had never been spoken since the first procession of relatives. None of them could bring themselves to sit down and put their arm around her and say, "How has it been all these years, with him going in and out of hospitals? How many years has he actually been crazy?" Tracy Lynn Giovanni, she had recited to herself, alone in the mind and now in the world, the woman who was never a child, born knowing there is the hint of wind in the flesh, wind that blows away the tiny structure of reason and logic, understanding that the great social conventions were nothing more than a fragrance that wafts through the mind to leave it either unsettled or strengthened. What was the perfume that drew her father's mind to a life that didn't exist in physics and couldn't be sketched in architecture? She had sat in a proper black dress, no make-up, no veil, no gloves to protect her hands from the thorns of the three dozen roses she held as others would clutch a stuffed bear. When they lowered his casket into the ground, she had stood at the foot of the grave, without even the cavalier and understanding arm of her friend Maggie who had moved away years ago. Her distant relatives stood to the sides, either from some sense of hierarchy, she surmised later, or from fear she might raise her hand and point at the guilt they wore between the stripes of their pressed lapels. She slowly lowered herself to her knees and pulled the roses from their ribbon, dropped them into the grave. But her gesture was not a fond farewell, instead, a message to bury with him, that the yellow roses were the taint on her life, the stain of living with no one, of being her father's keeper, the holder of the envelope of sanity, a yellowed and brittle paper in the cluttered drawer of

their life together. The yellow roses were a reminder of the
sickly color that her dreams would be, romantic and hopeful
but always with that stain of a silent pathology. They were
yellow for the friend she never had, the child inside herself
who had never once been able to say, "what does it mean,
Daddy?" and be sure of the answer.

'Just be sad,' Patricia had said to her, but that wasn't
possible. Sad was to let the walls fall down, to admit that
something missing could never be found, never created, to
let the world win. Sad would prove that her father's reality
didn't exist on any plane, anyplace. It wouldn't bring him
back, or make him sane, or bring her closer to him. It
wouldn't give her a childhood. Patricia was right. Not even
beach life in Mexico. No activity on her part would make her
father's death a fact that didn't hurt her every day. It didn't
work, not this way, and it wouldn't work even if she pulled a
canoe from the cement piles and set off down the very
stream her father had taken to die.

"Fall through me, then," Trout said, the night and
exhaustion pushing on her brain. "Kick me aside, Patricia,
that's the only way you'll get to death's door, you hear me?
I'm fighting you for the door handle. Break my arms to get
there," she growled, crawling onto the gurney and straddling
Patricia, her hands gripping her lover's shoulders. Trout
leaned into Patricia's face. "You'll have to tear through my
body," she said, twisting Patricia's hospital gown in her fists.
"Pull my skin aside and crawl through my lungs, girl. I can't
watch it. I won't, so blind me. You're not going!" she said,
shaking Patricia violently, pushing her into the mattress.
"You do not have my blessing to give up," she screamed.
Trout leaned her forehead against Patricia's and sobbed,
slowly climbing off the bed. She crawled under the gurney
and let Patricia's blankets fall around her like tent flaps. You
want to get down there, then dive through my chest, she
thought. For God's sake, don't go.

Cherice pressed herself against the wall as if it might hold her up. She had had to push her way into the hospital through a side door, while a Guardsman checked someone else's papers, all to look for Jacob, and why was she looking? Who knew? But here she was. She had pulled the lapels of her suit jacket together as she looked into rooms, turned down corridors.

That's when she saw Trout, disheveled and dirty, that wild hair of hers all matted, gripping the front of someone's pajamas. Patricia, Cherice had thought, and closed her eyes. She had watched Trout sobbing, saw her lift the blankets and climb under the gurney. She had cautiously walked down the corridor, and now that she was standing inches away from Patricia, feeling as if her toes were grazing Trout's head this very minute, she turned, palms against the wall as if to keep herself from falling. Who were these people? How had they managed to figure it out, all this devotion stuff? Trout had picked up Patricia's hand, held it to her cheek. Cherice's breath stopped in her throat, tears came to her eyes. You tell everyone it makes you sick, but this is what it means, you idiot, she admonished herself. Sitting on a damn folding chair clutching the only thing that matters. Sleeping on the floor just to be close. Monica wouldn't have done that for her, Cherice thought, letting her head drop against the wall, her arms stiffly at her side, and she wouldn't have done it for Monica. Fight for someone? Shit. She wouldn't even water plants. Monica had sloped down the street toward another set of tits at the first sign of trouble, and Cherice had boarded a plane to wander around on the arms of faceless men. In Amsterdam, she had made love to Patricia until her vision was foggy and her knees could hardly hold her up, but she fled the whole damn city just to stay away from her. And Jacob? What about him? He hadn't asked for anything. Just talked about himself, his pain, listened to her pain, and still she'd dumped him in the hospital and rushed off for martinis. She closed her eyes. What did she know about love? What did she even know about friendship? She reached out her hand to Patricia's face but jerked it back, turned and strode down the hall, peering over the bodies of the other coma victims.

"Sorry ol' man," she said under her breath as she separated a second blanket from the base of his bed.

She returned to Patricia, dropped to the floor and carefully lifted the flaps of Trout's tent. She slid the blanket over her tucked-up legs. Trout opened her eyes with a start. Cherice hesitated, then covered her with the blanket.

"Thank you," Trout said, puzzled. Cherice gave a quick nod, dropped the covering between them and scrambled toward the wall.

Cherice struggled through the halls, bursting into waiting rooms, looking into corners and behind plants. Jacob stood against a wall, his foot propped up on a planter.

"Jacob," she said with relief.

"Cherice," he said, surprised, then smiled. "They ran out of crutches. I was just storing up the energy to hop home on one foot."

Who was this guy, anyway? she thought. How could he be as much a misfit as she? A white boy, disenfranchised? He'll say something stupid, he's bound to. But maybe there was something there. Some way to have a friend. Nothing committed. Nothing sexual. She didn't know what it was, but maybe she didn't have to throw it away this time.

Cherice looked around for something to stand on, put a small crate at his feet and climbed onto it. She stood eye to eye with him and put her arms around his neck.

"You know these damn dykes," she said, smiling, "have to have everything equal."

"Yeah?" he said. "Must be what I like about you . . . damn dykes. What are you, looking for friends?"

Cherice dropped her arms, looked away, shrugged her shoulders.

"You looking for crutches?"

Jacob nodded.

"Well, come on, then," she said, jumping off the crate and kicking it aside, putting her arm around his waist and readying herself for his weight.

"You're such a bossy thing," he said with mock disgust, then smiled at her.

"Decisive, Peaches," she said, looking up, "just decisive."

*T*rout woke with a start at the sound of shoes and boots moving on the floor. It was morning. Scrambling from under the bed she touched Patricia, expecting her to open her eyes, wave a finger. Patricia hadn't moved. Trout turned her back and leaned on the side of the bed. Nothing. She put her head in her hands, felt her knees buckle under her. There was no change in Patricia's condition. She had done nothing, could do nothing. "There's nothing to do but wait," she heard the nurse say on the first day she entered the hospital. Ineffective. Incapable. Trout sunk to her knees, breathing heavily, still with her hands over her eyes. She hadn't been able to watch as they wheeled her father away. She had been unable to make a life for him that he wanted to live in. She had been unable to say goodbye. Trout opened her eyes and leaned her head against the gurney. What was she then? An animal that wandered aimlessly, nothing but tissue that lives, dies, then turns to fodder? The hall was filled with strangers avoiding each other's glances, and Trout immediately looked down for fear people would see the terror she felt, the animal cravings in her eyes. She rose, furtively kissed her lover and left the hospital, pushing her way into the street.

Roaming the streets last night, she had almost begun to believe in magic. If she couldn't create life for someone else, then could she make offerings to them to help them do it themselves? Could she decorate the Buddha, as Lynn would say, hiding her desire to be the cause of the effect, cloaking her wish to be effective behind the guise of anything she could get her hands on? What would she do if there were things in life she could do, and things that were neither her burden nor her business? The idea shot a pain through Trout's chest. Center stage or off stage: those, she had always believed, were the only two choices. Worse yet, what would she do with things that hadn't been said, were lost, never to get found again? All the bitter, angry things she had never been able to say to her father, all the kind loving things that neither of them had said with any sincerity, a childhood that she knew now wasn't filled with love, it wasn't love. She had taken care, she had tended and protected, but never loved, and she had been relied upon, but never really loved in return. What to do with a pain like that, that didn't go away, and couldn't be mended?

"Trout!" She turned and saw Henry.

"No place else to be," he said, holding up his hands. "I figured . . . you might need a nurse. Hey, are you all right?"

Trout looked up at him, tears covering her face. She opened her mouth to speak but could only shake her head slowly, raise a hand and drop it. Henry took her in his arms, held her face against his chest.

At the hospital, Henry summarily announced to the National Guard that he was Patricia's husband and took up residence at her side, launching into a constant gab. He talked about his job, his new boots, and when Patricia didn't respond, discussed his plans to move to Chicago.

Trout aimlessly wandered the streets, from Portrero up 24th Street to Sabito's on 17th and back again, weaving in and out of the side streets and alleyways. Trout looked up and saw a woman turn a corner.

"Lynn?" she shouted, and started down the street, jogging until she got to the corner, then turning nearly into Lynn's chest.

"Lynn," Trout said, pronouncing the name as if the finality of it, the precision of it, were something to clutch.

"Rope," Lynn said.

Trout stood silently, unflinching. She ran away from me once; she's not doing it again.

"Sit down with me here, Lynn," Trout said softly. She grasped Lynn's arm tentatively and guided her onto the sidewalk.

"Smoke?" Trout said, offering Lynn a cigarette.

And what about this one, Lynn thought? Was she a rope, or a net? Lynn looked over at Trout's tear-stained, grimy face, at the tight jaw. A rope, she decided. A single skein thinking it has to hold up under the pressure. I slept in a net last night, she wanted to say to Trout, and it taught me something about the difference between a rope and a net. She couldn't explain it.

Trout looked at Lynn's face. Lynn was clearly thinking about the cigarette. Neither of them smoked, hadn't for years, but caution had already been thrown to the wind. She had made a trade on the bridge, and this was no time to foolishly throw things away. It was such a worldly concern, smoking. Trout put the cigarette to her own lips and pulled it from the pack, lit it, offered the pack again.

"I don't smoke," Lynn said calmly.

Trout took a shallow drag and grimaced. There was something comforting in having Lynn around. Lynn wouldn't question the smell of fear coming off her body. What type of family did she have left, anyway?

"You know where people went?" Lynn said, wiping her nose across the back of her hand. "Into the stock exchange to sell their shares of insurance companies, invest in construction firms, even in the middle of it."

"Seems like a reasonable investment decision to me," Trout said, tiredly.

Trout was startled by the look in Lynn's eyes. I've got her, Trout thought.

"This city will be a great place to invest," Trout said, warming to her plan. "Bank loans all over the place, low interest." This plan didn't make sense and Trout knew it, but did Lynn? she wondered.

"Yeah, really cheap loans," Trout continued, "and then your property will be worth twice what it was before."

"That's ridiculous," Lynn said softly. Trout needed to hear about the net.

"What?" Trout asked, trying not to sound too sure or excited about the conversation. She took another drag on her cigarette.

"Competition for bank loans will be incredible," Lynn said under her breath.

"No. Easy. Rebuilding all over the place. The banks'll love it," Trout said, tilting her head back in exhaustion.

"Very few people will qualify because the banks won't need to qualify many," Lynn said sternly, sounding like herself despite the filthy clothes. "And with the devastation of the economic foundation of the city—its white-collar financial district—employment will mean everything. A very good time for foreign investors and property management firms."

Back into reality, Trout thought.

"That and an enormous amount of money down. No home equity loans," Lynn said. "They'll write tough new foreclosure clauses if they have any brains. Essentially we're looking at the demise of the San Francisco middle-class."

Trout smiled to herself. Wouldn't you know it would be financial theories that would bring her back. She should have given up trying to soothe Lynn's emotions the last time and gone straight for her pocketbook.

"Besides," Lynn continued, "buildings that collapsed because they were built either on landfill or on the subterranean rivers won't be salable, no matter how much money you put into the building. Or the land. They won't sell for years. Not 'til people forget again."

Trout exhaled, stubbed her cigarette out and glanced sideways at Lynn. "Welcome back."

Lynn just shook her head, looked around her.

"How many years were we lovers?" Lynn asked.

"Don't start that," Trout said irritably.

"No, seriously, how many years?" Lynn turned to her.

"You know yourself. We were together six years, which means you've been a lesbian for eleven, OK? Just to continue to thwart the idea that you're not responsible for it yourself."

"I'm over that now," Lynn said. "I know you didn't make me a lesbian."

"Give you the yarn, will you make one for me?" Trout said.

"That's an old joke."

"Well that's big of you, Lynn," Trout said sarcastically.

"I don't know what I'm going to do without a job," Lynn said softly.

"Well," Trout said with resignation, "you're about to find out."

"I've never done anything else except work fifty hours a week," Lynn said.

"Good riddance to it," Trout said wearily.

"No. No, not at all," Lynn said with growing nervousness. "You can't imagine the volume of paper that went sailing out those windows. All those years building something, sucked into a huge . . . vacuum cleaner."

"I like that image, Lynn," Trout said with a grim smile, "cleaned up like toe jam and fur balls."

"No. It was everything."

"So build something else," Trout said flippantly.

"I've been found out, can you understand?" Lynn said. "They've never known that I was Chinese, but I can't take it anymore."

"What, did they get racist on you again?" Trout said.

"Yeah. Only this time I can't ignore it," Lynn said, wondering why the years had gone by and other comments had not phased her. Because there was no other choice this time, she thought. Unlike Trout's company, which could place its West Coast office in a hundred other locations, her company needed to be in San Francisco for the export business and would rebuild immediately. There was opportunity for advancement out of all of this, but only if she announced herself as Chinese.

"I have to find food and . . . get back to Patricia," Trout said, exhausted. "You wanna come with?"

Lynn stood up and sighed.

"Or you could go to Sabito's," Trout said. "There are all kinds of women putting together committees and things. You know how the girls get."

Trout watched Lynn think about it and wondered why she was waiting, why she was leading Lynn back to Sabito's. Well, Henry was standing guard over Patricia. She was the one who needed food, and so what if she went to Sabito's to find it, and perhaps a beer or two? Was this escape? How could she be walking down the street now with Lynn, knowing she wasn't going back to the hospital just yet, heading instead toward a place where everyone was intact and making plans? Running away, was that what she was doing? Last night had proven that she was useless, and Trout had walked here with the stooped-over gait of someone who had been beaten across the shoulders, flogged with her own foolish belief that her determination, her will and effort, her little bits of glass or even her body under the bed could prevent Patricia from making her own decision about life and death. What she thought she had, but didn't possess in the slightest, was control, and wasn't that the cardinal sin for a middle-class girl? she wondered. Hard work yields results, and wasn't that, at its core, a belief that cause and effect was the infallible, supreme force? The middle-class didn't believe in luck, let alone bad luck, nor fate nor whim nor chance. Things do not just 'happen' and people aren't powerless. Life has predictable activities, measurable advances, reasons, conclusions, always a reaction stemming from a plan, and a scheme governing everything from the tiniest physical ailment to global winds. There she had been, in the hospital at Patricia's bedside, she thought with a tightening in her chest, grasping at any possible cause, desperate for an effect, refusing to believe that there could be an instance when one should let go and simply hope. Hope had always meant going into something blind, trusting things that were not trustworthy, believing women when they said they were safe drivers or good for a loan. Risk was something you did with shaky investments, or when you let your father take back his canoe. Relationships were carefully calculated ventures, involving compatibilities and opinions and things that could be decided with the mind, like politics and lifestyles and whether one appreciated dogs. Obviously, the careful calculations meant nothing now, and probably never had.

In that respect, Trout thought as she led Lynn in the direction of Sabito's, she was very much like Beth. This punk with no future in fact had no hope, but neither did she. She did not trust nor make the leap of faith into hope, but worked doubly hard at control. She didn't believe in the world either, or she would have had more faith, would have ended her ceaseless activity of prevention, would have abandoned her regime. What was control, then, but cynicism made practical?

Trout kicked a smashed paper punch and a spatula out of her path. I'll have just one beer, she thought. Trout held the door open for Lynn when they reached Sabito's.

"There's a shower hook-up in the back," Trout said, "why don't you go do something about your hair?"

"Thanks."

Anything but thanks, Trout thought wearily. She should tell me to mind my own business or something, but for

God's sake don't be willing to take it from me. It isn't worth anything anyway. It doesn't mean anything, and there isn't any more to give. Besides, you left me for offering the last time, remember? she thought as she watched Lynn disappear into the kitchen.

*L*ouise, how about a beer?" Trout climbed onto a barstool. "Any food for sale?"

"Flea market at the back tables," Louise said, pulling a beer from the cooler. "Backpacks are at a premium. Books are goin' cheap."

"Yeah, I'll bet," she said softly. "How'd you get to be such a cynic?"

"It's in my jeans," Louise said, slapping her thighs.

That and what else, Trout wondered, looking at the solidity of the woman as if she might be a tree trunk to lean on.

"You look lousy, Trout," Louise said softly, leaning on the bar in front of her.

"Patricia's in a coma," she said as if they were the last words she had the energy to mutter.

"Oh Jesus. Not her." Louise put her head down on the bar in front of Trout. Trout closed her eyes. Don't anybody else crumble in front of me. Louise had straightened and was looking at her when she opened her eyes. Hold me, she thought.

"Twelve-year-old Scotch is in the back. C'mon," Louise said, holding out her hand. Trout stood as if commanded and put herself into the woman's grasp.

Louise shut the door behind them in the little office/storeroom, so narrow and cluttered they could not stand side by side. Trout looked at the shelves of boxes, the cramped and battered desk, the blankets on a tiny army cot that was wedged against the back wall. Louise reached around the back of several boxes of beer and pulled out the Glenlivet, opened her desk drawer and withdrew a single glass.

"Not used to company," Louise said, rubbing the glass on the front of her shirt and pouring it half full. Trout took a large swallow, grimaced, and passed the glass. Louise refilled it before drinking. The two drained the glass and Trout held it out for more. Louise looked at her, cradled the hand holding the glass as she poured. Don't drop your hand, Trout thought, looking at the expansiveness of the palm against her own. She took a step toward Louise, ran her hand down the forearm that clutched the bottle by the neck, and wrapped her fingers around Louise's wrist. She drank from the glass and offered it but Louise set it on the desk, put the bottle next to it. Trout leaned against her chest and Louise encircled her with her arms, running her hand up to her hair. Trout kept her arms and hands against Louise's chest like a child, wishing she could lose herself in the breadth of the woman.

"Let me give you something," Louise said, tightening her grasp. Trout turned her face up to be kissed. Her skin grew warm, her arms passively resting on Louise. Louise moved her to the bed and laid her down slowly, kissing her neck and ears with the smoothness of one used to being in charge. Let me live here, Trout thought, under someone's direction, hiding under the blankets. I'm no one now, no decisions or abilities. Let me fall under the weight and touch of someone else, Trout thought, as Louise opened her blouse, then reached for the buttons on her pants. Just hold me 'til you block out the light. Trout kept her eyes closed, feeling the hands and tongue of someone who required nothing.

Louise left Trout sleeping naked under the covers, grabbed the Glenlivet by the neck and went back into the bar. Better the girls think she had been hitting the bottle alone than expose Trout. As she reached for a glass above the bar, she saw her hands shaking and looked around to see if anyone noticed. It wasn't like her, none of this. She didn't sleep with lesbians and certainly not with the wives of her friends. But this hadn't been like the others. Christ, Trout had just wanted a little comfort, not an entire life change. She hadn't dumped the specter of lousy dicks at her door and asked her to make it all better, and there wasn't going be some damn scene where the woman showed up pretending to "explain" how she couldn't really be a lesbian, or insult Louise enough to reassure herself that she wasn't queer. Louise cleared her throat. She didn't like bedding another butch's woman but, hell, she'd done less reputable things than that. Still, she didn't know why she was shaking.

Trout woke up and dressed with the motions of a sleepwalker, went into the kitchen and showered with a few other women who only spoke after they had their clothes on again. Trout went into the bar and sat down at the first stool, glanced at Louise and looked away. Infidelity seemed like the cigarettes, so normal a thing to worry about, a regular day-to-day type of concern, compared with the enormity of a city turned to dust and her power exposed as oatmeal.

"What can I get you?" Louise said in a businesslike tone. Trout had a reason to pretend, Louise thought, hearing a tenderness behind her question that she didn't reserve for the blue-moon women, as she called them.

"Oh. . ." Trout stammered, looking around.

"How 'bout a Scotch with a water back. A big water back." Trout nodded with a tiny smile.

"Tracy," Lynn said behind her. Trout jumped.

"I got you some food. I can take it to Patricia and Henry for you if you want to hang out here," Lynn said.

"I can take it," Trout said.

"I don't mind."

"I'd rather you didn't, OK?" Trout said.

"Why?"

"What's with you, anyway?" Trout said, then turned away. Louise delivered her Scotch.

"You," Lynn said. How to explain it? How to tell her the connectedness she had learned sleeping in the net of the jungle-gym. How to show her that she was part of the net whether she understood that or not. "I've always wanted to repay you for taking care of me all those years, but you wouldn't let me. So I thought, maybe I could find you and Henry some dinner. You'd see it wasn't so hard to accept something from me, that it wouldn't mean anything other than a little gift between friends. Christ, Tracy," Lynn said, putting the grocery bag on the bar, "what would happen if someone just wanted to give you something?"

"I'd lay down and die for it, Lynn," Trout said, resting her head on the bar, knowing she was thanking Louise for her tenderness. She sounded cavalier, she knew, and the statement had a false ring to it. It was a new idea, and she'd made a muck of her attempts to secure things for herself so far.

"Then let me look in on Patricia. Just rest for Christsake. Let me pass myself off as you."

Trout sighed. "All right, go ahead. Be me," she said without raising her face from the bar. "I can't do it anymore. I've run out of . . . everything." Trout reached into her back pocket and turned over the Power of Attorney papers. Lynn arranged to get them back in one hour.

"C'mon sweetie," Lynn called. The dark-haired woman who had seen the factory workers die clambered up from the floor and came to Lynn's side, looping her arm through Lynn's.

"Sweetie?" Trout whispered to Louise. "When did that happen?"

"Shit if I know," Louise said and slapped her hand on the bar. "There's all kinda duets I don't know about 'til they hit the door." She picked up the cocktail spigot and poured Trout more water.

"Louise," Trout said softly, "thank you, too."

"Oh now, don't say it more than once. I'm not much good with the gifts either."

Louise and Trout looked at each other and sighed.

*P*atricia woke slowly, focusing her eyes and taking several short, panicked breaths, then closing her eyes again. She heard a voice, but it seemed to be a man's. When she opened her eyes again, she saw more clearly. It was a man all right, a mustache and everything, but in a little Candy Striper hat and lipstick.

"Who . . . ?" she said softly.

"Oh goodness, back from the nearly departed," he said. "It's Henry. You remember me?"

Patricia said nothing, fell asleep for another hour.

"Well, then, do you remember you? Who are you, darling?" Henry asked when she awoke.

"Patricia," she said slowly, then closed her eyes. "Patricia Hanson. How long . . . ?"

"Two days now. Trout is beside herself, let me tell you," Henry said.

"Where is she?" Patricia sighed.

"Playing The Lone Ranger in the streets looking for food," he said, crossing his legs at the knee. "It's a Grade B Western out there. I found her in the rubble of your house looking for the Power of Attorney papers."

"The safe . . ." she stopped and rested, "Henry, what are you doing . . . in drag?"

"Oh this," he said, laughing. "You like this? The Frank Nightingale look. I couldn't help it: everybody's praying their little hearts out around here. You know how I get around piety."

Patricia tried to smile, then closed her eyes. Henry touched his eyebrows with the tip of his middle finger. "Besides, people are selling everything right here in the hospital and the cosmetics were going for nothing. Every other woman is the Avon lady."

"Oh God," Patricia whispered, sighing deeply.

"Don't worry, Trout will be along any minute now. See all this junk all over the bed? It's some kind of lesbian voodoo, I've decided. You know, that Earth Mother crystal stuff."

"Racist." Crystals and Garbage Bring Headless Woman Second Chance, she thought.

"Oh good Lord, who would have thought your politics would come out of the coma-closet before the rest of you? Trout's tried everything. Been watching you like the kettle that won't boil."

Henry took his nurse's cap off. "Christ, she's gonna be happy you're alive," he whispered, half to himself.

"My turn," Lynn said, standing at Henry's shoulder. She set her bag of food on the floor, offered him a sandwich and a beer.

"A beer! Aren't you resourceful!" he said.

"You're awake," she said to Patricia.

"Just now," Henry said. "Try to get her to solve math problems. Dissect world politics or some such. She'll be right as rain in no time. I'm going to the little boy's room."

Lynn sat in the folding chair.

"Where's . . . Trout?" Patricia asked softly.

Lynn sighed, looked down. "She's off wondering how to live in the world now that she couldn't make you better."

"I am better."

"Yes, but she didn't make you that way. She didn't fix it," Lynn said.

"No . . . she didn't," Patricia said with weary anger, remembering the glib excitement Trout had found in the city.

"She doesn't have to fix everything," Lynn said with irritation. "Have you ever considered that?"

Patricia said nothing.

"You don't even know what you've got, do you?" Lynn said. Maybe for the first time she'd give Trout something that she wouldn't get credit for, Lynn thought. "Sorry to launch into you, but the city has no patience with small-talk right now. Besides, what makes you think Suzie Sunshine has to clear away all the clouds in your sky? Why do you constantly make her prove that she loves you, instead of just trusting that she does?" Lynn continued. "You know what Tracy's problem is? She doesn't know how to take."

Patricia shifted uneasily in her bed.

"Not without feeling that she has to repay it a thousand times over," Lynn said. "I always thought she was constantly taking care of me because she loved me, and then because she wanted some kind of hold over me, but after I left her, I saw it was because she was afraid of receiving. And you know who lost the most in that arrangement? She did. So she's out there, completely lost now that she can't give you your life. She feels like a failure. And she's scared."

Patricia sighed. "You . . . seem better," she said with difficulty.

"Yeah, well, nothin' like analyzing your ex- to bring you back to reality," Lynn said. There was no point going into her discovery: she had been praying long enough. "I always wanted to give her something, Patricia. I wanted her to rely on me for something. But I couldn't do it when we were together, I didn't understand it. You're the closest thing to a partner she's ever had. She needs you now. She needs to know it's all right to need you."

The thought of Trout and Beth out in the mess of the city made Patricia very tired. Trying to avoid looking at the people streaming through the halls at her bedside, she wondered why she wasn't crazy with worry, or even able to cry, not over the walls torn down in the city but from the walls still standing around her mind, her heart, the walls that stopped her voice in her throat.

She looked at the magazine Henry had left open on her chest, displaying a photo exhibit that had been in San Francisco at the time and now was probably destroyed. "Boat Bites Bay" by Schaeffer, a broken boat, not floating, nor junk on the lake bed. Patricia thought it was beautiful, or maybe just an image that seemed to give her solace because that was the way she felt, not down, not up, resigned in a state between float and sink. Sinking was the real terror, she thought, knowing she had come very close. Floating in splendor might not be possible in a world like this, but the real nightmare was ultimately being beaten down by the world. Patricia breathed heavily and closed her eyes again, afraid to look at her thoughts, afraid to think, for fear the idea would become real and she'd be lost like a beetle bug, curled up at the sound of danger into something that resembles a stone, a little piece of glass.

How had it gotten this far? Patricia wondered. The desire to take Lynn in her arms had been surprising to her, she thought guiltily. It was a shock to feel a woman's body other than Trout's. She had wanted Lynn to get well, and when she first reached out, she hadn't known if she was going to shake Lynn by the shoulders or embrace her. Patricia had surveyed Lynn's face just before she rushed back into the fog. She looked for a sign of reality and wasn't sure what she saw, but Lynn had left Patricia with a feeling she hadn't had in years: wishing for change, for improvement. Why had she lost the desire to make a difference to Trout, she wondered, because Trout didn't need her like that? Patricia thought that Trout had had it all sewn up, her optimism and confidence like little tin soldiers all in a row. How could Trout need reassurance and passion when she had her staunchly defended happiness? She seemed so sure of the sunshine and flowers in life. If what Lynn said was true and it had all been a mask, how had she tolerated this in Trout for so long? Patricia smiled bitterly. Why didn't it matter to her that she didn't show her own strength and hope? When had she begun to feel that her lover could live without her passion and contribution? How was Trout able to tolerate her? Always demanding that Trout prove her love by doing things, taking care of things, managing their lives. How sad, she thought. Sad to simply let go, to stop giving, and how lonely for both of them. No wonder it had been so easy to slip her arms around Lynn, so easy to call up that feeling of giving pleasure, of giving anything at all. And Trout, too, she realized. Wanting so much to give up, and yet still managing to come up with a scheme, a plan for their lives, to keep loving her in the old way. Why wouldn't she want to run away to Mexico if she thought she had to reconstruct not just her own life, but Patricia's as well? Who should ever shoulder that much of a burden? All these years, their relationship had seemed solid as a rock. What was coming out of all this rubble, both of the city and the inside of her mind? The idea that she had to accept her own task of reconstruction, of rebuilding the connection between herself and Trout? Invent her own hope?

It made her tired. This time she knew it was a physical tiredness, not the emotional fatigue that she had fallen prey to for years. Everything in Amsterdam had been coated with a sheen of ice, including Patricia, her heart, and the fiery night with Cherice. Stroking the covers of her gurney, she felt that way now, as if she were trying her best to pump through something ugly and cold that seemed to lay not just on top of her, not just on her skin, but three inches deep. She pushed against it with everything she had.

Henry returned.

"Clueing her in on the state of the world?" Henry asked.

"More like stirring up the muck, I'm afraid." Lynn said. "I'll leave this food here. There's someone waiting for me outside to take the ID papers back to Trout. I've gotta go. Get better, eh?"

Patricia nodded and wished she could think of something to say.

*T*rout turned the corner to the long hall of the comatose with a tightness in her chest. At the sight of Henry talking animatedly, she stood still for a moment. Had she looked the way he did, like a bag lady talking to herself for two days? Had she seemed like one of the desperate, railing at nothing in public places? Trout saw Patricia's hand move, and she rushed down the hall and stood behind the folding chair, gripping the back as if it could hold her up.

Patricia smiled, then closed her eyes. Trout clutched Patricia's hand, brought it to her lips and held it.

Patricia had done it, Trout thought, with joy and a surprising pain. It wasn't the sound of her voice or her love that had brought Patricia back. She had awakened, on her own, to see Henry, of all people. The feat had been accomplished without her assistance or even her presence. Trout sat speechless, dry-eyed, her mouth slightly open and her brow furrowed, witnessing something she couldn't comprehend. Trout felt frozen, immobilized. If she couldn't run away into her father's world, if she couldn't do anything that was effective, then what could she do? Nothing, a voice inside her exclaimed, she could do nothing.

"So, you think the little butch here is hungry?" Henry asked, dipping into the paper bag for a newspaper-wrapped sandwich.

"I'm so tired, Trout," Patricia said softly. "Can you hold it for me?"

"Hold it? Yes," Trout said vaguely.

"Tear it into little pieces," Henry said.

"Tear it, yes yes," Trout said.

"I'll be going," Henry said.

"Why?" Trout exclaimed, standing abruptly, still clutching the sandwich.

"To find the boys, of course," Henry said, with a gaiety that Trout could see through.

"Don't go," Trout said softly. "I don't want to . . . lose you."

"There's been quite enough loss around here, my dear," Henry said tenderly. "I don't expect there'll be much more. Besides, all the AIDS patients have been moved to Edison High School. I knew they'd quarantine us one of these days." He handed her his nurse's cap and walked slowly down the hall.

Trout watched him go, then sat down again and turned to Patricia. She picked up Patricia's hand and held it against her chest, letting the sandwich drop into her lap. She's back, Trout recited to herself.

*H*ave you found the right place!" a man said, regarding Henry. The man stood in tight black pants and a loose flowered shirt, strands of Christmas tinsel around his neck, a clip earring high on one ear.

"You wanna volunteer?" the man said softly, looking at Henry's face, then down at the sidewalk when he saw the pain in his eyes. "Gloves are at the top of the stairs. You can deliver water, shuttle supplies, or just entertain. Look for the guys with the flowers on their shirts. They'll direct you," he said, and getting no response, just nodded to Henry to join the encampment.

Henry slowly passed the Romanesque archway that framed the man, up the stairs of Edison High School to the blacktop playground that stretched a city block on Dolores Street. Generators whined in the background, supplying oxygen and weak lights for the gurneys that covered the basketball court and the jump rope area, stretched across the hopscotch grid and the volleyball arena. Men moved slowly between the beds, dipping water out of buckets, holding cigarettes to lips, smoothing damp cloths against foreheads. A cluster of men in the shadows circled around each other, dipping into the shadows, emitting a sad laugh, a rumble of conversation. A man on roller skates, as if fulfilling his traditional Sunday task of entertaining the brunch crowd on Market Street, wove in and out of the maze of beds, flapping his bright red cape and waving his arm above his tattered, feathered cap.

So now the Angel of Death wears roller skates, Henry thought, turning from the crowd and leaning over the cement wall to look down on the people wandering Dolores Street.

"You wanna see the roof fallen in on people?" Henry shouted into the street. "Here you go! We're the experts, darling," he snarled.

The man in the flowered shirt looked up, then out at the people on the street who now stepped off the sidewalk into the boulevard to avoid Henry's gaze.

"You think you've seen tragedy? Bring the news cameras over here, you lily-ass bastards! We've been pulling our lives from the wreckage for a long time."

The skater turned a slow circle. The men working in the encampment turned to listen, but no one moved to stop him.

"You think the world's fallen apart? Live it for five, ten years! And it isn't pretty, honey, it isn't over in fifteen seconds with all your high-dollar crystal shattered around you. It's torture. You call your momma and tell her you're dying. Try that little trembler on for size. You don't know," he sneered.

"What did you lose, huh, lady, your cat? Your fondue forks? Well, don't call Burroughs for the remedy, that's for sure," Henry screamed, starting to cry.

"You got it bad?" Henry sobbed, crumpling against the wall and sitting on the blacktop. "Times ten, baby, times ten."

*P*atricia's back, but I'm gone, Trout thought. Undefined, a
sheath of a being, insubstantial, without plans or flesh.
Who could love a woman who has no opinions, no clues, no
solace or structure to give? No one could. She would lose
her, not to the deathly walk toward a tunnel of light, not to a
pipe that fell from a beam, she would lose her to the wide
world of real people. Patricia would gather her strength and
step over her, kicked aside with an inattentive boot heel,
discarded like the empty wrapper that she was. It was only
right, she thought, what possible use did she have? She
couldn't love. She couldn't move. If she was frozen,
immobilized by the ugly knowledge that she had never
controlled the things that mattered, then what was she? She
was a Dayrunner made flesh and since that's not a person,
who was she? One's personality could not be described by
the things one did for others, she thought forlornly.

So what was her personality? Efficient. That is not a
personality trait. That's a mode of action. And if she couldn't
describe her own personality, then what of her life? How
would she run her life, what would it look like if she wasn't
running others', if she hadn't spent her childhood and now
her adulthood marshaling the world into order? Trout looked
away, shamefully. And she couldn't pretend the plan to go to
Mexico was really an escape. It was just another in her series
of schemes to put other people into places where she
thought they would be out of harm's way. Another sorry
action by a woman who believed that she could only have
what she wanted after everyone else was safely taken care of.

She felt as she had when she stared at her apartment:
This was an obscenity. This was a naked woman, not just
exposed, breasts and butt crying for a wrap, but a woman
who had hollow spaces and broken boards where the solid
construction of trust and commitment should be. The sun
shone on her mockeries of sheltering love, her rubble for a
heart.

Oh, she had learned to love all right, to feel the emotion
that poured into you like warm milk. It was the simpler
emotion, it could fill you up when you met a cat, or watched
a baby throw sand. But trust? No. She had developed a

sense of vigilance. And devotion? She had consistency. Efficiency. My God, she thought, someone throw a cloth over her, cover her grotesqueness.

She could feign abilities only one more time.

"Is there anything . . . I can do for you, my darling," Trout said softly.

Beth returned, saw the tears running down Trout's face and put her hand on Trout's shoulder for a moment.

"Whoa," Beth said, tears welling in her own eyes. "She talks, soon she'll walk. She's a real Ma." Beth smiled, and took Patricia's hand.

Beth explained that she would be returning to the ducks in the morning. They needed her.

Patricia smiled slightly over the determination in her daughter's voice.

"All right. That's fair enough," Patricia said.

"What?" Beth said.

"It's . . . reasonable," Patricia said, trying the words on for size. "We're going to stay in your house, if it's still there. We'll leave a note telling you where we go . . . when we find somewhere else."

Beth smiled, wiped her chin with the back of her hand, straightened her shoulders.

"Of course . . . we may get rid of some of that junk you've got in there," Patricia said sternly.

Beth smiled.

"You gonna do the dishes too, Ma?" she said, teasing, stuffing her hands back into her jacket.

Patricia snorted, then smiled. "Maybe. Maybe I'll even do the dishes." Patricia reached out and signaled her daughter to come closer. "I love you. Very much. Don't you ever forget that."

Beth bit her lip. "Forget? You callin' me stupid? Hey." Beth took her mother's hand. "Bye, Ma. Bye Trout."

"Goodbye . . . sweetheart," Trout said vaguely, trying to shake what felt like a sudden frostbite, a numbness in the temples. "And . . . thank you."

Trout sat down, looked away, turned back to Patricia.

"I'm sorry about Mexico," Trout said tearfully. "Not one of my better ideas."

"It's OK," Patricia said softly, reaching out for Trout's hand. Trout put her palm against Patricia's. "You were just trying too hard. And . . . I guess I haven't been trying hard enough. So, I think we should build a house."

Trout said nothing.

"All right," Patricia said, "we take a vacation to Mexico, couple months, then we come back and build a house. How's that for a plan?"

She should turn away, right this minute, Trout thought. She should jump up from the chair and save them both from the agony of the discovery: she couldn't be loved, she didn't have anything to give. She would leave Patricia. She had to.

"Hey," Patricia said, yanking on her hand. "Come back here."

Trout took a deep breath, looked down at her lap. She couldn't meet Patricia's eyes.

"Look," Patricia said, "I'm not good at these kinds of things, but I owe you, well . . . an apology. I've left a lot of the details to you for a long time, and . . . that's not fair."

"I don't know how to build a house," Trout said weakly.

"You don't have to. You're not alone, remember? That's my strong suit."

"I'm not good for anything right now," Trout said, swallowing back her tears.

"Trout . . ." Patricia said softly, "I don't love you for what you do." Now, she thought with chagrin, maybe before, but not now. "I love you."

"But there's no way to . . . measure that and I can't risk it, I can't risk that you won't."

"But we have to," Patricia said, as if practicing the words for herself. "We have to risk it."

The rope that binds, Trout heard Lynn chant, can also be the cords of a fishing net, flung outward, connected yet venturing. Come back? Trout wondered. Was all her calling to Patricia in her coma also to herself? To learn to expose herself like the sides of her raggedy flat, bare-chested and without a plan, standing in the light of day challenging the world to love her? Daring the world to say "come back, we have something to offer you." Was that the normalcy Patricia talked about?

"All right," Trout said softly, smiling with a sad and frightened face. "But no white couches. You hear me? Nothing fucking white at all!"

Patricia smiled, and pulled Trout downward to kiss her.

Other Books from Third Side Press

Two Willows Chairs **Jess Wells** Superbly crafted short
stories of lesbian lives and loves. $8.95 1-879427-05-2
 "All the stories are gems." —*Seattle Gay News*

The Dress/The Sharda Stories **Jess Wells** Rippling with
lesbian erotic energy, this collection includes one story Susie Bright
calls "beautifully written and utterly perverse." $8.95 1-879427-04-4

Hawkwings **Karen Lee Osborne** A novel of love, lust, and
mystery, intertwining Emily Hawk's network of friends, her
developing romance with Catherine, and the search throughout
Chicago for the lover of a friend dying of AIDS. $9.95 1-879427-00-1
 *American Library Association
1991 Gay & Lesbian Book Award Finalist*

Cancer As a Women's Issue: Scratching the Surface
 Midge Stocker, editor Personal stories of how cancer affects
us as women, individually and collectively. $10.95 1-879427-02-8
 *"If you are a woman, or if anyone you love is a woman, you
 should buy this book."* —*Outlines*

SomeBody To Love: A Guide To Loving The Body You Have
 Lesléa Newman A chance to look at ourselves as beautiful,
powerful, and lovable—challenging what society teaches us.
Includes activities that empower women to rethink our
relationships with food and with people. $10.95 1-879427-03-6
 *"very useful and very, very important. This book will change
 many women's lives."* —*Jewish Weekly News*

To order any of the books listed above, or to receive a free
catalog, write to us at 2250 W. Farragut, Chicago, IL
60625-1802. Please include $2 shipping for the first book and
.50 for each additional book.

Third Side Press publishes lesbian fiction and women's
nonfiction (particularly health) from a feminist perspective.
Our name, Third Side Press, comes from the concept that every
issue has more than two sides, and the difficulty of generally
holding a point of view outside those that prevail in the main
stream of U.S. culture.

JESS WELLS has published six volumes of writing, including two collections of short stories (*The Dress/The Sharda Stories* and *Two Willow Chairs*). Her work has also been published in eleven anthologies, including *Woman on Woman, Lesbian Love Stories, Word of Mouth: Women Write the Erotic,* and *When I Am An Old Woman I Shall Wear Purple.*

Her work "The Dress" was the first piece to herald the new discovery of femme-drag; her stories "The Succubus" and "Morning Girls" are cited as among the earliest and best of lesbian erotica; her story "Two Willow Chairs," widely reprinted, is now included in university curriculum and textbooks.

Wells resides in the San Francisco Bay area.